Christmas 1911

To Erik ♡   P9-BIZ-472

from Mrs. Simmons.

FIVE LITTLE PEPPERS MIDWAY

"Now I'm going to drive you down in my gig,"
Dr. Fisher said to Polly. — *Page* 112.

FIVE LITTLE PEPPERS MIDWAY

By MARGARET SIDNEY

ILLUSTRATED BY ARTHUR BECHER

BOSTON

HOUGHTON MIFFLIN COMPANY

The Riverside Press Cambridge

1937

TO

MY LITTLE MARGARET

WHO IS PHRONSIE PEPPER TO ALL
WHO KNOW HER

THIS BOOK IS LOVINGLY INSCRIBED

CONTENTS

Five Little Peppers Midway

CHAPTER I.

PHRONSIE'S PIE.

"JEFFERSON," said Phronsie, with a grave
uplifting of her eyebrows, " I think I will
go down into the kitchen and bake a pie; a
very little pie, Jefferson."

"Bless you, Miss," replied the cook, showing his white teeth in glee, " it is the making
of the kitchen when you come into it."

"Yes, Jefferson," said Phronsie slowly, " I
think I will go down and make one. It must
be very, very full of plums, you know," looking up at him anxiously, " for Polly dearly
loves plums."

11

"It shall be that plummy," said Jefferson convincingly, "that you'd think you never saw such a one for richness. O my! what a pie that shall be!" exclaimed the cook, shutting up one eye to look through the other in a spasm of delight at an imaginary pie; "so it's for Miss Mary, is it?"

"Yes," said Phronsie, "it is. Oh, Jefferson, I'm so glad you like to have me make one," she clasped her hands in silent rapture, and sat down on the lowest stair to think it over a bit, Jefferson looking at her, forgetful that the under cook was fuming in the deserted domains over his delay to return. At last he said, bowing respectfully, "If you please, Miss, it's about time to begin. Such a pie ain't done without a deal of care, and we'd best have it a-baking as soon as may be."

"Yes," said Phronsie, getting off from her stair, and surrendering her hand to his big black palm, "we ought to go right this very minute. But I must get my apron on;" she stopped and looked down at her red dress.

"Oh! you can take one of my aprons," said the cook, "they're as fine, and big, and white, and I'll just put you in one of 'em and tie you up as snug; you'll come out as clean and sweet when we're through, as you are now, Miss."

"Tie me up?" laughed Phronsie in glee. "Oh! how nice, Jefferson. Do you know I love you very much, Jefferson, you're so very good to me?"

The big fellow drew a long breath. "No, Miss, I'm big and black, and just fit to stay down-stairs," he managed to say.

"But I love you better because you are black, Jefferson," insisted Phronsie, "a great deal better. You are not like everybody else, but you are just yourself," clinging to his hand.

"Well, Miss, I ain't just fit for a lily to touch and that's the truth," looking down at his palm that the small white hand grasped closely. "It's clean, Miss," he added with pardonable pride, "but it's awful black."

"I like it better black, Jefferson," said Phronsie again, "really and truly I do, because then it's your very, very own;" in a tone that thrilled him much as if a queen had knighted him on the spot.

This important declaration over, the two set
forth on their way toward the kitchen, Phronsie
clinging to his hand, and chatting merrily over
the particular pie in prospect, with varied re-
marks on pies in general, that by and by would
be ventured upon if this present one were a
success — and very soon tied up in one of the
cook's whitest aprons she was seated with due
solemnity at the end of the baking table, the
proper utensils and materials in delightful confusion before her, and the lower order of
kitchen satellites revolving around her, and
Jefferson the lesser sphere.

"Now all go back to your work," said that
functionary when he considered the staring and
muttered admiration had been indulged in long
enough, "and leave us."

"I want you," said his assistant, touching
his elbow.

"Clear out," said Jefferson angrily, his face
turned quite from Phronsie.

But she caught the tone and immediately
laid down the bit of dough she was mould-
ing.

"Do go," she begged, "and come back

quickly," smiling up into his face. "See, I'm going to pat and pat and pat, oh! ever so much before you come back."

So Jefferson followed the under cook, the scullery boy went back to cleaning the knives, Susan, the parlor maid who was going through the kitchen with her dustpan and broom, hurried off with a backward glance or two, and Phronsie was left quite alone to hum her way along in her blissful culinary attempt.

"Bless me!" exclaimed a voice close to her small ear, as she was attempting for the fifth time to roll out the paste quite as thin as she had seen Jefferson do, "what is this? Bless my soul! it's Phronsie!"

Phronsie set down the heavy rolling-pin and turned in her chair with a gleeful laugh.

"Dear, dear Grandpapa!" she cried, clasping her floury hands, "oh! I'm so glad you've come to see me make a pie all by myself. It's for Polly, and it's to be full of plums; Jefferson let me make it."

"Jefferson? And where is he, pray?" cried Mr. King irately. "Pretty fellow, to bring you down to these apartments, and then go off

and forget you. Jefferson!" he called sharply,
" here, where are you?"

"O, Grandpapa!" exclaimed Phronsie in
dire distress, "I sent him; Jefferson didn't
want to go, Grandpapa dear, really and truly,
he went because I asked him."

"If you please, sir," began Jefferson, hurrying up, "I only stepped off a bit to the cellar.
Bassett sent down a lot of turnips, they ain't
first-rate, and "—

"All right," said Mr. King, cutting him
short with a wave of his hand, " if Miss Phronsie sent you off, it's all right; I don't want to
hear any more elaborate explanations."

"Little Miss hasn't been alone but a few
minutes," said Jefferson in a worried way.

"And see," said Phronsie, turning back to
her efforts, while one hand grasped the old
gentleman's palm, "I've almost got it to look
like Jefferson's. Almost, haven't I?" she
asked, regarding it anxiously.

"It will be the most beautiful pie," cried Mr.
King, a hearty enthusiasm succeeding his irri-
tability, "that ever was baked. I wish you'd
make me one sometime, Phronsie."

" Do you? " she cried in a tremor of delight, " and will you really have it on the table, and cut it with Aunt Whitney's big silver knife? "

" That I will," declared Mr. King solemnly.

" Then some day I'll come down here again, Jefferson," cried Phronsie in a transport, " and bake one for my dear Grandpapa.   That is, if this one is good.   Oh! you do suppose it will be good, don't you? " appealingly at him.

" It shall," said Jefferson stoutly, and seizing the rolling-pin with extreme determination. " You want a bit more butter worked in, here," a dab with skillful fingers, and a little manipulation with the flour, a roll now and then most deftly, and the paste was laid out before Phronsie.   " Now, Miss, you can put it in the dish."

" But it isn't my pie," said Phronsie, and, big girl as she felt herself to be, she sat back in her chair, her lower lip quivering.

" Not your pie? " repeated the cook, bringing himself up straight to gaze at her.

" No," said Phronsie, shaking her yellow head gravely, " it isn't my pie now, Jefferson. You put in the things, and rolled it."

" Leave your fingers off from it, can't you? "

cried Mr. King sharply. "Goodness! this pie isn't to have a professional touch about it. Get some more flour and stuff, whatever it is you make a pie of, and let her begin again. There, I'll sit down and watch you; then there'll be some chance of having things straight." So he drew up a chair to the side of the table, first calling off Pete, the scullery boy, from his knives to come and wipe it off for him, and Mrs. Tucker who was in kitchen dialect "Tucker," to see that the boy did his work well.

"Lor' bless you, sir," said Tucker, bestowing a final polish with her apron, "'twas like satin before, sir — not a wisp of dust."

"I don't want any observations from you," said the old gentleman, depositing himself in the chair. "There, you can go back to your work, Mrs. Tucker, and you too, Pete. Now I'll see that this pie is to your liking, Phronsie."

But Phronsie still sat back in her chair, thoughtfully surveying Jefferson.

"Grandpapa," she said at last slowly, "I think I'd rather have the first pie, I really would, Grandpapa, may I?" She brought her yellow head forward by a sudden movement, and looked deep into his keen eyes.

"Bless my soul! Rather have the first pie?" repeated the old gentleman in astonishment, "why, I thought you wanted to make one all yourself."

"I think I'd rather do part of it," said Phronsie with great deliberateness, "then Polly'll like it, and eat it, and I'll do yours, Grandpapa dear, just as Jefferson fixed mine, all alone. Please let me." She held him fast with her eyes, and waited for his answer.

"So you shall!" cried Mr. King in great satisfaction, "make mine all alone. This one would better go as it is. Put away the flour and things, Jefferson; Miss Phronsie doesn't want them."

Phronsie gave a relieved little sigh. "And, Jefferson, if you hadn't showed me how, I couldn't ever in all this world make Grandpapa's. Now give me the little plate, do."

"Here 'tis, Miss," said the cook, all his tremor over the blunder he had made, disappearing, since, after all, things were quite satisfactory. And the little plate forthcoming,

Phronsie tucked away the paste lovingly in its depths, and began the important work of concocting the mixture with which the pie was to be filled, Mr. King sitting by with the gravity of a statue, even to the deliberate placing of each plum.

"Where's Phronsie?" called a voice above in one of the upper halls.

"Oh! she's coming, Polly is!" cried Phronsie, deserting a plum thrust in endwise in the middle of the pie, to throw her little sticky fingers around Jefferson's neck; "oh! do take off my apron; and let me go. She'll see my pie!"

"Stop!" cried Mr. King, getting up somewhat stiffly to his feet, "I'll take off the apron myself. There, Phronsie, there you are. Whew! how hot you keep your kitchen, Jefferson," and he wiped his face.

"Now we'll run," said Phronsie softly, "and not make a bit of noise, Grandpapa dear, and, Jefferson, please put on my top to the pie, and don't let it burn, and I'll come down very, very soon again, and bake one all alone by myself for Grandpapa."

The old gentleman kept up very well with the soft patter of her feet till they reached the foot of the staircase. "There, there, child," he said, "there's not the least need of hurry now."

"But she will come down," said Phronsie, in gentle haste pulling at his hand, "then if she should see it, Grandpapa!"

"To be sure; that would indeed be dreadful," said Mr. King, getting over the stairs very creditably. "There, here we are now. Whew! it's terribly warm in this house!"

But there was no danger from Polly; she was at this very instant, not being able to find Phronsie, hurring off toward the library in search of Mrs. Whitney.

"We want to do the very loveliest thing!" she cried, rushing in, her cheeks aflame. "Oh! pray excuse me;" she stopped short, blushing scarlet.

"Don't feel badly, Polly dear," said Mrs. Whitney, over in the dim light, where the divan was drawn up in the east window, and she held out her hand and smiled; the other lady whose *tête-à-tête* was thus summarily disturbed was elderly and very tall and angular. She put up

her eyeglass at the intrusion and murmured
" Ah ? "

" This is Polly Pepper," said Mrs. Whitney,
as Polly, feeling unusually awkward and shy,
stumbled across the library to get within the
kind arms awaiting her.

" One of the children that your kindness received in this house ? " said the tall lady, making
good use of the eyeglass.   The color mounted
steadily on Polly's already rosy cheek, at the
scrutiny now going on with the greatest free-
dom.

" One of the dear children who make this
house a sunny place for us all," said Mrs. Whitney distinctly.

" Ah ?   I see.   You are extremely good to
put it in that way."   A low, well-bred laugh
followed this speech.   Its sound irritated the
young girl's ear unspeakably, and the brown
eyes flashed, and though there was really no
occasion to feel what was not addressed to her,
Polly was quite sure she utterly disliked the
lady before her.

" My dear Mrs. Chatterton," said Mrs. Whitney in the gentlest of accents, " you do not

comprehend; it is not possible for you to understand how very happy we all are here. The
house is quite another place, I assure you, from
the abode you saw last before you went
abroad."

Mrs. Chatterton gave another low, unpleasant laugh, and this time shrugged her shoulders.

"Polly dear," said Mrs. Whitney with a
smile, "say good-morning to Mrs. Chatterton,
and then run away. I will hear your wonderful plan by and by. I shall be glad to, child,"
she was guilty of whispering in the small ear.

"Good-morning, Mrs. Chatterton," said
Polly slowly, the brown eyes looking steadily
into the traveled and somewhat seamed countenance before her.

"Good-morning," and Polly found herself
once more across the floor, and safely out in the
hall, the door closed between them.

"Who is she?" she cried in an indignant
spasm to Jasper, who ran up, and she lifted her
eyes brimming over with something quite new
to him. He stopped aghast.

"Who?" he cried. "Oh, Polly! what has
happened?"

" Mrs. Chatterton.   And she looked at me
— oh! I can't tell you how she looked; as if I
were a bug, or a hateful worm beneath her,"
cried Polly, quite as much aghast at herself.
" It makes me feel horridly, Jasper — you can't
think."

" Oh! that old " — He stopped, pulling himself up with quite an effort.   " Has she come
back — what brought her, pray tell, so
soon? "

" I don't know, I am sure," said Polly, laughing at his face.   " I was only in the room a
moment, I think, but it seemed an age with that
eyeglass, and that hateful little laugh."

" Oh! she always sticks up that thing in her
eye," said Jasper coolly, " and she's everlastingly ventilating that laugh on everybody. She
thinks it high-bred and elegant, but it makes
people want to kill her for it."   He looked and
spoke annoyed.   " To think you fell into her
clutches! " he added.

" Well, who is she? " cried Polly, smoothing
down her ruffled feathers, when she saw the
effect of her news on him.   " I should dearly
love to know."

"Cousin Algernon's wife," said Jasper briefly.

"And who is he?" cried Polly, again experiencing a shock that this dreadful person was a relative to whom due respect must be shown.

"Oh! a cousin of father's," said Jasper. "He was nice, but he's dead."

"Oh!" said Polly.

"She's been abroad for a good half-dozen years, and why she doesn't stay there when everybody supposed she was going to, astonishes me," said Jasper, after a moment. "Well, it will not be for long, I presume, that we shall have the honor; she'll be easily tired of America, and take herself off again."

"She doesn't stay in this house, does she, Jasper?" cried Polly in a tone of horror.

"No; that is, unless she chooses to, then we can't turn her off. She's a relative, you know."

"Hasn't she any home?" asked Polly, "or any children?"

"Home? Yes, an estate down in Bedford County — Dunraven Lodge; but it's all shut up, and in the hands of agents who have been trying for the half-dozen years she was abroad, to sell it for her. She may have come back to settle down there again, there's no telling what she will do. In the meantime, I fancy she'll make her headquarters here," he said gloomily.

"Oh, Jasper!" exclaimed Polly, seizing his arm, feeling that here was need of comfort indeed, "how very dreadful! Don't you suppose something will happen to take her away?"

"I don't see what can," said Jasper, prolonging the gloom to feel the comfort it brought. "You see she has nobody who wants her, to step in and relieve us. She has two nephews, but oh! you ought to see them fight!"

"Fight?" repeated Polly aghast.

"Yes; you can't dignify their skirmishes by any other name," said Jasper, in disgust. "So you see our chances for keeping her as long as she condescends to stay, are really very good."

Polly clung to his arm in speechless dismay. Meanwhile conversation fast and brisk was going on between the two shut up in the library.

"It is greatly to your discredit, Marian," said Mrs. Chatterton in a high, cold voice, "that you didn't stop all this nonsense on your father's part, before the thing got to such a pass as to install them in this house."

" On the contrary," said Mrs. Whitney with a little laugh, " I did everything I could to further the plan that father wisely made."

" Wisely! " cried Mrs. Chatterton in scorn. "Oh, you silly child! don't you see what it will all tend to? "

" I see that it has made us all very happy for five years," said Mrs. Whitney, preserving her composure, " so I presume the future doesn't hold much to dread on that score."

" The future is all you have to dread," declared Mrs. Chatterton harshly. " The present may be well enough; though I should think existence with that low, underbred family here, would be a " —

" You may pause just where you are, Mrs. Chatterton," said Marian, still with the gentlest of accents, but with a determination that made the other look down at her in astonishment, " not another word shall you utter in that strain, nor will I listen to it." And with fine temper undisturbed in her blue eyes, she regarded her relative.

" Dear me, Marian ! I begin to notice your
age more now. You shouldn't fly into such
rages; they wear on one fearfully; and especially for a stranger too, and against your own
people — how can you ? "

Mrs. Chatterton drew out a vinaigrette,
then a fan from a silken bag, with clasps that
she was always glad to reflect were heirlooms.
" It's trying, I must confess," she declared,
alternately applying the invigorating salts and
waving the combination of gauze and sandal
wood, " to come home to such a reception.
But," and a heavy sigh, " I must bear it."

" You ought to see father," cried Mrs. Whitney, rising. " I must go at once and tell him of
your arrival."

" Oh ! I don't know that I care about seeing
Cousin Horatio yet," said Mrs. Chatterton carelessly. " He will probably fall into one of his
rages, and my nerves have been upset quite
enough by you. I think I'll go directly to my
apartments." She rose also.

" Father must at once be informed of your
arrival," repeated Marian quietly. " I'll send
him in to see you."

"And I shall go to my apartments," declared Mrs. Chatterton determinedly.

"Hoity-toity!" exclaimed Mr. King's voice, and in he came, with Phronsie, fresh from the kitchen, clinging to his hand.

CHAPTER II.

PHRONSIE dropped one small hand by her side, and stood quite still regarding the visitor.

"O my goodness me," ejaculated Mrs. Chatterton, startled out of her elegance, and not pausing to adjust the glass, but using her two good eyes to the best advantage.

"Hoity-toity! So you are back again!" exclaimed Mr. King by way of welcome. "Well, and if I may ask, what brought you now, Eunice?"

Mrs. Chatterton gathered herself up and smiled in a superior way.

"Never mind my reasons, Cousin Horatio. What a fine child you have there;" now the glass came into play; "pray tell me all about her."

30

"You have well said," observed Mr. King, seating himself with the utmost deliberateness, and drawing Phronsie to her accustomed place on his knee, where she nestled, regardless of his immaculate linen and fine waistcoat, "Phronsie Pepper is indeed a fine child; a very fine child, Madam."

"O my, and O my!" cried Mrs. Chatterton, holding up her hands, "to think that you can so demean yourself; why, she's actually mussing your shirt-front with her dirty little hands!"

"Phronsie Pepper's hands are never dirty, Madam," said the old gentleman gravely. "Sit still, child," as Phronsie in a state of alarm, struggled to slip down from his lap, thrusting the two members thus referred to, well out before her.

Mrs. Chatterton burst into a loud laugh. "To think I have come to see Horatio King in such a state! Jasper Horatio King!" she repeated scornfully. "I heard about it through the Bascombs' letters, but I wouldn't believe it till I used my eyes. It's positively dreadful!"

Mr. King put back his head and laughed also; so heartily, that Phronsie ceased to struggle, and turned to regard him in silent astonishment; and Mrs. Whitney, charmed that the rage usually produced by conversation with Cousin Algernon's wife was not forthcoming, began to laugh, too, so that the amusement of the tall lady was quenched in the general hilarity.

"What you can find in my words to cause such an unseemly outburst, I cannot see," she cried in a passion.

"I'm under the impression that you led off the amusement yourself," said Mr. King, wiping his eyes. "Phronsie, it's all very funny, isn't it?" looking down into the little wondering face.

"Is it really funny?" asked Phronsie. "Does the lady like it?"

"Not particularly, I suspect," said Mr. King carelessly.

"And that you can talk with that chit, ignoring me, your cousin's wife, is insufferable." Mrs. Chatterton now arose speedily from the divan, and shook out a flounce or two with great venom. " I had intended to make you a visit. Now it is quite impossible."

" As you like," said the old gentleman, also rising, and placing Phronsie on her feet, observing ostentatious care to keep her hand. " My house is open to you, Eunice," with a wave of his disengaged hand in old-time hospitality, " but of course you must suit yourself."

" It's rather hard upon a person of sensibility, to come home after a six years' absence," said Cousin Eunice with a pathetic sniff, and once more seeking her vinaigrette in the depths of the silken bag, " to meet only coldness and derision. In fact, it is very hard."

" No doubt, no doubt," said the old gentleman hastily, " I can imagine such a case, but it has nothing to do with you. Now, if you are going to stay, Eunice, say so at once, and proceed to your room. If not, why you must go, and understand it is no one's fault but your own."

He drew himself up and looked long and hard into the thin pale face before him. Phronsie pulled at his hand.

"I want to ask the lady to stay, Grandpapa dear."

"She doesn't need urging," said old Mr. King quite distinctly, and not moving a muscle.

"But, Grandpapa dear, she isn't glad about something."

"No more am I."

"Grandpapa," cried Phronsie, moving off a bit, though not deserting his hand, and standing on her tiptoes, "I want her to stay, to see me. Perhaps she hasn't any little girls"

"To see you?" cried Mr. King irately. "Say no more, child, say no more. She's been abusing you right and left, like a pickpocket."

"What is a pickpocket?" asked Phronsie, getting down from her tiptoes.

"Oh! a scoundrel who puts his hands into pockets; picks out what doesn't belong to him, in fact."

Phronsie stood quite still, and shook her head gravely at the tall figure. "That was not nice," she said soberly.

"Now do you want her to stay?" cried the old gentleman.

"Insufferable!" repeated Mrs. Chatterton between her teeth, "to mix me up with that chit!"

"Yes, I do," said Phronsie decidedly, "I do, Grandpapa. Now I know she hasn't any little girls — if she had little girls, she wouldn't say such very unnice things; I want the poor lady to stay with me."

Mrs. Chatterton turned and went abruptly off to the door; hesitated, and looked back.

"I see your household is in a very chaotic state, Cousin Horatio. Still I will remain a few days," with extreme condescension, "on condition that these Peppers are not thrust upon my attention."

"I make no conditions," said the old gentleman coolly. "If you stay, you must accept my household as you find it."

"Come, Marian," said Mrs. Chatterton, holding out her hand to Mrs. Whitney. "You may help me to my apartments if you like. I am quite unstrung by all this," and she swept out without a backward glance.

"Has she gone?" cried Jasper, hurrying in with Polly running after. "It's 'stay,' isn't it, father?" as he saw the old gentleman's face.

"Yes," said Mr. King grimly, "it is 'stay' indeed, Jasper."

"Well, now then, you've a piece of work on your hands about the biggest you ever did yet, Polly Pepper!" cried Jasper, "to make things comfortable in this house. I shall be just as cross as can be imagined, to begin with."

"You cross!" cried Polly.

"Cross as a bear; Marian will fight against the prevailing ill wind, but it will finally blow her down to a state of depression where her best friend wouldn't recognize her, and " —

"You don't mention me, my boy," said Mr. King dryly.

Jasper looked into his father's eyes, and they both laughed.

"And if you, Polly Pepper, don't keep things bright, why, we shall all go to the dogs," said the old gentleman, sobering down. "So mind you do, and we'll try to bear Cousin Algernon's relict."

" I will," said Polly stoutly, though " relict "
sounded very dreadful to begin with.

" Give us your hand, then," said Jasper's
father, putting out his palm. " There! " releasing it, " now I'm much more comfortable about
matters."

" And give me your hand, Polly," cried Jasper, his own brown hand flying to meet hers.
" There! and now I'm comfortable too! So
it's a compact, and a sure one! "

" And I want to give my hand," cried Phronsie, very much aggrieved. " Here, Jasper."

" Bless my soul, so you must! " cried old
Mr. King; " to think we didn't ask you first.
There — and there! "

" And, Phronsie darling," cried Polly in a
rapture, " you must promise with me, after you
have with the others. I couldn't ever get along
in all this world without that."

So the ceremony of sealing the compact having been observed with great gravity, Phronsie drew a long breath, and now felt that the
" poor lady " might come down at any time
to find all things prepared for her.

" Now tell our plan," cried Jasper to Polly,

"and put this disagreeable business out of our heads. It's a fine one," he added to his father.

"Of course it is," cried the old gentleman.

"Well, you know Joel and Davie and Van and Percy are coming home from school next week for the Christmas holidays," began Polly, trying to still the wild beating of her heart.

"Bless me! so they are," said Mr. King. "How time flies, to be sure! Well, go on, Polly."

"And we ought to do something to celebrate," said Polly, "at least don't you think so?" she asked anxiously, looking up in his face.

"To be sure I do," cried the old gentleman heartily. "Well, what would you do, Polly child, to show the youngsters we're proud of them, and glad to get them back — hey?"

"We want to get up a little play," said Polly, "Jasper and I, and act it."

"And have music," cried Jasper. "Polly shall play on the piano. The boys will be so delighted to see how she has improved."

"And Jasper will play too," cried Polly eagerly. "Oh, Jasper! will you play that concerto, the one you played when Mary Gibbs was here at tea last week? Do, Jasper, do."

"That nearly floored me," said Jasper.

"No; you said it was Mary's watching you like a lynx — you know you did," said Polly, laughing merrily.

"Never mind," said the old gentleman. "What next, Polly? The play is all right."

"I should think it was," cried Jasper. "It's the Three Dragons, and the Princess Clotilde."

"O my goodness," exclaimed Mr. King, "What a play for Christmas Eve!"

"Well, you'll say it's a splendid hit!" cried Jasper, "when you see it from the private box we are going to give you."

"So you are intending to honor me, are you?" cried his father, vastly pleased to find himself as ever, the central figure in their plans. "Well, well, I dare say it will all be as fine as can be to welcome these young scapegraces home. What next, Polly?"

"It must be kept a perfect surprise," cried Polly, clasping her hands while the color flew

over her face. "No one must even whisper it
to each other, the day before Christmas when
the boys get here, for Joel is so very dreadful
whenever there is a secret."

"His capacity certainly is good," said Mr.
King dryly. "We will all be very careful."

"And Phronsie is to be Princess Clotilde,"
cried Jasper, seizing her suddenly, to prance
around the room, just like old times.

"Oh, Jasper! I'm eight years old," she
cried. struggling to free herself.

"Nonsense! What of it — you are the
baby of this household." But he set her on
her feet nevertheless, one hand still patting the
soft yellow waves over her brow. "Go on,
Polly, do, and lay the whole magnificence before father. He will be quite overcome."

"That would be disastrous," said Mr. King;
"better save your effects till the grand affair
comes off."

"Jasper is to be one of the dragons," announced Polly, quite in her element, "that is,
the head dragon; Ben is to be another, and
we haven't quite decided whether to ask Archy
Hurd or Clare to take the third one."

"Clare has the most 'go' in him," said Jasper critically.

"Then I think we'll decide now to ask him," said Polly, "don't you, Jasper?"

"A dragon without 'go' in him would be most undesirable, I should fancy. Well, what next do you propose to do, Polly?" asked Mr. King.

"Now that we know that you will allow us to have it," cried Polly in a rapture, "why, we can think up splendid things. We've only the play written so far, sir."

"Polly wrote the most," said Jasper.

"Oh, no, Jasper! I only put in the bits," said Polly. "He planned it — every single bit, Jasper did."

"Well, she thought up the dragons, and the cave, and " —

"Oh! that was easy enough," said Polly, guilty of interrupting, "because you see something has to carry off the Princess Clotilde."

"Oh, now! you are not going to frighten my little girl," cried Mr. King. "I protest against the whole thing if you do," and he put out his hand. " Come, Phonsie," when, as of old, she hurried to his side obediently.

" Oh! we are going to show her the boys, and how we dress them up just like dragons," cried Polly, " and while they are prancing around and slashing their tails at rehearsal, I'm going to keep saying, ' That's nothing but Jasper and Ben and Clare, you know, Phronsie,' till I get her accustomed to them. You won't be frightened, will you, pet, at those dear, sweet old dragons? " she ended, and getting on her knees, she looked imploringly into Phronsie's blue eyes.

" N-no," said Phronsie, slowly, " not if they are really Jasper and Ben and Clare."

" They really will be," cried Polly, enchanted at her success, " Jasper and Ben and Clare; and they will give you a ride, and show you a cave, oh! and perfect quantities of things; you can't think how many! "

Phronsie clapped her hands and laughed aloud in glee.

" Oh! I don't care if they are true dragons, Polly, I don't," she cried, dreadfully excited.

" Make ' em real big live ones, do; do make them big, and let me ride on their backs."

" These will be just as real," said Polly comfortingly, " that is, they'll act real, only there will be boys inside of them. Oh! we'll have them nice, dear, don't you fear."

" But I'd really rather have true ones," sighed Phronsie.

CHAPTER III.

THE REHEARSAL.

"NOW, Phronsie, said Polly, on her knees before the Princess, who was slowly evolving into "a thing of beauty," "do hold still just a minute, dear. There," as she thrust in another pin, then turned her head critically to view her work, "I do hope that is right."

Phronsie sighed. "May I just stretch a wee little bit, Polly," she asked timidly, "before you pin it up? Just a very little bit?"

"To be sure you may," said Polly, looking into the flushed little face; "I'll tell you, you may walk over to the window and back, once; that'll rest you and give me a chance to see what is the matter with that back drapery."

So Phronsie, well pleased, gathered up the embyro robe of the Princess and moved off, a bewildering tangle of silver spangles and float-

44

ing lace, drawn over the skirt of one of Mrs. Whitney's white satin gowns.

"There ought to be a dash of royal purple somewhere," said Polly, sitting on the floor to see her go, and resting her tired hands on her knees. "Now where shall I get it, and where shall I put it when I do have it?" She wrinkled up her eyebrows a moment, lost in thought over the momentous problem. "Oh! I know," and she sprang up exultingly. "Phronsie, won't this be perfectly lovely? we can take that piece of tissue paper Auntie gave you, and I can cut out little knots and sashes. It is so soft, that in the gaslight they will look like silk. How fine!"

"Can't I be a Princess unless you sew up that purple paper?" asked Phronsie, pausing suddenly to look over her shoulder in dismay at Polly.

"Why, yes, you can be, of course," said Polly, "but you can't be as good a one as if you had a dash of royal purple about you. What's a bit of tissue paper to the glory of being a Princess?" she cried, with sparkling eyes. "Dear me, I wish I could be one."

" Well, you may have it, Polly," said Phronsie with a sigh, " and then afterwards I'll rip it all off and smooth it out, and it will be almost as good as new."

" I think there won't be much left of it when the play is over," cried Polly with a laugh; " why, the dragons are going to carry you off to their cave, you know, and you are to be rescued by the knight, just think, Phronsie! You can't expect to have such perfectly delightful times, and come out with a quantity of tissue paper all safe.   Something has to be sacrificed to royalty, child."

Phronsie sighed again.   But as Polly approved of royalty so highly, she immediately lent herself to the anticipations of the pleasure before her, smothering all lesser considerations.

" When you get your little silver cap on with one of Auntie's diamond rings sewed in it, why, you'll be too magnificent for anything," said Polly, now pulling and patting with fresh enthusiasm, since the " purple dash " was forthcoming.

" Princesses don't wear silver caps with diamond rings sewed in them," observed Phronsie wisely.

"Of course not; they have diamonds by the bushel, and don't need to sew rings in their caps to make them sparkle," said Polly, plaiting and pinning rapidly, "but in dressing up for a play, we have to take a poetic license. There, turn just one bit to the right, Phronsie dear."

"What's poetic license?" demanded Phronsie, wrenching her imagination off from the bushel of diamonds to seize practical information.

"Oh! when a man writes verses and says things that aren't so," said Polly, her mind on the many details before her.

"But he ought not to," cried Phronsie, with wide eyes, "say things that are not so. I thought poets were always very good, Polly."

"Oh! well, people let him," said Polly, carelessly, "because he puts it into poetry. It would never do in prose; that would be quite shocking."

"Oh!" said Phronsie, finding the conversation some alleviation to the fitting-on process.

"Now this left side," said Polly, twisting her head to obtain a good view of the point in question, "is just right; I couldn't do it any better if I were to try a thousand times. Why won't this other one behave, and fall into a pretty curve, I wonder?"

Phronsie yawned softly as the brown eyes were safely behind her.

"I shall gather it up anyway, so," and Polly crushed the refractory folds recklessly in one hand; "that's the way Mary Gibbs's hat trimmings look, and I'm sure they're a complete success. Oh! that's lovely," cried Polly, at the effect. "Now, that's the treatment the whole drapery needs," she added in the tone of an art connoisseur. "Oh!"

A rushing noise announced the approach of two or three boys, together with the barking of Prince, as they all ran down the wide hall.

"O dear, dear!" exclaimed Polly, hurriedly pulling and pinning, "there come the boys to rehearse. It can't be four o'clock," as the door opened and three members of the cast entered.

"It's quarter-past four," said Jasper, laughing and pulling out his watch; "we gave you an extra fifteen minutes, as you had such a lot to do. Dear me! but you are fine, Phronsie. I make my obeisance to Princess Clotilde!" and he bowed low to the little silver and white figure, as did the other two boys, and then drew off to witness the final touches.

"It's a most dreadful thing," cried Polly, pushing back the brown waves from her brow, as she also fell off to their point of view, "to get up a princess. I had no idea it was such a piece of work."

"You have scored an immense success," said Jasper enthusiastically. "Oh, Phronsie! you will make the hit of the season."

"You'll think it is even much nicer when it is done," said Polly, vastly relieved that Jasper had given such a kind verdict. "It's to have a dash of royal purple on that right side, and in one of the shoulder knots, and to catch up her train."

"That will be very pretty, I don't doubt," said Jasper, trying to resolve himself into the cold critic, "but it seems to me it is almost perfect now, Polly."

"Oh! thank you so much," she cried, with blooming cheeks. "How do you like it, Clare and Bensie?"

"I can't tell," said Ben, slowly regarding the Princess on all sides; "it's so transforming."

"It's tiptop!" cried Clare. "It out-princesses any princess I've ever imagined."

"Well, it's a perfect relief," said Polly, "to have you boys come in. I've been working so over it that I was ready to say it was horrid. It's too bad, isn't it, that Dick can't be here to-day to rehearse his part?"

"To be sure," exclaimed Jasper, looking around, "where is the Princess's page?"

"He's gone to the dentist's," said Polly, making a wry face. "Auntie had to make the appointment for this afternoon, and we couldn't put off the rehearsal; Clare can't come any other time, you know."

Phronsie turned an anxious face to the window. "I hope he's not being hurt very much," she said slowly.

"I don't believe he is," Polly made haste to answer most cheerfully, "it was only one tooth, you know, Phronsie, to be filled. Auntie says Dr. Porter told her the rest are all right."

But a cloud rested on the Princess's face. "One tooth is something," she said.

"Just think how nice it will be when it is all over, and Dick comes scampering in," cried Jasper, with great hilarity.

"Do climb up on the sofa, Phronsie," urged Polly, looking into the pale little face, "you must sit down and rest a bit, you're so tired."

"I will read the prologue while she rests," said Jasper.

"So you can," said Polly. "Take care, child," in alarm, "you mustn't curl up in the corner like that; princesses don't ever do so."

"Don't they?" said Phronsie, flying off from the lovely corner, to straighten out again into the dignity required; "not when they are little girls, Polly?"

"No, indeed," said Polly, with a rescuing hand among the silver spangles and lace; they must never forget that they are princesses, Phronsie. There now, you're all right."

"Oh!" said Phronsie, sitting quite stiffly,

glad if she could not be comfortable, she could be a princess.

"Gentle ladies and brave sirs," began Jasper in a loud, impressive tone, from the temporary stage, the large rug in front of the crackling hearth fire.

Clare burst into a laugh. "See here now," cried Jasper, brandishing his text at him, "if you embarrass me like that, you may leave, you old dragon!"

"You ought to see your face," cried Clare. "Jap, you are anything but a hit."

"You'll be yet," declared Jasper with a pretended growl, and another flourish of the manuscript.

"Go on, do," implored Polly, "I think it is lovely. Clare, you really ought to be ashamed," and she shook her brown head severely at him.

"If I don't quench such melodrama in the outset," said Clare, "he'll ruin us all. Fair ladies and brave sirs," mimicking to perfection Jasper's tones.

"Thank you for a hint," cried Jasper, pulling out his pencil. "I didn't say 'fair'; that's better than 'gentle.' I wish critics would always be so useful as to give one good idea. Heigho! here goes again:

> "'Fair ladies and brave sirs,
>   The player's art is to amuse,
>   Instruct, or to confuse
>   By too much good advice,
>   But poorly given:
>   That no one follows, because, forsooth,
>   'Tis thrown at him, neck and heels.
>   The drama, pure and simple, is forgot
>   In tugging in the moral'"—

"I thought you were going to alter 'tugging in' to something more elegant," said Polly.

"Lugging in," suggested Clare, with another laugh.

"Morals are always tugged in by the head and shoulders," said Jasper. "Why not say so?"

"We should have pretty much the whole anatomy of the human form divine, if you had your way," cried Clare. "Listen!

"'Because, forsooth, 'tis thrown at him, neck and heels' and 'Tugging in the moral, head and shoulders.' Now just add 'by the

pricking of my thumbs,' etc., and you have
them all."

Jasper joined as well as Polly and Ben in
the laugh at the prologue's expense, but Phronsie sat erect winking hard, her royal hands
folded quite still in her lap.

"You're bound for a newspaper office, my
boy," said Jasper at length. "How you will
cut into the coming poet, and maul the fledg-
ling of the prose writer! Well, I stand corrected.

> "'The drama pure and simple,
> Is forgot, in straining at the moral.'

"Is that any better?" (To the audience.)

"Yes, I think it is," said Polly, "but I do
believe it's time to talk more elegantly, Jasper.
It is due to the people in the private boxes, you
know."

"Oh! the boxes are to have things all right
before the play is over; never you fear, Polly,"
said Jasper.

> "'A poor presentment,
> You will say we give;
> But cry you mercy, Sirs, and'" —

"I don't like ' cry you mercy,' " announced Ben slowly, " because it doesn't seem to mean anything."

"Oh! don't cut that out," exclaimed Polly, clasping her hands and rushing up to Ben. " That's my pet phrase; you mustn't touch that, Bensie."

"But it doesn't mean anything," reiterated Ben in a puzzled way.

"Who cares?" cried Jasper defiantly. " A great many expressions that haven't the least significance, are put in a thing of this sort. Padding, you know, my dear sir."

"Oh!" said Ben literally, " I didn't know as you needed padding. All right, if it is necessary."

"It's antique, and perfectly lovely, and just like Shakespeare," cried Polly, viewing Ben in alarm.

"Oh! let the Bard of Avon have one say in this production," cried Clare. " Go on, do, with your ' cry you mercy.' What's next, Jap?"

"Are you willing, Ben?" asked Jasper, with a glance at Polly.

"Ye-es," said Ben, also gazing at the rosy face and anxious eyes, "it can go as padding, I suppose."

"Oh! I am so glad," exclaimed Polly in glee, and dancing around the room. "And you won't be sorry, I know, Bensie; the audience will applaud that very thing I'm almost sure," which made Jasper sternly resolve something on the spot.

"Well, I shall never be through at this rate," he said, whirling over the manuscript to find his place. "Oh! here I am:

"'But cry you mercy, Sirs and ladies fair,
We aim but to be dragons,
Not mortals posing for effect.
We have a princess, to be sure'"—

"I should think we have," interrupted Clare with a glance over at the sofa. "Goodness me, she's fast asleep!"

"Poor little thing, she is tired to death," cried Polly remorsefully, while they all rushed over to the heap of lace and spangles, blissfully oblivious of "prologues."

"Do let her sleep through this piece of

stupidity," said Jasper, bundling up another satin skirt that Mrs. Whitney had loaned for Polly to make a choice from. "There," putting it under the yellow head, "we'll call her when the dragons come on."

"Take care," cried Polly, with intercepting hand, "that's Auntie's lovely satin gown."

"Beg pardon," said Jasper, relinquishing it speedily. "Here's the sofa pillow, after all," dragging it from its temporary retirement under the theatrical débris. "Now let's get back to work; time is going fast." In a lowered voice:

> "'We have a princess, to be sure,
> A sweet and gracious Clotilde,
> And a knight who does her homage;
> But the rest of us
> Are fishy, scaly,
> Horny and altogether horrid,
> And of very low degree
> Who scarce know why we are upon the boards,
> Except for your amusement,
> So prithee'"—

"Hold!" cried Clare, "what stuff."

"Give me an inch of time," cried Jasper, hurrying on, "and I'll end the misery:

"'So prithee, be amused;
  We're undone, if you are not,
  And all our labor lost.
  Pray laugh, and shake your sides,
  And say "'tis good;
  I' faith, 'tis very good."
  And we shall say
"Your intellects do you credit."
  And so we bid you a fond adieu,
  And haste away to unshackle the dragons,
  Who even now do roar without.'"

Clare threw himself into the part of the dragons, and forgetful of Phronsie, gave a loud roar. Polly clapped her hands and tossed an imaginary bouquet as Jasper bowed himself off.

"Hush!" said Ben, "you'll wake up Phronsie," but it was too late; there she sat rubbing her eyes in astonishment.

"Oh! you darling," cried Polly, running over to her, to clasp her in her arms, "I'm so sorry I tired you all out, Phronsie dear, do forgive me."

"I'm not tired," said Phronsie, with dewy eyes. "Has Jasper got through reading? What was it all about, Polly?"

"Indeed and I have finished," he cried with a yawn and throwing the manuscript on the table, "and I don't know in the least what it is all about, Phronsie."

"Just a lot of dreadful words," said Clare, over in the corner, pulling at a heap of costumes on the floor. "Never mind; the horrible spell is broken; come on, you fellows, and tumble into your dragon skins!"

With that the chief dragon deserted Phronsie, and presently there resounded the rattle of the scales, the clanking of chains, and the dragging about of the rest of their paraphernalia.

"Now, Phronsie," said Jasper, coming back, half-within his dragon skin and gesticulating, "you see that it's only I in this thing. Look, dear! here goes in my head," and he pulled on the scaly covering, observing great care to smile reassuringly the last thing before his countenance was obscured.

Phronsie screamed with delight and clapped her hands. "Oh, Jasper! let me have one on, do, Jasper! I'd much rather be a dragon than a princess. Really and truly I would, Jasper."

"I don't agree with you," said Jasper, in a muffled voice. "Phew! this is no end stuffy, fellows. I can't stand it long."

"I'm all coming to pieces," said Ben, turning around to regard his back where the scales yawned fearfully.

"I'll run and ask Mamsie to come and sew you up," cried Polly, flying off. "She said she would help, if we wanted her."

CHAPTER IV.

WELCOME HOME!

"MARION," said old Mr. King, putting his head in at the door of her little writing-room, " can't you get her comfortably out of the way this morning? I want your services without interruption."

" She's going down to Pinaud's," said Mrs. Whitney, looking up from the note she was writing.

" Capital! when she once gets there, she'll stay the morning," declared Mr. King, greatly pleased. " Now, then, after she's cleverly off, you may come to me."

" I will, father," said Marian, going back with a smile to her correspondence.

Half an hour later Thomas, with the aid of the horses and the shopping coupé having carried off Mrs. Chatterton, Mrs. Whitney pushed

aside her notes, and ran down to her father's
study.

She found him in his velvet morning-gown
seated before his table, busy with a good-sized
list of names that was rapidly growing longer
under his pen.

"Oh! I forgot," he said, looking up; "I
intended to tell you to bring some of your
cards and envelopes. I want some invitations
written."

"Are you going to give a dinner?" asked
Marian, looking over his shoulder. "Oh, no!
I see by the length of your list it's an evening
affair, or a musicale."

"You run along, daughter," said the old
gentleman, "and get what I tell you. This is
my affair; it's a musicale and something else
combined. I don't just know myself." And
he laughed at the sight of her face.

"If father is only pleased, I don't care what
it is," said Mrs. Whitney to herself, hurrying
over the stairs and back again, never once
thinking of Polly's and Jasper's surprise for
the boys.

"You see, Marian," said Mr. King as she

sat down by the table and laid the cards and envelopes in front of him, " that I'm going to help out that affair that Jasper and Polly are getting up."

" Oh, father! how good of you! " exclaimed Mrs. Whitney in a delighted tone, which immensely pleased the old gentleman, to begin with.

" They've been working very hard, those two, at their studies this autumn. I've seen them," cried Mr. King with a shrewd air, " and I'm going now to give them a little pleasure."

Marian said nothing, but let him have the comfort of doing all the talking, which he now enjoyed to his heart's content.

" Whether the other chaps have done well, I don't know. Davie may have kept at it, but I suspect the rest of the boys haven't killed themselves with hard study. But they shall have a good home-coming, at any rate."

Mrs. Whitney smiled, and he proceeded:

" Now I'm going to send out these invitations " — he pushed the list toward her — " I shall have the drawing-room and music-room floors covered. and all extra seats arranged, give Turner *carte blanche* as to flowers, if he can't furnish enough out of our own conservatories — and the evening will end with a handsome ' spread,' as Jasper calls it. In short, I shall recognize their attempt to make it pleasant for the boys' holiday, by helping them out on the affair all I can." The old gentleman now leaned back in his big chair and studied his daughter's face.

" And you'll never regret it, father," she cried, with an enthusiasm that satisfied him, " for these young people will all repay you a thousand-fold, I do believe, in the time to come."

" Don't I know it? " cried Mr. King, getting out of his chair hastily to pace the floor. "Goodness me! they repay me already. They're fine young things, every one of them — Whitneys, Peppers and my boy — as fine as they are made. And whoever says they're not, doesn't know a good piece of work when it's before his eyes. Bless me! " pulling out his handkerchief to mop his face violently, " I don't want to see any finer."

" I hope I shall have a sight of Jasper's and

Polly's faces when you tell them what you intend to do," said Mrs. Whitney; "where are your cards, father?"

"Tell them? I sha'n't tell them at all," cried the old gentleman; "I'm going to have a surprise, too. No one must know it but you and Mrs. Pepper."

"Oh!" said Mrs. Whitney. "It was very stupid in me not to understand that. It will be all right, father; Mrs. Pepper and I will keep our secret, you needn't fear."

"If you can only keep *her* out of the way," exclaimed Mr. King, pointing irascibly in the direction of Mrs. Chatterton's apartments, "all will be well. But I doubt if you can; her meddlesome ears and tongue will be at work as usual," he added in extreme vexation.

"Here comes Jasper," exclaimed Mrs. Whitney, which had the satisfactory result of bringing her father out of his irritation, into a flutter over the concealment of the party preparations.

"Jasper," cried Polly that evening, as they ran into the music-room to play a duet, "we're all right about everything now, as your father

says we may invite the girls and your
friends."

"And he said when I asked him if we ought
not to have cake and coffee, 'I'll attend to
that,'" said Jasper, "so everything is all
straight as far as I can see, Polly."

"The private boxes trouble me, I must confess," said Polly, drumming absently on the
keys, while Jasper spread the sheet of music
on the rack. "You know there must be two;
one for dear Mr. King and one for the boys as
guests of honor. Now how shall we manage
them?"

She took her hand off suddenly from the
keys and folded it over its fellow on her knee,
to study his face anxiously.

"It's pretty hard to get them up, that's a
fact," said Jasper truthfully, "but then, you
know, Polly, we've always found that when a
thing had to be done, it was done. You know
the little brown house taught us that."

"So it did," said Polly, brightening up.
"Dear little old brown house, how could I
ever forget it! Well, I suppose," with a sigh,

" it will come to us as an inspiration when it's time to fix them."

" I suppose so too," said Mrs. Pepper, passing the door, as usual with her mending basket, " and when two people start to play a duet, I think they much better put their minds on that, and not waste precious time on all sorts of questions that will take care of themselves when the time comes."

" You are right, Mrs. Pepper," cried Jasper with a laugh, and seating himself before the piano. " Come, Polly!"

" Mamsie is always right, isn't she, Jasper?" cried Polly with pride, putting her hands down for the first chords.

" Indeed she is," responded the boy heartily. " Here now, Polly, remember, you slipped up a bit on that first bar. Now!"

The twenty-first of December came all too soon for Polly and Jasper, whose school duties had engrossed them till two days before, but after hard work getting up the stage properties, and the many rehearsals, everything was at last pronounced ready, the drawing-room and music-room locked, the keys given to Mrs.

Whitney who promised faithfully to see that no one peeped in who should not, and Polly hurried into her hat and jacket, to go to the station with Jasper to meet the boys.

Thomas drove furiously, as they were a bit late, and they arrived only a minute before the train puffed in.

" Here they are! " cried Polly, and " Here they are! " cried Jasper, together, in great excitement, on the platform.

" Halloo, Polly! " cried Joel, prancing out of the car first, and " How d'ye do, Polly? " as they all hurried after. " Halloo, Jasper! "

" Oh, Polly! it's good to see you! " The from Davie, not ashamed to set a kiss on her red lips.

Van and Percy looked as if they wanted to, but contented themselves with wringing her hand nearly off, while Joel declared he would look after the luggage.

" No, I will," cried Van, dropping Polly's hand.

" You forget," said Percy quietly, " I hold the checks, I'll attend to it myself." He unclosed his brown traveling glove, and Van, at sight of them, turned back.

"Go along, do, then," he cried; "I don't want to, I'm sure; I'd much rather stay with Polly. How d'ye do, Thomas?" he called carelessly to the coachman on his box, who was continually touching his hat and indulging in broad smiles of content.

Polly was tiptoeing in very delight, holding Davie's hand closely while her eyes roved from one to the other of the boys, and her tongue ran fast indeed. A group of girls, who had also come down to the station to meet friends, stopped a bit as they came laughing and chatting by.

"How d'ye, boys?" they said carelessly to the three home-comers. "Oh, Polly! won't it be entrancing to-night?" cried one of them, seizing her arm as she spoke.

"Hush!" said Polly, as she tried to stop her.

"May I bring Elsie Fay? she's come on the train to stay over Christmas with her aunt. May I, Polly?" begged another girl eagerly.

"Yes, yes." said Polly in a paroxysm of fear

lest Joel, who was crowding up between them, should catch a word; " do be still," she whispered. " Bring anybody; only stop, Alexia."

" He won't hear," said Alexia carelessly; " that boy doesn't mind our talking; his head's full of skating and coasting."

" You're going to have something to-night that you don't want me to know about," declared Joel, his chubby face set defiantly, and crowding closer; " so there; now I'm going to find out what it is."

" If we don't want you to know, you ought not to try to find out, Joel Pepper," cried Alexia. " And you sha'n't, either."

" There, now you see," cried Polly, unable to keep still, while her face grew red too. " O dear! what shall we do? "

" You are — you are," cried Joel, capering up and down the platform, his black eyes shining with delight. " Now I know for certain, and it's at our house, too, for you asked Polly if you might bring some other girl, Elsie somebody or other, so! Oh! I'll soon know."

" Joel," exclaimed Jasper suddenly, clapping

him on the shoulder, "I'm going round to the gymnasium; want to go with me?"

Joel stopped his capering at once, this new idea thrusting out the old one.

"Don't I, though!" he cried, with a nod at Polly and her friends. "But I'll find out when I do get home," the nod declared plainly.

But Jasper also nodded. He said, "He won't get home till late; depend on me." And then "Come on, Joe," he cried; "I'm going to walk," and they were off.

Alexia pinched Polly's gray woollen jacket sleeve convulsively. "What an escape," she breathed.

"Here comes Percy," cried Polly nervously, and she broke away from her and the other girls, and ran to meet him, and the two boys following.

"Where's Jasper?" asked Percy, rendered quite important in air and step, from his encounter with the baggage officials.

"Oh! he isn't going home with us," said Polly. "Come, do let us get in," and she scampered off to the carriage and climbed within.

"That's funny," said Percy, jumping in after.

Van opened his lips to tell where Jasper had gone, but remembering Percy's delight in such an expedition, he closed them quickly, and added himself to the company in the carriage. Davie followed, and closed the door quickly.

"Stop! where's Joel?" asked Percy. "Thomas, we've forgotton Joe," rapping on the glass to the coachman.

"No, we haven't; he isn't going to drive," said Polly.

"Oh!" and Percy, thinking that Joel had stolen a march on them on his good strong legs, now cried lustily, "Go on, Thomas; get ahead as fast as you can," and presently he was lost in the babel of laughter and chatter going on in the coach.

"I've a piece of news," presently cried Van in a lull. "Davie's bringing home a prize; first in classics, you know."

"Oh, Davie!" screamed Polly, and she leaned over to throw her arms around him; "Mamsie will be so glad. Davie, you can't think how glad she'll be!"

Davie's brown cheek glowed. "It isn't much," he said simply, "there were so many prizes given out."

"Well, you've taken one," cried Polly, saying the blissful words over and over. "How perfectly elegant!"

Van drummed on the carriage window discontentedly. "I could have taken one if I'd had the mind to."

"Hoh-oh!" shouted Percy over in his corner. "Well, you didn't have the mind; that's what was wanting."

"You keep still," cried Van, flaming up, and whirling away from his window. "You didn't take any, either. Polly, his head was under water all the time, unless some of the boys tugged him along every day. We hardly got him home at all."

"No such thing," contradicted Percy flatly, his face growing red. "Polly, he tells perfectly awful yarns. You mustn't believe him, Polly. You won't, will you?" He leaned over appealingly toward her.

"Oh! don't, don't," cried Polly, quite dismayed, "talk so to each other."

" Well, he's so hateful," cried Van, " and the airs he gives himself! I can't stand them, Polly, you know " —

"And he's just as mean," cried Percy vindictively. " Oh! you can't think, Polly. Here we are," as Thomas gave a grand flourish through the stone gateway, and up to the steps.

" I'll help you out," and he sprang out first.

" No, I will," declared Van, opening the door on the other side, jumping out and running around the carriage. " Here, Polly, take my hand, do."

" No, I got here first," said Percy eagerly, his brown glove extended quite beyond Van's hand.

" I don't want any one to help me, who speaks so to his brother," said Polly in a low voice, and with her most superb air stepping down alone, she ran up the steps to leave them staring in each other's faces.

Here everybody came hurrying out to the porch, and they were soon drawn into the warm loving welcome awaiting them.

" Oh, Félicie! I don't want that dress," said Polly as she ran into her room after dinner, to

Mrs. Whitney's French maid, "I'm going to wear my brown cashmere."

"Oh, Mademoiselle!" remonstrated Félicie, adjusting the ruffle in the neck of the white nun's veiling over her arm.

"Oh, no, Polly! I wouldn't," began Mrs. Pepper, coming in, "the white one is better for to-night."

"Mamsie!" cried Polly, breaking away from the mirror where she was pulling into place the bright brown waves over her forehead, "how lovely! you've put on your black silk; and your hair is just beautiful!"

"Madame has ze fine hair," said Félicie, "only I wish zee would gif it to me to prepaire."

"Yes, I have good hair," said Mrs. Pepper, "and I'm thankful for it. No one looks dressed up, in my opinion, with a ragged head. The finer the gown, the worse it makes careless hair look. No, Polly, I wouldn't wear the brown dress to-night."

"Why, Mamsie!" exclaimed Polly in surprise, "I thought you'd say it was just the thing when only the girls and Jap! friends are coming to the play. Besides, I don't want to look too dressed up; the Princess ought to be the only one in a white gown."

"You won't be too conspicious," said her mother; adding slowly, "you might wear the nun's veiling well enough as you haven't any part in the play, Polly," and she scanned the rosy face keenly.

"I don't want any part," cried Polly; "they all play better than I do. Somebody must see that everything goes off well behind the scenes; that's my place, Mamsie. Besides, you forget I am to play my sonata."

"I don't forget," said her mother; "all the more reason you should wear the white gown, then."

"All right," cried Polly, merrily dashing across the room to Félicie, "put it over my head, do. Well, I'm glad you think it is right to wear it, Mamsie," as the soft folds fell around her. "I just love this dress. Oh, Auntie! how perfectly exquisite!"

Mrs. Whitney came in smilingly and put a kiss on the tall girl's cheek. "Do I look nicely ? " she asked naively, turning around under the chandelier.

" Nicely ? " exclaimed Polly, lifting her hands, " why you are fresh from fairyland. You are so good to put on that lovely blue moiré and your diamond cross, just for the boys and girls."

" I am glad you like it," said Mrs. Whitney hastily. " Now, Polly, don't you worry about anything; I'll see that the last things are done."

" Well, I am worrying," confessed Polly, quite in a tremble; " I must see to one corner of the private box for the boys. You know the last India shawl you lent me wasn't pinned up straight and I couldn't fix it, for Van wanted me just then, and I couldn't get away without his suspecting something. Oh, Auntie! if you would see to that."

" I will," said Mrs. Whitney, not daring to look at Mrs. Pepper, " and to all the other things; don't give a thought to them, Polly."

" How good you are," cried Polly with a sigh of relief. " Oh, Auntie! we couldn't do anything without you."

" And you don't need to go into the drawing-room at all," said Mrs. Whitney, going to the door   " Just keep behind the scenes, and get your actors and Phronsie ready, and your mother and I will receive your friends. Come, Mrs. Pepper."

" That is splendid," cried Polly, left behind with the maid, " now I can get ready without flying into a flurry, Félicie; and then for Phronsie and the rest! "

" There is a dreadful commotion in there among the audience," said Jasper, out in the green room; " I imagine every one who had an ' invite,' has come. But I don't see how they can make such a noise."

" Oh! a few girls and boys make just about as much confusion as a good many," observed Polly. " Jasper, wouldn't you like to see Joel's eyes when Aunt Whitney leads him into the private box? " she allowed herself time to ex- claim.

" Yes," laughed Jasper, pulling out his watch from beneath his dragon-skin; " well, we have only five minutes more, Polly. We must have the curtain up sharp."

" O dear, dear! " cried Polly, flying here and

there to bestow last touches on the different members of her cast. "Now, Clare, you must remember not to give such a shriek when you go on, mustn't he, Jappy? Just a dull, sullen roar, your part is."

"Well, I'm nearly dead under here," cried Clare, glaring beneath his dragon face. "I'll shriek, or roar, just as I like, so!"

"Very well," said Polly, "I don't know but it's as well, after all, that you are cross; you'll be more effective," she added coolly. "Let me see — oh! the door of the cave wants a bit more of gray moss; it looks thin where it hangs over. You get it, will you, Hannah?" to one of the maids who was helping.

"And just one thing more," scanning hastily the stage setting, "another Chinese lantern is needed right here," going toward the front of the stage, "and that green bush is tumbling over; do set it straight, somebody; there now, I believe everything is all ready. Now let us peep out of the curtain, and get one good look at the audience. Come, Phronsie, here's a fine place; come, boys!"

The different members of the cast now applied their eyes to as many cracks in the curtain as could be hastily managed.

There was a breathing space.

"What, what?" cried Polly, gazing into the sea of faces, and the dragons nearly knocked the Princess over as Mr. King gave the signal for the band stationed in the wide hall, to send out their merriest strains.

CHAPTER V.

AFTER THE PLAY.

IT was all over. Phronsie had been swept off, a vision of loveliness, to the cave; the dragons had roared their loudest, and the gallant knight had covered himself with glory in the brilliant rescue of the Princess; the little page had won the hearts of all the ladies; Mr. King had applauded himself hoarse, especially during the delivery of the prologue, when " I cry you mercy, sirs, and ladies fair," rang out; the musical efforts of Polly and Jasper in the " Wait " between the two acts were over, and the crowded house, in every way possible, had expressed itself delighted with all things from beginning to end.

" Phronsie, Phronsie, they're calling you," whispered Polly excitedly, out in the green room.

"Come, Princess." The head dragon held out his hand. "Hurry dear! See the flowers!"

"They can't be for me," said Phronsie, standing quite still; "Polly has done all the work; they're hers."

"Nonsense, child!" cried Polly, giving her a gentle push forward. "Go on, and take them."

"Polly, you come too," begged Phronsie, refusing to stir, and holding her by the gown.

"I can't, Phronsie," cried Polly in distress; "don't you see they haven't called me. Go on, child, if you love me," she implored.

Phronsie, not being able to resist this, dropped Polly's gown and floated before the footlights.

"Thank you," she said, bowing gravely to the sea of faces, as her hands were filled with roses, "but I shall give these to Polly, because we couldn't any of us have done it without her." And so she brought them back to put into dismayed Polly's lap.

"The authors — the authors of the play!" cried a strong voice, privately urged on by Mr. King.

"There, now's your turn," cried Clare to Polly. "And go ahead, old dragon," to Jasper, "make your prettiest bow."

So the chief dragon led up blushing Polly to the front of the stage, to hear a neat little speech from Mr. Alstyne, thanking them for the pleasure of the evening and congratulating them on its success; and the band played again, the camp chairs were folded up and removed, the green-room and stage were deserted, and actors and audience mingled in a gay, confusing throng.

Phronsie, in her little silver and white gown and gleaming cap, began to wander among the guests, unconscious that she had not on the red cashmere dress she had worn all day. Groups stopped their conversation to take her into their midst, passing her on at last as one might hand over a precious parcel to the next waiting hands. Polly, seeing that she was well cared for, gave herself up to the enjoyment of the evening.

"Well, sir, how did you like it?" asked Jasper, with a small pat on Joel's back.

"Well enough," said Joel, "but why didn't

you make more of it? You could have crawled up on top of the cave, and slashed around there; and you old dragons were just three muffs in the last act. I'd rather have had Polly in the play; she's twice the 'go' in her."

"So would we all have preferred Polly," cried Jasper, bursting into a laugh, "but she wouldn't act — she directed everything; she was all the play, in fact."

Polly meanwhile was saying to Pickering Dodge, "No, not to-night; you must dance with one of the other girls."

"But I don't choose to dance with anybody but you," said Pickering, holding out his hand. "Come, Polly, you can't refuse; they're forming the Lancers. Hurry!"

Polly's feet twitched nervously under her white gown, and she longed more than ever after the excitement she had passed through, to lose herself in the witching music, and the mazy dance. She hesitated a bit, but just then glancing across the room, "Come," she said, "I want you to dance with Ray Simmons. You can't refuse," using his own words; and before he was conscious how it was done, he was by Ray's side, and asking for the pleasure of the dance.

Polly stood quite still and saw them go away and take the last places in the set, and a sorry little droop fell upon the curves of the laughing mouth. She was very tired, and the elation that had possessed her over the success of the evening was fast dropping out, now that everybody was enjoying themselves in their own way, leaving her alone. She felt left out in the cold; and though she fought against it, a faint feeling of regret stole over her for what she had done. She almost wished she was standing there by the side of Pickering Dodge, one of the bright group on whom the eyes of the older people were all turned, as they waited for the first figure to begin.

"Well, Polly" — it was Mr. Alstyne who spoke, and he acted as if he had come to stay by her side — "you've covered yourself with glory this evening."

"Have I, sir?" asked Polly absently, wishing there had been less of the glory, and a little more fun.

"Yes, indeed," said Mr. Alstyne, his keen eyes searching her face. "Well, now, Polly, your dragons, although not exactly like any living ones extant, made me think of some I saw at the Zoo, in London. Do you want me to tell you how?"

"Oh! if you please," cried Polly, her color coming back, and beginning to forget the dance and the dancers.

"Let us sit down here, then," said Mr. Alstyne, drawing her off to two chairs in a corner, "and you shall have the tale. No pun, Polly, you know." And he plunged into it at once.

"Yes, Alstyne has her all right," Mr. King was saying at the further end of the drawing-room to Mrs. Pepper; he spied the whole thing; "he'll take care of her, you may depend."

And two more people had seen; one was Jasper. Nevertheless his partner, Alexia Rhys, thought it necessary to enlighten him.

"Just think, Polly's given up her chance with the best dancer in the room, and sent

Pickering Dodge off with that horrid Ray Simmons."

Jasper pretended not to hear. " This is our figure," he said hastily, and they whirled off, finished it, and were back again.

" Isn't she a goose? " as he fanned her, and tried to introduce another subject.

" I suppose she best pleases herself," said the boy indifferently. " Why should any one else interfere in the matter? "

" But some one else ought to interfere," cried Alexia, with a little pout, provoked at his indifference; " that's just the way she does in school all the time. Oh! I'm vexed at her, I can tell you. She's so silly — dear me, it's our turn again."

By the next interim she had forgotten all about Polly and whether she was having a nice time or the stupidest one imaginable, for Joel, who held dancing in great contempt, sauntered up.

" Aren't you glad now that you didn't find out about the secret? " cried Alexia radiantly. " Oh! you are such a nuisance, Joey," she added frankly.

" Phooh! " exclaimed Joel, " it wasn't worth finding out, that old secret.   But it's as good as girls ever get up," he finished with a supercilious air.

" It was a perfectly splendid play! " cried Alexia, " and much too good for a lot of boys. Goodness, Joey, I wouldn't celebrate if you four were coming home from school to our house.   I'd have the jollification the night before you went back."

" I wouldn't go home if 'twas to your house," declared Joel with equal candor.   " I'd run off to sea, first."

" Come, come, you two, stop sparring," cried Jasper, holding out his hand; " its our turn again, Alexia.   Joel, take yourself off."

Alexia flashing Joel a bright, making-up smile, dashed off into the figure.

" Good-by," said Joel with a smile as cheery, for he really liked her the best of all Polly's girl friends.

After the dance, supper was announced, and everybody marched out to the supper room; the dancers with their partners following.

" Will you allow me? " Mr. Alstyne seeing

the movement, got out of his chair and offered his arm to Polly with a courtly bow.

"Oh! don't think of me, sir," she began, blushing very hard. "Joel will look out for me."

"I much prefer waiting upon Miss Polly Pepper to any other lady in the room," said Mr. Alstyne, with another bow, courtlier than the first, "since Mrs. Alstyne is provided for. See, Polly, Mr. King is taking her out. And your mother has her cavalier, in Mr. Cabot; and Mrs. Whitney has already gone out with Mr. Fairfax. So if you don't accept my services, I shall be entirely left out in the cold" He stood offering his arm, and Polly, laughing merrily, put her hand within it.

"It's very good of you, sir," she said simply, as they fell into step and joined the procession.

"I'm afraid if you had trusted to Joel's tender mercies, you would have fared hardly," said Mr. Alstyne, laughing. "Look, Polly, over yonder in the corner." They were just passing into the supper room, and now caught sight of Joel chatting away to a very pretty little creature, in blue and white, as busily and unconcernedly as if he had done that sort of thing for years.

"Why!" cried Polly quite aghast, "that can't be Joel. He just hates girls, you know, Mr. Alstyne, and never goes to parties."

"He seems to be able to endure it all very well to-night," said her companion dryly. "Shall I get you an ice, Miss Polly?"

"Yes, thank you," said Polly absently, not being able to take her eyes from Joel and his friend. At last, by the force of attraction, he turned and looked at her. But instead of showing self-consciousness, his round eyes surveyed her coolly, while he went on talking and laughing with the little blue-and-white thing.

"Polly, Polly," exclaimed Alexia Rhys, hurrying up, while Jasper was storming the supper table for her, "do look at Joel Pepper! He actually brought in a girl to supper!"

"I see," said Polly, gazing at the two in a fascinated way.

"On the other hand," said Alexia, sending swift, bird-like glances around the supper room, "there are Van and Percy moping off by themselves as if they hadn't a friend in the world. What a pity; they used to be so lively at parties."

Polly wrenched her gaze away from the astonishing sight on which it had been fixed, and following Alexia's glance, took a keen look over at the young Whitneys. "Oh! oh! I must go to them," she cried remorsefully. "Tell Mr. Alstyne, please, when he comes back, where I am," and without another word she dashed back of some gaily dressed ladies just entering the supper room, and was out of the door.

"If I ever did!" cried Alexia irritably to herself, "see anything so queer! Now she thinks she must race after those boys. I wish I'd kept still. Jasper, she's just as funny as ever," as he came up with a plate of salad, and some oysters.

"Who?" said the boy; "is this right, Alexia?" offering the plate.

"Why, Polly," said Alexia; "yes, that's lovely," with a comforted glance at the plate and its contents. "Oh! she's gone off, Mr. Alstyne," to that gentleman, approaching with

Polly's ice. "You can't expect her to stay for the goodies," beginning to nibble at her own.

"Where is she?" cried Mr. Alstyne, laughing, and sweeping the room with his brown eyes. "Oh! I see," his glance lighting on the Whitney boys' corner.

"Yes, she told me to tell you," said Alexia, between her mouthfuls of salad and oyster, "where she is," as he started.

"Oh, Percy and Van!" Polly was whispering hurriedly, "I'm sorry I hurt your feelings, only it was so very dreadful, you know, to hear you go on so to each other."

"We didn't mean anything," said Percy, pushing one foot back and forth in an embarrassed way, and looking as if he did not know what to do with his hands, which confused him more than anything else, as he had been quite sure of them on all previous occasions.

Van thrust his into his pockets, and seemed on the point of whistling, but remembering where he was, took his lips speedily out of their curves, and looked the other way.

Just then Mr. Alstyne came up.

"Oh!" cried Polly suddenly, the color rushing over her face. "Could you, Mr. Alstyne, give that to some one else? Percy and Van are going to wait upon me."

"Yes, indeed," said Mr. Alstyne in a flash, "nothing easier;" and he disappeared as suddenly as he came.

"Now, boys," said Polly, turning back to them and whispering busily, "I know you won't ever say such perfectly dreadful things to each other again. And so I'm going to ask you both to get me something to eat, will you?"

"How do you know we won't?" cried Percy slowly. He was sorry enough for the episode in the coach, yet couldn't resist the temptation to show he was not to be driven.

"Because I shall then have nothing whatever to eat," said Polly merrily, "for of course I can't take a bit from anybody else after refusing Mr. Alstyne's kindness. Don't you see? Oh, Percy! you wouldn't quite do that?"

Van laughed. "She's got us, Percy," he

said, " quite fast. You know you won't fight, and I won't again; we both said so a little while back; so what's the good of holding out now? "

Percy drew himself up very slowly and decidedly. " I won't trouble you so again, Polly," holding out his hand. " Now would you like oysters? " all in the same breath.

" And here's mine," cried Van, extending his brown one. " Can't I bring you some salad? "

" Yes, yes," cried Polly gaily, and she released their hands after a cordial grasp. " You may bring me everything straight through, boys," as they rushed off, heads erect, to the crowded supper-table.

" You've had a good time? " asked Mrs. Pepper slowly, with a keen glance into the flushed face and sparkling eyes, as they turned up the gas in Polly's bedroom. " Dear me! it is half-past eleven."

" Splendid," said Polly, shaking herself free from the white gown and beginning to braid her hair for the night. " Percy and Van were perfectly lovely, and Mr. Alstyne was so good to me. And oh! Mamsie, isn't dear Mr. King just the dearest dear, to give all this to the boys? We haven't thanked him half enough."

"He is indeed," said Mrs. Pepper heartily. "Why, where is Phronsie?" looking around the room.

"She was right back of you," said Polly. "She wanted to take off her things herself. Did you ever see such a sweet "— she began, but Mrs. Pepper did not stop to hear, hurrying out to the adjoining room, shared by the mother and her baby.

"She isn't here," Polly heard her say in bewildered tones. So Polly, her long hair blown about her face, ran in, brush in hand.

"Why, where " — she began laughingly.

"She wouldn't go down-stairs, I don't think," said Mrs. Pepper, peering in all the corners, and even meditating a look under the bed.

"No, no," cried Polly, "the lights are all turned out," investigating all possible and impossible nooks that a mouse could creep into. "Where can she be? Phronsie — Phronsie!"

"Well, of course she is down-stairs," declared Mrs. Pepper at last, hurrying out of the room.

"Take a candle, Mamsie, you'll fall," cried Polly, and throwing on her bath wrapper, she seized the light from the mantel and hurried after her.

Half-way down she could hear Phronsie's gay little laugh, and catch the words "Good-night, my dear Grandpapa," and then she came slowly out from Mr. King's sitting-room, and softly closed the door.

"Phronsie!" exclaimed Polly, sitting down on the middle of the stairs, the candle shaking ominously, "how could" —

"Hush!" said Mrs. Pepper, who had fumbled her way along the hall. "Don't say anything. Oh, Phronsie dear, so you went down to bid Grandpapa good-night, did you?"

Phronsie turned a glance of gentle surprise on her mother, and then looked up at Polly.

"No, not exactly to bid him good-night," she said slowly. "I was afraid he was sick; I heard him coughing, so I went down."

"He is quite well, isn't he?" asked Mrs.

Pepper. "Here, give me your hand, child; we must get up to bed."

"Oh, yes! he is quite really and truly all well," declared Phronsie, breaking into another glad little laugh. "He said he never had such a beautiful time in his life, and he is just as well as he can be. Oh, Polly!" as she picked up her Princess gown and prepared to ascend the stairs, "how funny you look sitting there!"

"Funny?" said Polly grimly. "I dare say, and I feel funny too, Phronsie."

CHAPTER VI.

THE LITTLE BROWN HOUSE.

THEY were all sitting around the library fire; Polly under the pretext of holding Phronsie's head in her lap, was sitting on the rug beside her, the boys on either hand; old Mr. King was marching up and down the long room, and looking at them. The merriest of stories had been told, Polly urging on all the school records of jolly times, and those not so enjoyable; songs had been sung, and all sorts of nonsense aired. At last Joel sprang up and ran over to pace by the old gentleman's side.

"Christmas was good enough," said the boy, by way of beginning conversation.

"Hey?" responded the old gentleman, looking down at him, "I should think it was. Well, and how about the wonderful play on the

98

twenty-first? And that was good enough, too, I dare say."

"That was well enough," said Joel indifferently, "I don't care for such stuff, though."

"Tut — tut!" cried Mr. King in pretended anger, "now I won't have anything said against that wonderful production. Not a thing, sir, do you hear?"

Joel laughed, his chubby face twinkling all over in secret amusement. "Well, I know something better, if you'll only let us do it, sir, than a hundred old plays."

"And pray what is it?" demanded Mr. King, "let's have it at once. But the idea of surpassing the play! Oh, no, no, it can't be done, sir!"

"It's to go and see the Little Brown House," said Joel, standing up on his tiptoes to a level with the old gentleman's ear, and one eye looking backward to see that nobody heard.

Mr. King started, pulled his handsome moustache thoughtfully, looked at Joel sharply, and then over at the group in the firelight.

"They don't know anything about it," cried the boy in a whisper, "don't tell them, it's my secret, and yours," added generously. "Oh! if we might only go and look at it."

"It's winter," observed the old gentleman, and stepping to the window he put aside the draperies, to peer out into the black evening. "Yes, it really is winter," he added with a shiver, to the boy who was close behind, and as if no longer in doubt about it, he added most emphatically, "it really is winter, Joel."

"Well, but you never saw anything like it, how magnificent winter is in Badgertown," cried Joel in an excited whisper. "Such hills to coast down; the snow is always crisp there, sir, not like this dirty town mud. And the air is as dry as punk," he added artfully. "Oh! 'twould be such a lark;" he actually clasped his hands.

"Badgertown isn't so very far off," said Mr. King thoughtfully, "I'll think about it and see if we can manage it."

"Ugh-ow!" squealed Joel, utterly forgetful of his caution of secrecy, "we can, we can; we can open the little brown house, and build great fires there, and " —

But he got no further. Into the midst of

Van's liveliest sally, came the words " little brown house," bringing all the young people to their feet, Phronsie running to the old gentleman's side, with, " What is it, Grandpapa? He said little brown house."

" Get away! " cried Joel crossly to the besiegers, each and all wildly clamoring. " What is it? What are you talking about? It's my secret," he cried, " and his," pointing with a dismayed finger to Mr. King.

" Well, it isn't a secret any longer," cried Polly, flushing with excitement. " You said ' little brown house,' we heard you just as plainly; and you're getting up something, I know you are."

" People don't usually select a roomful of listeners, and then shout out their secrets," said Jasper. " You are in for it now, Joe, and no mistake. Go ahead, old fellow, and give us the rest of it."

Joel whirled away from them all in desperation.

" You might as well," laughed the old gentleman, " the mischief is done now, and no mistake."

So Joel, thus set upon, allowed the whole beautiful plan to be wrung from him, by slow and torturing installments; how they all were to go to Badgertown, open the little brown house, and stay there — here he glanced at Mr. King — "perhaps a week," he brought out suddenly, filling the time with all sorts of frolics, and playing they were there again, and really and truly living in the old home.

At last it was all out, to be received in different ways by the listeners.

"Oh, Joe!" cried Davie with shining eyes. "We never could come away again if we once get there, never!"

Polly stood quite still, a mist gathering before her glad eyes, out of which she dimly saw the little brown house arise and beckon to her.

Phronsie jumped up and down and clapped her hands in glee. "Oh, Grandpapa, Grandpapa!" she screamed, "please take us to the little brown house, please!"

That settled it. "I do not think we need to consider it longer," said Mr. King, glancing at Ben, whose face told what he thought, "children, we will go — that is, if Mrs. Pepper says yes."

"I will ask her," cried Joel with a howl, springing off.

"Come on," cried Jasper, "let's all 'be in at the death.'" And the library was deserted in a twinkling.

But mother was nowhere to be found. "Upstairs, down-stairs, and in the lady's chamber," they sought her wildly and thoroughly.

"Oh! I forgot," exclaimed Polly, when at last they gathered in the wide hall, disposing themselves on the chairs and along the stairs, all tired out. "She has gone to evening meeting with Auntie. How stupid in me not to remember that."

"Well, I declare!" cried a voice above them, and looking up they met the cold blue eyes of Mrs. Chatterton regarding them over the railing. "Cousin Horatio, do you keep a menagerie, or a well-ordered house, I beg to inquire?"

"A menagerie," said Mr. King coolly, leaning on the balustrade at the foot of the stairs, and looking up at her. " All sorts of strange animals wander in here, Cousin."

" Hum; I understand. I'm not so dull as you think. Well, you've changed, let me tell you, vastly, and not for the better either, in the last six years. Who would ever suppose I see before me fastidious Horatio King!" she exclaimed, lifting her long thin hands to show him their horror-stricken palms.

" I dare say, I dare say, Cousin Eunice," assented Mr. King carelessly, " but I consider all you say as a compliment."

" Compliment?" she repeated disdainfully, and added with a rising note of anger, forgetting herself, " there's no fool like an old fool."

" So I think," said Mr. King in the same tone as before. " Children, come into my room now, and close the door." And Cousin Eunice was left to air further opinions to her own ear.

But when Mother Pepper and Mrs. Whitney did come home from the meeting, oh! what a time there was. They all fell upon her, as soon as the door opened, and the whole air was filled with "Little brown house." "May we — may we?" "A whole week." "Two days, Mamsie, do say yes," and Phronsie's glad little chirp "Grandpapa wants to go, he does!" ending every other exclamation.

"What a babel," cried Mrs. Pepper, her black eyes roving over the excited group. "Now what is it all about? Baby, you tell mother first."

Phronsie was not too big to jump into the comfortable lap, and while her fingers played with the bonnet strings, she laid the whole delightful plan open, the others hanging over them in ill-suppressed excitement.

"Well, you see, Mamsie," she began deliberately.

"Oh! you are so slow, Phronsie," exclaimed Polly, "do hurry."

"Let her take her own time," said Mr. King, "go on, child."

"Dear Grandpapa," proceeded Phronsie, turning her yellow head to look at him, her hand yet among the bonnet strings, "is going to take us all, every sin-gle one, to see the little brown house, and just touch it once, and be sure it's there, and peek in the doors and windows and " —

"No, no," roared Joel, "we're going to stay, and a week too," hopping confidently up and down.

"Oh, Joe! not a week," corrected Polly with glowing cheeks, "perhaps two days; we don't know yet."

"Three — three," begged Van, pushing his head further into the centre of the group. "Mrs. Pepper, do say you want to stay three days," he begged.

"I haven't said I wanted to go yet," she answered with a smile.

"Now, every one of you keep quiet," commanded Mr. King, raising his hand, "or you'll spoil the whole thing. Phronsie shall tell her story as she likes."

Thereupon the rest, with the shadow of his warning that the whole might be spoiled, fell back to a vigorous restraint once more.

"Perhaps," cried Phronsie with shining eyes, and grasping the strings tighter she leaned forward and pressed her red lips on the mother's mouth, " we'll go in and stay. Oh, Mamsie!"

That " Oh, Mamsie!" carried the day, and every one hanging on the conversation, knew as soon as they heard it, that a victory had been won.

" It's no use to contend against the Fates," said Mrs. Whitney, laughing, " Mrs. Pepper, you and I know that."

" That's so," cried old Mr. King, " and whoever finds it out early in life, is the lucky one. Now, children, off with you and talk it over," he cried, dismissing them as if they were all below their teens. " I want to talk with Mrs. Pepper now."

And in two days they were ready to go. Mrs. Chatterton with nose high in the air, and plentiful expressions of disgust at such a midwinter expedition, taking herself off to make a visit of corresponding length to some distant relatives.

" I hope and pray this may not get into a society paper," she cried at the last, as she was seated in the carriage, " but of course it will; *outré* things always do.   And we shall be disgraced for life. One comfort remains to me, I am not in it."

Mr. King, holding the carriage door, laughed long and loudly. "No, Cousin Eunice," he said, "you are not in it. Take comfort in that thought. Good-by," and the carriage rolled off.

Mother Pepper and the "five little Peppers" were going back to the little brown house. "Really and truly we are," as Phronsie kept saying over and over again with every revolution of the car-wheels, in a crooning fashion, and making it impossible for Mr. King to shiver in apprehension at the step he was taking. Were not two cases of blankets and household comforts safely packed away in the luggage car? "It's not such a dreadful risk," said the old gentleman gruffly to himself, "it's quite a common occurrence nowadays to take a winter outing in the country. We're all right," and he re-enforced himself further by frequent glances at Mrs. Pepper's black bonnet, two seats off.

It was to be a three-days' frolic, after all. Not that the whole party were to stay in the little brown house. O dear, no! how could

they? It was only big enough for the Peppers.
So Mrs. Whitney and her three boys, with Mr.
King, and Jasper, who concealed many disappointed feelings, planned to settle down in
the old hotel at Hingham.

And before anybody imagined they could
reach there so soon, there they were at Badgertown Centre, to find Mr. Tisbett waiting
there on his stage-box as if he had not stirred
from it for five years.

"Sho, now!" he called out from his elevated position to Mrs. Pepper, as she stepped
down from the car, "it's good to see you,
though. Land! how many of ye be there?
And is that Phronsie? Sho, now!"

"Did you get my letter?" exclaimed Mother
Pepper to Mrs. Henderson, who was pressing
up to grasp her hand, and preparing to fall on
the young folks separately. The parson stood
just back, biding his time with a smile.

"Is it possible?" he exclaimed; "are these
tall boys and girls the five little Peppers? It
can't be, Mrs. Pepper," as at last he had her
hand. "You are imposing on us."

And then the village people who had held

back until their pastor and his wife paid their respects, rushed up and claimed their rights, and it was high holiday indeed for Badgertown

"My goodness!" exclaimed Mr. King at a little remove and viewing the scene with great disfavor, "this is worse than the danger of taking cold. Have they no sense, to carry on like this?"

"They're so glad to see the Peppers again, father," said Mrs. Whitney with bright eyes. "You took them away from all these good people, you know; it's but fair to give them up for one day."

The old gentleman fumed and fretted, however, in a subdued fashion; at last wisely turning his back, he began to stalk down the platform, under pretense of examining the landscape.

"Your friends will stay with us," Mrs. Henderson was saying in a gently decisive manner, "the old parsonage is big enough," she added with a laugh.

"Oh! you are so good and thoughtful, dear Mrs. Henderson," cried Mrs. Pepper with de-

light at the thought of the homelike warmth
of the parsonage life awaiting the old gentleman, for whom she was dreading the dreary
hotel.

"I'm good to ourselves," declared the parson's wife gaily.

Jasper gave a shout when the new arrange-
ment was declared, as it presently was by Percy
and Van, who flung themselves after him as
he was seeing to the luggage with Ben, and
his face glowed with the greatest satisfaction.

"That is jolly," he exclaimed, "and that's
a fact! Now, Ben, we're but a stone's throw
apart. Rather different, isn't it, old fellow,
from the time when I used to race over from
Hingham with Prince at my heels?"

Dr. Fisher's little thin, wiry figure was now
seen advancing upon the central group, and
everybody fell away to let him have his chance
to welcome the Peppers.

"I couldn't get here before," he cried, his
eyes glowing behind his spectacles. "I've left
a very sick patient. This is good," he took
them all in with a loving glance, but his hand

held to Polly. "Now I'm going to drive you down in my gig," he said to her at last. "Will you come?"

"Yes, indeed," cried Polly in delight, as her mother smiled approval, and she ran off to let him help her in. "It's only yesterday since you took me to drive, Dr. Fisher, and you gave me my stove — is it?" And so she rambled on, the little doctor quite charmed to hear it all.

But Mr. Tisbett had a truly dreadful time placing his party in the old stage, as the townsfolk, fearful that so good a chance for seeing the Peppers would not happen during the three days' stay, insisted on crowding up close to the ancient vehicle, and getting in everybody's way, thereby calling forth some exclamations from Mr. King that could not be ragarded as exactly complimentary. And quite sure that he was a frightful tyrant, they fell back with many a pitying glance at the Pepper family whom he was endeavoring to assist into their places.

At last it was all accomplished in some way, and Mr. Tisbett cracked his whip, Mrs. Pepper and Phronsie leaned out of the window to

bow right and left into smiling faces, Ben and
Davie did the same over their heads.

"Good-by," sang out Joel, whom the stage
driver had taken up beside him. Here we are,
off for the 'little brown house.' G'lang!"

CHAPTER VII.

OLD TIMES AGAIN

"DON'T let me look — oh! don't let me look," cried Polly in the old gig, and twisting around, she hid her face against the faded green cloth side. "I ought not to see the little brown house before Mamsie and the others do."

"I'll turn down the lane," said the little doctor, "so"; and suiting the action to the word, Polly could feel that they were winding down the narrow little road over toward Grandma Bascom's. She could almost smell the violets and anemones under the carpet of snow, and could scarcely restrain herself from jumping out for a riotous run.

"Don't go too far away," she cried in sudden alarm. "We must be there by the time the stage does." And she applied her eye to the little circular glass in the back of the gig. "Will it never come — oh! here it is, here it is, dear Dr. Fisher." And with a quick flourish around of the old horse, they were soon before the little brown house, and helping out the inmates of the stage, who with more speed than grace were hurrying over the steps.

Joel was down before Mr. Tisbett had fairly drawn up in front of the gate. "Hold on," roared the stage driver, "I don't want you to break your neck with me."

"It's really here!" cried Phronsie with wide eyes, standing quite still on a hummock of frozen snow, with her eyes riveted on the house. "It really is!" Polly had raced up the winding path, and over the flat stone to drop a kiss on the little old door.

"Oh! oh! Mamsie, do come!" she cried to Mrs. Pepper on the path.

"Hum! I think, Jasper, you and I will let them alone for a few moments," said Mr. King, who was still within the stage. "Here, my good fellow," to Mr. Tisbett, "you say it's all comfortable in there for them?"

"Yes, yes, sir," said Mr. Tisbett heartily.

" Good land! Mis' Henderson had her boys come down airly this mornin' and make the fires; and there's a mighty sight of things to eat." The stage-driver put one foot on the hind wheel to facilitate conversation, and smacked his lips.

" All very well. Now you may drive us down the road a bit," said Mr. King, withdrawing his head to the depths of the lumbering old vehicle again.

" Ain't goin' in?" cried Mr. Tisbett, opening his round eyes at him in astonishment.

" Get up and drive us on, I say," commanded the old gentleman, " and cease your talking," which had the effect to send honest Mr. Tisbett clambering expeditiously up to the box, where he presently revenged himself by driving furiously over all the hard frozen ruts he could quickly select, determined not to stop till he was obliged to.

" Goodness!" exclaimed Mr. King within, holding to the strap at the side, as well as to the leather band of the swinging seat in front. " What an abominable road!"

" The road is well enough," said Jasper, who

couldn't bear to have a word uttered against Badgertown, "it's the fellow's driving that makes it rough. Here, can't you be a little more careful to keep the road?" he called, thrusting his head out of the window. But he only narrowly escaped losing his brown traveling cap for his pains, as the stage gave a worse lurch than before, to introduce a series of creakings and joltings hitherto unparalleled.

"I cannot endure this much longer," said old Mr. King, growing white around the mouth, and wishing he had strength for one-half the exclamations he felt inwardly capable of. Outside, honest Mr. Tisbett was taking solid comfort in the reflection that he was teaching a rich city man that he could not approach with anything less than respect, a citizen of Badgertown.

"Ain't I as good as he?" cried Mr. Tisbett to himself, with an extra cut to the off horse, as he spied a sharp ragged edge of ice along the cart track in front of him. "Now that's good; that'll shake him," he added cheerfully. "Land! but I hain't been spoke to so since I was sassed at school by Jim Bently, and then I licked him enough to pay twice over. G'lang there — easy! "

The first thing he knew, one of the glass windows was shivered to fragments; the bits flying off along the quiet road, to fall a gleaming shower upon the snow.

"Whoa! " called Mr. Tisbett, to his smoking horses, and leaning over, he cried, " What's the matter in there? "

"The matter is," said Jasper, putting his face out, " that as I could not possibly make you hear my calls, I chose to break the window. Have the goodness to let my father and me at once out of this vehicle."

Mr. Tisbett got down slowly over the wheel. " Beg your pardon," he said awkwardly, pulling open the door, " ain't you goin' to ride back? "

"Heavens! " cried Mr. King. He was glad to find he could ejaculate so much as he tremblingly worked his way out to *terra firma*. " Nothing on earth would tempt me to step foot inside there again."

"Here is the money for your window," said Jasper, putting a bill into the fur mitten, covering Mr. Tisbett's brawny right hand. "Kindly bring our traps to the little brown house; here, father, take my arm," and he ran after the tall figure, picking its way along the frozen road.

"Hey — what's this?" exclaimed Mr. Tisbett, looking into the center of his fur mitten, "five dollars! Gee — thumps! I ain't a-goin' to take it, after shaking that old party almost to pieces."

He stood staring at the bill in stupid perplexity till the uneasy movements of his horses warned him that his position was not exactly the proper one for a stage-driver who was on his box from morning till night, so he clambered over the wheel, full of vexed thoughts, and carefully tucked the bill under the old cushion before he took his seat.

"I'll give it back to him, that's cert'in," he said, picking up the reins, "and p'raps they've had enough walkin' so they'll let me pick 'em up," which raised him out of his depression not a little.

But the stern faces of the old gentleman, and the tall boy, smote him with a chill, long before he passed them, and he drove by silently, well knowing it would not do to broach the subject by so much as a look.

Not daring to go near the little brown house without the occupants of the stage who had driven down the road with him, Mr. Tisbett drew up miserably to a convenient angle, and waited till the two came up. Then without trusting himself to think, he sprang to the ground, and with shame written all over his honest face, called out, " See here, you young chap, I want to speak to you, when you've got him in the house."

" I will see you then," said Jasper, as the two hurried on to meet the Peppers rushing out from the little brown house, and down the small path.

" I've made an awful mess for 'em all, and they just come home," groaned Mr. Tisbett; drawing his fur mitten across his eyes, and leading his horses, he followed at a funeral pace, careful not to stop at the gate until the door was closed, when he began furiously to unload.

A footstep crunching the snow, broke into the noise he was making. " Hoh! well," he exclaimed, pausing with a trunk half-off the rack, " it's a mighty awkward thing for a man to say he's sorry, but you bet I be, as cert'in as my name's John Tisbett." His face became so very red that Jasper hastened to put his young shoulder under the trunk, a movement that only added to the stage-driver's distress.

" It don't pay to get mad, now I tell you," declared Mr. Tisbett, dumping the trunk down on the snow, and then drawing himself to his full height; " fust place, your pa sassed me, and " —

" He didn't intend to," cried Jasper eagerly, " and I'll apologize for him, if that's what you want." He laid his strong right hand in the old fur mitten.

" Good land! Tain't what I want," cried honest John, but he gripped the hand nevertheless, a fact that the boy never forgot; " I say I'm sorry I shook up your pa."

" His age ought to have protected him," said the boy simply.

" Sho! that's a fact," cried Mr. Tisbett, sinking in deeper distress, " but how is anybody to remember he's so old, when he steps so almighty high, as if he owned all Badgertown — say!"

"I think we shall be good friends, Mr. Tisbett," said Jasper cordially, as he turned to wave his hand toward the little brown house; simultaneously the door opened, and all the young Peppers and Whitneys rushed out to help in the delightful unloading.

It was well along in the afternoon. The dusk of the December twilight shut down speedily, around the little brown house and its happy occupants, but no one wanted the candles lighted till the last moment.

"Oh, Polly!" cried Joel, who was prancing as of old over the kitchen floor, "don't you remember that night when you said you wished you had two hundred candles, and you'd light them all at once?"

"I said a good many silly things in those days," said Polly meditatively, and smoothing Phronsie's yellow hair that was lying across her lap.

"Some silly ones, and a good many wise ones," observed Mother Pepper, over in her little old rocker in the west window, where she

used to sit sewing up coats and sacks for the
village storekeeper. "You kept us together
many a time, Polly, when nothing else
could."

"Oh! no, I didn't, Mamsie," protested Polly,
guilty of contradicting, "you and Bessie did.
I just washed dishes, and swept up, and " —

"Baked and brewed, and fussed and
stewed," finished Joel, afraid of being too sen-
timental.

"Polly was just lovely in those days," said
Davie, coming across the room to lay a cool
cheek against her rosy one. " I liked the rainy
days best when we all could stay in the house,
and hear her sing and tell stories while she was
working."

"She was cross sometimes," cried Joel, determined not to let reminiscences become too
comfortable; "she used to scold me just awfully, I know."

Polly broke into a merry laugh; yet she
exclaimed "You poor Josey, I suppose I was
dreadful! "

"You didn't catch one half as bad scoldings
as belonged to you," put in Ben, thrusting an-

other stick in the stove. "You were a bad lot, Joe, in those days."

"And not over good in these," cried old Mr. King, ensconced in the snuggest corner in the seat of honor, the high-backed rocker, that comforted Phronsie after her little toe was hurt. "There, now, my boy, how's that?" with a grim smile.

"Do you remember when the old stove used to plague you, Polly?" cried Joel, suddenly changing the conversation. "And how Ben's putty was everlastingly tumbling out? Hoh — hoh!"

"And you two boys were always stuffing up the holes for me, when Ben was away," cried Polly, with affectionate glances at Davie and Joel.

"I didn't so much," said Joel honestly, "Dave was always giving boot-tops and such things."

"Boot-tops!" repeated Mr. King in astonishment. "Bless me, I didn't know that they had anything in common with stoves."

"Oh! that was before we knew you," said Joel, ready in advance of any one else with the explanation; "it wasn't this stove. Dr Fisher gave Polly this one after she had the measles; but it was a lumbering old affair that was full of holes that had to be stopped up with anything we could get. And leather was the best; and Davie saved all the old boot-heels and tops he could find, you know."

"Oh!" said the old gentleman, wondering if other revelations would come to light about the early days of the Peppers.

"Isn't Dr. Fisher lovely?" cried Polly, with sparkling eyes, " just the same as ever. Mamsie, I ought to do something for him."

"He is as good as gold," assented Mrs. Pepper heartily. "You've done something, I'm sure, Polly. The medical books you bought out of your pocket money, and sent him, pleased him more than anything you could give him."

"But I want to do something now," said Polly. "Oh! just think how good he was to us."

"May we never forget it!" exclaimed Mrs. Pepper, wiping her eyes.

"But he's very unwise," said Mr. King, a

trifle testily, " not to take up with my offer to
establish him in the town.   A man like him
could easily hold a good practice, because the
fellow's got ability."

" Oh! Dr. Fisher wouldn't leave Badgertown," cried all the Peppers in a bunch.   " And
what would the poor people here do without
him? " finished Polly.

" Well, well, never mind, he won't come to
town, and that's enough," said the old gentleman quickly.   " Aside from that, he's a sensible
chap, and one quite to my liking."

" Oh, Polly! " cried Phronsie suddenly, and
lifting her head, she fastened her brown eyes on
the face above her, " wasn't Mamsie's birthday
cake good? "

" The flowers were pretty, but the cake was
heavy, don't you remember? " said Polly, who
hadn't recovered from that grief even yet.

" I thought it was just beautiful," cried Mrs.
Pepper hastily.   " No one could have baked it
better in the old stove you had.   I'm sure we
ate it all up, every crumb."

" We kept it in the old cupboard," cried Joel,
rushing over to the corner to swing the door

open. "And we never once peeked, Mamsie, so afraid you'd suspect."

"You kept staring at the cupboard door all the evening, Joe, you know you did," cried Ben; "you were just within a hair's breadth of letting the whole thing out ever so many times. Polly and I had to drag you away. We were glad enough when you went to bed, I can tell you."

"You were always sending me off to bed in those days," said Joel, taking his head out of the cupboard to throw vindictive glances over to the group around the stove.

"I wish we could do so now," said Ben.

"And those two," Joel went on, pointing to Polly and Ben, "used to go whispering around a lot of old secrets, that they wouldn't tell us. Oh! it was perfectly awful, wasn't it, Dave?" bestowing a small pinch on that individual's shoulder.

"I liked the secrets best not to know them till Polly and Ben got ready to tell us," said David slowly; "then they were just magnificent."

Phronsie had laid her head back in the waiting lap, and was crooning softly to herself.

"I want to go and see dear good Mr. Beebe," she said presently, "and nice Mrs. Beebe, can I, Mamsie?" looking over at her.

"To be sure," cried Mrs. Pepper, "you shall indeed, child."

"Beebe — Beebe, and who is he, pray?" demanded Mr. King.

"Oh! he keeps the shoe shop over in the Center," explained three or four voices, "and Phronsie's new shoes were bought there, you know."

"And he gave me pink and white candy-sticks," said Phronsie, and he was very nice; and I like him very much."

"And Mrs. Beebe gave us doughnuts all around," communicated Joel; "I don't know but that I liked those best. There was more to them."

"So you always bought your new shoes of the Beebes?" asked the old gentleman, a question that brought all the five Peppers around his chair at once.

"We didn't ever have new shoes that I can remember," said Joel quickly, "except Phronsie's, and once Ben had a new pair. He had to, because he was the oldest, you know."

" Oh! " said Mr. King.

" You see," said Phronsie, shaking her head gravely, while she laid one hand on his knee, " we were very poor, Grandpapa dear. Don't you understand? "

" Yes, yes, child," said old Mr. King; " there, get up here," and he took her within his arms.

" No, no, you're not going to talk yet," seeing Percy and Van beginning violent efforts to join in the conversation. " Let the Peppers have a chance to talk over old times first. See how good Jasper is to wait."

" I would much prefer to hear the Peppers talk forever," said Jasper, smiling down on the two Whitneys, " than to have the gates opened for a general flood. Go on, do, Polly and Ben, and the rest of you."

" Oh! there is so much," said Polly despairingly, clasping her hands, " we shouldn't get through if we talked ten years, should we, Ben? Mamsie," and she rushed over to her, " can we have a baking time to-morrow, just as we used to in the old days? Oh! do say yes."

"Yes, do say yes," echoed Jasper, also rushing to the side of the little rocking-chair. "You will, won't you, Mrs. Pepper?"

"Hoh! hoh!" cried the two Whitneys derisively, "I thought you could 'hear the Peppers talk forever.' That's great, Jasper."

"Well, when it comes to hearing a proposal for a baking frolic, my principles are thrown to the wind," said Jasper recklessly. "Why, boys, that's the first thing I remember about the little brown house. Do say yes, Mrs. Pepper!"

CHAPTER VIII.

SOME BADGERTOWN CALLS.

" WELL, I declare!" exclaimed Grandma
Bascom, opening the door and looking in, " I never!"

"Come in," cried Mr. King sociably. His
night over at the parsonage had been a most
fortunate experiment. "I haven't slept so
finely in ten years," he confided to Mrs. Whitney as they met at breakfast at the minister's
table. So now, his face wreathed with smiles,
he repeated his invitation. "Come in, do, Mrs.
Bascom; we're glad to see you."

"I never!" said "Grandma Bascom" once
more, for want of something better to say, and
coming close to the centre of operations.

Jasper, attired in one of Mrs. Pepper's long
aprons, which was fastened in the style of the
old days, by the strings around his neck, was

busily engaged in rolling out under Polly's direction, a thin paste, expected presently under the genial warmth of the waiting stove, to evolve into most toothsome cakes. Ben was similarly attired, and similarly employed; while Joel and David were in a sticky state, preparing their dough after their own receipt, over at the corner table, their movements closely followed by the three Whitneys.

Phronsie, before a board laid ocross two chairs, was enlightening old Mr. King who sat by her, into the mysteries of baking day.

"Do bake a gingerbread boy," he begged. "I never had anything half so good as the one you sent over to Hingham."

"You were my poor sick man then," observed Phronsie, with slow, even pats on her bit of dough. "Please, the rolling-pin now, Grandpapa dear."

"To be sure," cried the old gentleman; "here, Jappy, my boy, be so good as to hand us over that article."

"And you see," continued Phronsie, receiving the rolling-pin, and making the deftest of passes with it over the soft mass, "I couldn't send you anything better, though I wanted to, Grandpapa dear."

"Better?" cried Mr. King. "I should think not; you couldn't have made me anything that pleased me more, had you tried a thousand times."

Phronsie never tired of hearing this, and now humming a soft note of thanks, proceeded with her task, declaring that she would make the best gingerbread boy that could possibly be achieved.

"Grandma Bascom" was still reiterating "I never," and going slowly from one group to another to inspect operations. When she came to Phronsie, she stopped short, raising her hands in surprise. "Seems as ef 'twas only yesterday when the Peppers went away, though land knows I've missed 'em all most dretfully, 'an there sets that blessed child baking, as big as any of 'em. I never!"

"Have you any more raisins to give us, Grandma?" shouted Joel across the kitchen. "They were terribly hard," he added in his natural voice; "almost broke our teeth."

"Hey?" called "Grandma" back again.

"Raisins, Grandma, or peppermints," cried Joel.

"Oh, Joe, for shame!" called Ben.

"I'm going to have the fun of going after them," declared Joel, throwing down his dough-pat, and wiping his sticky fingers on his apron; "just like old times — so there!"

"I'll go over and get 'em," said Grandma; "you come along with me," looking admiringly up at the tall boy; so the two, Joel laughing and hopping by her side as if he were five years younger, disappeared, well-pleased with each other.

"Now I shall take his dough." declared Dick, rushing around the end of the table, to Joel's deserted place.

"No such thing," declared Van, flying out of his chair. "Leave your hands off, youngster! that's to be mine."

Polly looked up from the little cookies she was cutting with the top of a tin baking powder box and their eyes met.

"I didn't promise not to have it out with Dicky," said Van stoutly. "He's a perfect plague, and always under foot. I never thought of such a thing as not making him stand around, Polly."

But the brown eyes did not return to their task, as Polly mechanically stamped another cookey.

"I only promised not to have a bout with Percy," Van proceeded uncomfortably. And in the same breath, "Go ahead, if you want it, Dickey, I don't care."

"I do want it," declared Dick, clambering into Van's chair, while Van returned to his own, "and I'm going to have it too. I guess you think you'd better give it up now, sir; I'm getting so big."

"Softly there, Dicky," said Mrs. Whitney, over in the window-seat with her fancy work; "if Van gives up, you should thank him; I think he is very good to do it." And the bigger boy's heart warmed with the radiant smile she sent him.

Dick gave several vicious thrusts to his dough, and looked up at last to say very much against his will, "Thank you;" and adding brightly, "but you know I'm getting big, sir, and you'd better give up."

"All right," said Van, with that smile in his heart feeling equal to anything.

"Now," cried Jasper, with a flourish of his baking apron, "mine are ready. Here goes!" and he opened the oven door and pushed in a pan of biscuit.

"Jappy's always ahead in everything," grumbled Percy, laboring away at his dough. "How in the world do you make the thing roll out straight? Mine humps up in the middle."

"Put some more flour on the board," said Polly, running over to him. "There, now see, Percy, if that doesn't roll smooth."

"It does with you," said Percy, taking the rolling-pin again, to send it violently over the long-suffering dough, "and — I declare, it's going to do with me," he cried, in delight at the large flat cake staring up at him from the board. "Now, says I, I'll beat you, Jappy!" And presently the whole kitchen resounded with a merry din, as the several cakes and biscuits were declared almost ready for their respective pans.

"But, I can tell you, this gingerbread boy is going in next," declared Mr. King from

Phronsie's baking-board. "It's almost done, isn't it, child?"

"Not quite, Grandpapa," said Phronsie; "this eye won't stay in just like the other. It doesn't look the same way, don't you see?" pointing to the currant that certainly showed no inclination to do its duty, as any well-bred eye should. "Wait just a moment, please; I'll pull it out and stick it in again."

"Take another," advised the old gentleman, fumbling over the little heap of currants on the saucer. "There, here's a good round one, and very expressive, too, Phronsie."

"That's lovely," hummed Phronsie, accepting the new eye with very sticky fingers. "Now, he's all ready," as she set it in its place, and took the boy up tenderly. "Give me a pan, do, Polly."

"Did you cut that out?" cried Dick, turning around in his chair, and regarding her enviously, "all alone by yourself? Didn't Grandpapa help you just one teenty bit to make the legs and the hands?"

"No; she made it all herself," said the old gentleman, with justifiable pride. "There,

Phronsie, here's your pan," as Polly set it down before her with a " You precious dear, that's perfectly elegant ! "

Phronsie placed the boy within the pan, and gave it many a loving pat. " Grandpapa sat here, and looked at it, and smiled," she said, turning her eyes gravely on Dick, " and that helped ever so much. I couldn't ever have made it so nice alone. Good-by; now bake like a good boy. Let me put it in the oven all by myself, do, Polly," she begged.

So Phronsie, the old gentleman escorting her in mortal dread that she would be burned, safely tucked her long pan into the warmest corner, shut the door, and gravely consulted the clock. " If I look at it in twenty-one min-utes, I think it will be done," she said, " quite brown."

In twenty-one minutes the whole kitchen was so far removed from being the scene of a baking exploit as was possible. Everything was cleared away, and set up primly in its place, leaving only a row of fine little biscuits and cookies, with Phronsie's gingerbread boy in the midst, to tell the tale of what had been going on.   Outside there was a great commotion.   Deacon Brown's old wagon stood at the gate, for the Peppers and their friends; and, oh! joy, not the old horse between the shafts, but a newer and much livelier beast.   And on the straw laid in the bottom of the wagon, the seats being removed, disported all the merry group, Mr. King alone having the dignity of a chair.

Deacon Brown, delighted with his scheme of bringing the wagon over as a surprise for the Peppers to take a drive in, was on the side of the narrow foot-path, chuckling and rubbing his hands together.   " You won't have to drive so easy as you used to, Ben," he called out, " this fellow's chirk; give him his head. Sho! what you goin' that way for? " as Ben turned off down the lane.

" To Grandma Bascom's," shouted two or three voices.

" Joel's over there," sang out Polly.

" We couldn't go without him, you know," chirped Phronsie, poking a distressed little face up from the straw heap.

" 'Twould serve him just right if we did,"

said Van. "He's a great chap to stay over there like this."

"No — no," cried Dick in terror, "don't go without Joel; I'd rather have him than any of you," he added, not over politely.

Phronsie began to cry piteously at the mere thought of Joel's being left behind.

"He wanted to see Mr. Beebe," she managed to say, "and dear Mrs. Beebe. Oh! don't go without him." So Mr. King made them hand her up to him, and at the risk of their both rolling out, he held her in his lap until the wagon, stopping at the door of " Grandma Bascom's " cottage, brought Joel bounding out with a whoop.

"Jolly! where'd you get that, and where are you going? " all in one breath, as he swung himself up behind.

"Deacon Brown brought it over just now," cried Polly.

"As a surprise," furnished Percy. "Isn't he a fine old chap? Here's for the very jolliest go! "

"We're going to see dear Mr. Beebe, and dear Mrs. Beebe," announced Phronsie, smil-

ing through her tears, and leaning out of the
old gentleman's lap to nod at him.

"Hurrah!" screamed Joel. "Good-by,
Grandma," to the old lady, whose cap-frills
were framed in the small window. "I've had a
fine time in there," he condescended to say, but
nothing further as to the details could they
extract from him; and so at last they gave it
up, and lent their attention to the various things
to be seen as the wagon spun along. And so
over and through the town, and to the very
door of the little shoe-shop, and there, to be
sure, was Mr. Beebe the same as ever, to welcome them; and Joel found to his immense
satisfaction that the stone pot was as full of
sugary doughnuts as in the old days; and
Phronsie had her pink and white sticks, and
Mrs. Beebe "Oh-ed" and "'Ah-ed" over them
all, and couldn't bear to let them go when at
last it was time to say "good-by." And at last
they all climbed into the old wagon, and were
off again on their round of visits.

It was not till the gray dusk of the winter
afternoon settled down unmistakably, so that
no one could beg to stay out longer, that they

turned Deacon Brown's horse toward the " little brown house."

"It's going to snow to-morrow, I think," observed Jasper, squinting up at the leaden sky, "isn't it, father?"

"Whoop!" exclaimed Joel, "then we will have sport, I tell you!"

"It certainly looks like it," said old Mr. King, wrapping his fur-lined coat closer. "Phronsie, are you sure you are warm enough?"

"Yes, Grandpapa dear," she answered, curling up deeper in the straw at his feet.

"Do you remember how you would carry the red-topped shoes home with you, Phronsie?" cried Polly, and then away they rushed again into "Oh, don't you remember this, and you haven't forgotten that?" Jasper as wildly reminiscent now as the others, for hadn't he almost as good as lived at the little brown house, pray tell? So the Whitneys looked curiously on, without a chance to be heard in all the merry chatter; and then they drew up at the gate of the parsonage, where they were all to have supper.

When Phronsie woke up in the big bed by the side of her mother, the next morning, Polly was standing over her, and looking down into her face.

"Oh, Phronsie!" she exclaimed in great glee, "the ground is all covered with snow!"

"O-oh!" screamed Phronsie, her brown eyes flying wide open, "do give me my shoes and stockings, Polly, do! I'll be dressed in just one — minute," and thereupon ensued a merry scramble as she tumbled out of the big bed, and commenced operations, Polly running out to help Mamsie get the breakfast.

"Mush seems good now we don't have to eat it," cried Joel, as they all at last sat around the board.

"'Twas good then," said Mrs. Pepper, her black eyes roving over the faces before her.

"How funny," cried Percy Whitney, who had run over from the parsonage to breakfast, "this yellow stuff is." And he took up a spoonful of it gingerly.

"You don't like it, Percy; don't try to eat it. I'll make you a slice of toast," cried Polly, springing out of her chair, " in just one mo-ment."

" No, you mustn't," cried Dick, bounding in in time to catch the last words. " Mamma said no one was to have anything different, if we came to breakfast, from what the Peppers are going to eat. I like the yellow stuff; give me some, do," and he slid into a chair and passed his plate to Mrs. Pepper.

" So you shall, Dickey," she said hastily. " And you will never taste sweeter food than this," giving him a generous spoonful.

" Grandpapa is eating ham and fried eggs over at the minister's house," contributed Dick, after satsifying his hunger a bit.

" Ham and fried eggs!" exclaimed Mother Pepper, aghast. " Why, he never touches them. You must be mistaken, my boy."

" No, I'm not," said Dick, obstinately. " The minister's wife said it was, and she asked me if I wouldn't have some, and I said I was going over to the Peppers to breakfast; I'd rather have some of theirs. And Grandpapa said it was good — the ham and fried eggs

was — and he took it twice; he did, Mrs.
Pepper."

" Took it twice? " she repeated, faintly, with
troubled visions of the future. " Well, well,
the mischief is done now, so there is no use
in talking about it; but I'm worried, all the
same."

" Hurry up, Percy," called Joel across the
table, " and don't dawdle so. We're going to
make a double ripper, four yards long, to go
down that hill there." He laid down his spoon
to point out the window at a distant snow-cov-
ered slope.

Percy shivered, but recalling himself in time,
said " Splendid," and addressed himself with
difficulty to his mush.

" Well, you'll never be through at that
speed," declared Joel. " See, I've eaten three
saucersful," and he handed his plate up. " And
now for the fourth, Mamsie."

" Oh! baked potatoes," cried Ben, rolling
one around in his hand before he took off its
crackling skin. " Weren't they good, though,
with a little salt. I tell you, they helped us to
chop wood in the old times! "

"I really think I shall have to try one," said Percy, who deeply to his regret was obliged to confess that Indian meal mush had few charms for his palate.

"There's real milk in my mug now," cried Phronsie, with long, deep draughts. "Polly, did I ever have anything but make-believe in the little brown house; ever, Polly?"

Polly was saved from answering by a stamping of snowy boots on the flat doorstone.

"Hurrah, there!" cried Van, rushing in, followed by Jasper. "Hoh, you slow people in the little brown house, come on for the double ripper!"

CHAPTER IX.

A SUDDEN BLOW.

" MAMSIE," cried Polly, suddenly, and resting her hands on her knees as she sat on the floor before the stove," do you suppose there is any one poor enough in Badgertown to need the little brown house when we lock it up to-morrow?"

" Not a soul," replied Mrs. Pepper, quickly; " no more than there was when we first locked it up five years ago, Polly. I've been all over that with the parson last evening; and he says there isn't a new family in the place, and all the old ones have their homes, the same as ever. So we can turn the key and leave it with a clear conscience."

Polly drew a long breath of delight, and gazed long at the face of the stove that seemed to crackle out an answering note of joy as the wood snapped merrily; then she slowly looked around the kitchen.

" It's so perfectly lovely, Mamsie," she broke out at length, " to see the dear old things, and to know that they are waiting here for us to come back whenever we want to. And to think it isn't wicked not to have them used, because everybody has all they need; oh! it's so delicious to think they can be left to themselves."

She folded her hands now across her knees, and drew another long breath of content.

Phronsie stole out of the bedroom, and came slowly up to her mother's side, pausing a bit on the way to look into Polly's absorbed face.

" I don't think, Mamsie," she said quietly, " that people ought to be so very good who've never had a little brown house; never in all their lives."

" Oh, yes, they had, child," said Mrs. Pepper briskly; " places don't make any difference. It's people's duty to be good wherever they are."

But Phronsie's face expressed great incredulity.

"I'm always going to live here when I am a big, grown-up woman," she declared, slowly gazing around the kitchen, "and I shall never, never go out of Badgertown."

"Oh, Phronsie!" exclaimed Polly, turning around in dismay, "why, you couldn't do that. Just think, child, whatever in the world would Grandpapa do, or any of us, pray tell?"

"Grandpapa would come here," declared Phronsie decidedly; and shaking her yellow head to enforce her statement. "Of course Grandpapa would come here, Polly. We couldn't live without him."

"That's it," said Polly, with a corresponding shake of her brown head, "of course we couldn't live without Grandpapa; and just as 'of course' he couldn't leave his own dear home. He never would be happy, Phronsie, to do that."

Phronsie took a step or two into the sunshine lying on the middle of the old kitchen floor. "Then I'd rather not come, Polly," she said. But she sighed and Polly was just about saying, "We'll run down now and then perhaps, Phronsie, as we have done now," when the door was thrown open suddenly, and Joel burst in, his face as white as a sheet, and working fearfully.

"Oh, Polly! you must tell Mrs. Whitney — I can't."

Polly sprang to her feet; Mrs. Pepper, who had just stepped into the pantry, was saying, "I think, Polly, I'll make some apple dumplings, the boys like them so much."

"What is it, Joe?" cried Polly hoarsely, and standing quite still. Phronsie, with wide eyes, went up and took the boy's cold hand, and gazed into his face as he leaned against the door.

"Dick!" groaned Joel; "oh! oh! I can't bear it," and covering his face with one hand, he would have pulled the other from Phronsie's warm little palm, but she held it fast.

"Tell me at once, Joe," commanded Polly. "Hush! — mother" — but Mrs. Pepper was already out of the pantry.

"Joel," said Mrs. Pepper, "whatever it is, tell us immediately."

The look in her black eyes forced him to gasp in one breath, "Dick fell off the double ripper, and both of his legs are broken — may be not," he added in a loud scream

Phronsie still held the boy's hand. He was conscious of it, and that she uttered no word and then he knew no more.

"Leave him to me, Polly," said Mrs. Pepper through drawn lips, "and then do you run as you have never run before, to the parsonage Oh! if they should bring him there before the mother hears."

Phronsie dropped the hand she held, and running on unsteady little feet into the bedroom, came back with Polly's hood and coat.

"Let me go," cried Polly wildly, rushing away from the detaining hand to the door, "I don't want those things on. Let me go, Phronsie!"

"You'll be cold," said Phronsie. With all her care, her little white lips were quivering as she held out the things. "Please, Polly," she said piteously.

"The child is right; put them on," commanded Mrs. Pepper, for one instant taking her thought from her boy; and Polly obeyed, and was gone.

In the parsonage "best room" sat Mrs.
Whitney. Her rocking-chair was none of the
easiest, being a hair-cloth affair, its cushion
very much elevated in the world just where it
should have been depressed, so that one was in
constant danger of slipping off its surface;
moreover, the arms and back of the chair
were covered with indescribable arrangements
made and presented by loving parishioners and
demanding unceasing attention from the occu-
pant. But the chair was drawn up in the sunshine pouring into the window, and Mrs. Whitney's thoughts were sunny, too; for she smiled
now and then as she drew her needle busily
in and out through the bright wools.

"How restful it all is here, and so quaint
and simple." She glanced up now to the high-
backed mantel with its wealth of daguerreo-
types, and surprising collection of dried leaves
in tall china vases; and over the walls, adorned
with pine-cone framed pictures, to the center
table loaded with "Annuals," and one or two
volumes of English poetry, and then her gaze
took in the little paths the winter sunshine was
making for itself along the red and green in-

grain carpet. "I am so glad father thought to bring us all. Dear father, it is making a new man of him, this winter frolic. Why " —

She was looking out of the window now, and her hands fell to her lap as Polly Pepper came running breathlessly down the village street, her hood untied, and the coat grasped with one hand and held together across her breast. But it was the face that terrified Mrs. Whitney, and hurrying out of her chair, she ran out to the veranda as the girl rushed through the gateway.

"Polly, child," cried Mrs. Whitney, seizing her with loving arms and drawing her on the steps — "oh! what is it, dear?"

Polly's lips moved, but no words came.

"Oh!" at last, "don't hate us for — bringing you to the — little — brown house. Why did we come!" And convulsively she threw her young arms around the kind neck. "Oh, Aunty! Dicky is hurt — but we don't know how much — his legs, Joel says, but it may not be as bad as we think; dear Aunty, it may not."

Mrs. Whitney trembled so that she could

scarcely stand. Around them streamed the same winter sunshine that had been so bright a moment since. How long ago it seemed. And out of gathering clouds in her heart she was saying, " Polly dear, God is good. We will trust him." She did not know her own voice, nor realize when Polly led her mercifully within, as a farmer's wagon came slowly down the street, to stop at the parsonage gate; nor even when Dick was brought in, white and still, could she think of him as her boy. It was some other little figure, and she must go and help them care for him. Her boy would come bounding in presently, happy and ruddy, with a kiss for mamma, and a world of happy non-sense just as usual. It was only when Mrs. Henderson came in, and took her hand to lead her into the next room, that it all came to her.

" Oh, Dick! " and she sprang to the side of the sofa where he lay. " My child — my child! "

And then came Dr. Fisher, and the truth was known. One of Dick's legs was broken below the knee; the other badly bruised. Only Jasper and the mother remained in the room while the little doctor set the limb; and after what seemed an age to the watchers, the boy came out.

"He bore it like a Trojan," declared Jasper, wiping his forehead. "I tell you, Dick's our hero, after this."

"Now I should like to know how all this happened," demanded Mr. King. The old gentleman had remained at the parsonage to get a good morning nap while the snow frolic was in progress. And he had been awakened by the unusual bustle below stairs in time to hear the welcome news that Dicky was all right since Dr. Fisher was taking care of him. He now presented himself in his dressing-gown, with his sleeping cap awry, over a face in which anger, distress and impatience strove for the mastery. "Speak up, my boy," to Jasper, "and tell us what you know about it."

"Well, the first thing I knew of any danger ahead," said Jasper, "was hearing Dick sing out 'Hold up!' I supposed the double ripper all right; didn't you, Ben?"

"Yes," said Ben sturdily, "and it was all right; just exactly as we used to make them, we boys; there wasn't a weak spot anywhere in her, sir."

"Who was steering?" demanded old Mr. King almost fiercely.

"I was," said Van, beginning boldly enough, to let his voice die out in a tremulous effort.

"Humph — humph," responded Mr. King grimly. "A bad business," shaking his head.

"Van would" — began Percy, but his eye meeting Polly's he added, "We'd none of us done any better, I don't believe, sir, than Van."

Van was now choking so badly that the greatest kindness seemed to be not to look at him. Accordingly the little company turned their eyes away, and regarded each other instead.

"Well, so Dick rolled off?" proceeded the old gentleman.

"Oh! no, he didn't," said all three boys together; "he stuck fast to the double ripper; we ran into a tree, and Dick was pitched off head-first."

"But honestly and truly, father," said Jasper, "I do not think that it was the fault of the steerer."

"Indeed it was not," declared Ben stoutly; "there was an ugly little gully that we hadn't seen under the snow. We'd been down four or five times all right, but only missed it by a hair-breadth; this time the 'ripper' struck into it; I suppose Dick felt it bump, as it was on his side, and sang out, and as quick as lightning we were against that tree. It was as much my fault as any one's, and more, because I ought to have known that old hill thoroughly."

"I share the blame, Ben," broke in Jasper, "old fellow, if you pitch into yourself, you'll have to knock me over too."

"Come here, Vanny," said old Mr. King, holding out his hand. "Why, you needn't be afraid, my boy," aghast at the tears that no power on earth could keep back. "Now all leave the room, please."

"Where's Polly?" asked Ben, on the other side of the door.

"She's run home," said David, "I guess. She isn't here."

"And that's where I must be too," cried Ben, bounding off.

When Van was next seen he was with old

Mr. King, and wearing all signs of having received his full share of comfort. Phronsie,
just tying on her little hood, to go down to the
parsonage to ask after Dicky, looked out of the
window to exclaim in pleased surprise, " Why,
here comes dear Grandpapa," and then she
rushed out to meet him.

" Here's my little girl," cried the old gentleman, opening his arms, when she immediately
ran into them. " Now we're all right."

" Is Dicky all right? " asked Phronsie anxiously, as she fell into step by his side.

" Yes, indeed; as well as a youngster can
be, who's broken his leg."

Phronsie shivered. " But then, that's nothing," Mr. King hastened to add; " I broke
my own when I was a small shaver no bigger
than Dick, and I was none the worse for it.
Boys always have some such trifling mishaps,
Phronsie."

" Ben never broke his leg, nor Joel, nor
Davie," said Phronsie. " Must they yet,
Grandpapa? "

" O dear, no," declared Mr. King hastily;
" that isn't necessary. I only meant they must

have something. Now you see, Ben had the measles, you know."

"Yes, he did," said Phronsie, quite relieved to think that this trial could take the place of the usual leg-breaking episode in a boy's career. "And so did Joel, and Davie — all of them, Grandpapa dear."

"Exactly; well, and then Ben had to work hard, and Joel and Davie too, for that matter. So, you see, it wasn't as essential that they should break their legs, child."

"But Jasper and Percy and Van don't have to work hard; oh! I don't want them to break their legs," said Phronsie, in a worried tone. "You don't think they will, Grandpapa dear, do you? Please say they won't."

"I don't think there is the least danger of it," said Mr. King, "especially as I shall put an end to this 'double-ripper' business, though not because this upset was anybody's fault; remember that, Phronsie." Van's head which had dropped a bit at the last words, came up proudly. "Van here, has acted nobly " — he put his hand on the boy's shoulder — "and would have saved Dicky if he could. It was a pure accident, that nobody could help except by keeping off from the abominable thing. Well, here we are at the little brown house; and there's your mother, Phronsie, waiting for us in the doorway."

"Halloo!" cried Van, rushing over the flat stone, and past Mrs. Pepper, "where's Joel? Oh — here, you old chap!"

"Well, Mrs. Pepper," said the old gentleman, coming up to the step, Phronsie hanging to his hand, "this looks like starting for town to-morrow, doesn't it?"

"Oh! what shall we do, sir?" cried Mrs. Pepper, in distress. "To think you have come down here in the goodness of your heart, to be met with such an accident as this. What shall we do?" she repeated.

"Goodness of my heart," repeated Mr. King, nevertheless well pleased at the tribute. "I've had as much pleasure out of it all as you or the young people. I wan't you to realize that."

"So does anyone who does a kind act," replied Mrs. Pepper, wiping her eyes; "well, sir, now how shall we manage about going back?"

"That remains to be seen," said Mr. King slowly, and he took a long look at the winter sky, and the distant landscape before he ventured more. "It very much looks as if we all should remain for a few days, to see how Dick is to get on, all but the four boys; they must pack off to school to-morrow, and then probably Mrs. Whitney will stay over with the boy till he can be moved. Dr. Fisher will do the right thing by him. Oh! everything is all right, Mrs. Pepper."

Mrs. Pepper sighed and led the way into the house. She knew in spite of the re-assuring words, that the extreme limit of the "outing" ought to be passed on the morrow.

CHAPTER X.

"GOOD-BY to the little brown house!'
Joel and David, Percy and Van sang
out in doleful chorus, from the old stage coach;
two of the boys on the seat shared by John
Tisbett, the other two within as companions to
Mrs. Pepper and Jasper, who were going home
to start the quartette off to school.

"Ben and I will take good care of everything, Mamsie," said Polly for the fiftieth time,
and climbing up on the steps to tuck the traveling shawl closer. Thereupon Phronsie climbed
up too, to do the same thing. "Don't you
worry; we'll take care of things," she echoed.

"I sha'n't worry," said Mrs. Pepper in a
bright assured way. "Mother knows you'll
both do just right. And Phronsie'll be a good
girl too," with a long look into the bright eyes

162

peering over the window casing of the old coach.

"I'll try," said Phronsie. "Good-by, Mamsie," and she tried to stand on tiptoe to reach her mouth up.

"Goodness me!" cried Polly, "you nearly tumbled off the steps. Throw her a kiss, Phronsie; Mamsie'll catch it."

"If that child wants to kiss her ma agen, she shall do it," declared Mr. Tisbett; and throwing down the reins, he sprang to the ground, seized Phronsie, and swung her lightly over the window edge. "There you be — went through just like a bird." And there she was, sure enough, in Mrs. Pepper's lap.

"I should like to go with you," Phronsie was whispering under Mrs. Pepper's bonnet strings, "Mamsie, I should."

"Oh, no, Phronsie!" Mrs. Pepper made haste to whisper back. "You must stay with Polly. Why, what would she ever do without you? Be mother's good girl, Phronsie; you're all coming home, except Auntie and Dick, in a few days."

Phronsie cast one look at Polly. "Good-

by," she said slowly. "Take me out now,"
holding her arms towards Mr. Tisbett.

"Here you be!" exclaimed Mr. Tisbett merrily, reversing the process, and setting her carefully on the ground. "Now, says I; up I
goes," his foot on the wheel to spring to the
box.

"Stay!" a peremptory hand was laid on his
shaggy coat sleeve, and he turned to face old
Mr. King.

"When I meet a man who can do such a kind
thing, it is worth my while to say that I trust no
words of mine gave offense. Bless you, man!"
added the old gentleman, abruptly changing
the tone of his address as well as its form, "it's
my way; that's all."

John Tisbett had no words to offer, but remained, his foot on the wheel, stupidly staring
up at the handsome old face.

"We shall be late for the train," called
Jasper within the coach, "if you don't start."

"Get up, do!" cried Joel, who had seized
the reins, "or I'll drive off without you, Mr.
Tisbett," which had the effect to carry honest
John briskly up to his place. When there, he

took off his fur cap without a word, and bowed
to Mr. King, cracked his whip and they were
off, leaving the four on the little foot-path
gazing after them, till the coach was only a
speck in the distance.

"Mamma dear," said Dick, one afternoon
three weeks later (the little brown house had
been closed a fortnight, and all the rest of
the party back in town), "when are we going
home?"

"Next week," said Mrs. Whitney brightly;
"the doctor thinks if all goes well, you can be
moved from here."

Dick leaned back in the big chintz-covered
chair. "Mamma," he said, "your cheeks
aren't so pink, and not quite so round, but I
think you are a great deal nicer mamma than
you were."

"Do you, Dick?" she said, laughing.
"Well, we have had a happy time together,
haven't we? The fortnight hasn't been so long
for you as I feared when the others all went
away."

"It hasn't been long at all," said Dick
promptly, and burrowing deeper into the chair-

back; "it's just flown, mamma. I like Polly and Phronsie; but I'd rather have you than any girl I know; I had really, mamma."

"I'm very glad to hear it, Dick," said Mrs. Whitney, with another laugh.

"And when I grow up, I'm just going to live with you forever and ever. Do you suppose papa will be always going to Europe then?"

"I trust not," said Mrs. Whitney fervently. "Dicky, would you like to have a secret?" she asked suddenly.

The boy's eyes sparkled. "Wouldn't I mamma?" he cried, springing forward in the chair; "ugh!"

"Take care, darling," warned his mother. "You must remember the poor leg."

Dick made a grimace, but otherwise took the pain pluckily. "Tell me, do, mamma," he begged, "the secret."

"Yes, I thought it would be a pleasant thing for you to have it to think of, darling, while you are getting well. Dicky, papa is coming home soon."

"Right away?" shouted Dick so lustily that Mrs. Henderson popped her head in the door.

"Oh! beg your pardon," she said; "I thought you wanted something."

"Isn't it lovely," cried Mrs. Whitney, "to have a boy who is beginning to find his lungs?"

"Indeed it is," cried the parson's wife, laughing; "I always picked up heart when my children were able to scream. It's good to hear you, Dicky," as she closed the door.

"Is he — is he — is he?" cried Dick in a spasm of excitement, "coming right straight away, mamma?"

"Next week," said mamma, with happy eyes, "he sails in the *Servia*. Next week Dicky, my boy, we will see papa. And here is the best part of the secret. Listen; it has all been arranged that Mr. Duyckink shall live in Liverpool, so that papa will not have to go across any more, but he can stay at home with us. O, Dicky!"

That "O, Dicky!" told volumes to the boy's heart.

"Mamma," he said at last, "isn't it good that God didn't give boys and girls to Mr. Duyckink? Because you see if he had, why, then Mr. Duyckink wouldn't like to live over there."

"Mr. Duyckink might not have felt as your father does, Dicky dear, about having his children educated at home; and Mrs. Duyckink wants to go to England; she hasn't any father, as I have, Dicky dear, who clings to the old home."

"Only I wish God had made Mr. Duyckink and Mrs. Duyckink a little sooner," said Dick reflectively. "I mean, made them want to go to England sooner, don't you, mamma?"

"I suppose we ought not to wish that," said his mother with a smile, "for perhaps we needed to be taught to be patient. Only now, Dicky, just think, we can actually have papa live at home with us!"

"Your cheeks are pink now," observed Dick; "just the very pink they used to be, mamma."

Mrs. Whitney ran to the old-fashioned looking-glass hanging in its pine-stained frame, between the low windows, and peered in.

"Do I look just as I did when papa went away six months ago, Dicky?" she asked, anxiously.

"Yes," said Dick, "just like that, only a great deal nicer," he added enthusiastically.

His mother laughed and pulled at a bright wave on her forehead, dodging a bit to avoid a long crack running across the looking-glass front.

"Here's Dr. Fisher!" shouted Dick suddenly. "Now, you old fellow, you," and shaking his small fist at his lame leg, "you've got to get well, I tell you. I won't wait much longer, sir!" And as the doctor came in, "I've a secret."

"Well, then, you would better keep it," said Dr. Fisher. "Good morning," to Mrs. Whitney. "Our young man here is getting ahead pretty fast, I should think. How's the leg, Dicky?" sitting down by him.

"The leg is all right," cried Dick; "I'm going to step on it," trying to get out of the chair.

"Dicky!" cried his mother in alarm.

"Softly — softly now, young man," said Dr. Fisher. "I suppose you want me to cure that leg of yours, and make it as good as the other one, don't you?"

"Why, of course," replied Dick; "that's what you are a doctor for."

"Well, I won't agree to do anything of the sort," said the little doctor coolly, "if you don't do your part. Do you know what patience means?"

"I've been patient," exclaimed Dick, in a dudgeon, "for ever and ever so many weeks, and now papa is coming home, and I" —

And then he realized what he had done, and he turned quite pale, and looked at his mother.

Her face gave no sign, but he sank back in his chair, feeling disgraced for life, and ready to keep quiet forever. And he was so good while Dr. Fisher was attending to his leg that when he was through, the little doctor turned to him approvingly: "Well, sir, I think that I can promise that you can go home Saturday. You've improved beyond my expectation."

But Dick didn't "hurrah," nor even smile.

"Dicky," said Mrs. Whitney, smiling into his downcast face, "how glad we are to hear that; just think, good Dr. Fisher says we may go next Saturday."

" I'm glad," mumbled Dick, in a forlorn little voice, and till after the door closed on the retreating form of the doctor, it was all that could be gotten out of him. Then he turned and put out both arms to his mother.

" I didn't mean — I didn't mean — I truly didn't mean — to tell — mamma," he sobbed, as she clasped him closely.

" I know you didn't, dear," she soothed him. " It has really done no harm; papa didn't want the home people to know, as he wants to surprise them."

" But it was a secret," said Dick, between his tears, feeling as if he had lost a precious treasure entrusted to him. " O, mamma! I really didn't mean to let it go."

" Mamma feels quite sure of that," said Mrs. Whitney gently. " You are right, Dicky, in feeling sorry and ashamed, because anything given to you to keep, is not your own, but belongs to another; but, my boy, the next duty is to keep back those tears — all this is hurting your leg."

Dick struggled manfully, but still the tears rolled down his cheeks. At last he said, raising his head, "You would much better let me have my cry out, mamma; it's half-way, and it hurts to send it back."

"Well, I don't think so," said Mrs. Whitney, with a laugh. "I've often wanted to have a cry out, as you call it. But that's weak, Dicky, and should be stopped, for the more one cries, the more one wants to."

"You've often wanted to have a cry out?" repeated Dick, in such amazement that every tear just getting ready to show itself, immediately rushed back again. "Why, you haven't anything to cry for, mamma."

"Indeed I have," she declared; "often and often, I do many things that I ought not to do "—

"Oh! never, never," cried Dick, clutching her around the neck, to the detriment of her lace-trimmed wrapper. "My sweetest, dearingest mamma is ever and always just right."

"Indeed, Dick," said Mrs. Whitney earnestly, "the longer I live, I find that every day I have something to be sorry for in myself.   But God, you know, is good," she whispered softly.

Dick was silent.

" And then when papa goes," continued Mrs. Whitney, " why, then, my boy, it is very hard not to cry."

Here was something that the boy could grasp; and he seized it with avidity.

" And you stop crying for us," he cried; " I know now why you always put on your prettiest gown, and play games with us the evening after papa goes.   I know now."

" Here are three letters," cried the parson, hurrying in, and tossing them over to the boy.   " And Polly Pepper has written to me, too."

Dick screamed with delight.   " Two for me; one from Ben, and one from Grandpapa!"

" And mine is from Phronsie," said Mrs. Whitney, seizing an epistle carefully printed in blue crayon.

But although there were three letters from home, none of them carried the news of what was going on there.   None of them breathed a syllable that Cousin Eunice Chatterton was ill with a low fever, aggravated by nervous prostration; and that Mrs. Pepper and Polly were having a pretty hard time of it. On the contrary, every bit of news was of the cheeriest nature; Jasper tucked on a postscript to his father's letter, in which he gave the latest bulletin of his school life. And Polly did the same thing to Ben's letter. Even Phronsie went into a long detail concerning the new developments of a wonderful kitten she had left at home, to take her visit to Badgertown, so the two recipients never missed the lack of information in regard to the household life, from which they were shut out.

Only once Mrs. Whitney said thoughtfully, as she folded her letter and slipped it back into its envelope, " They don't speak of Mrs. Chatterton. I presume she has changed her plans, and is going to remain longer at her nephew's."

" I hope she'll live there always," declared Dick, looking up savagely from Ben's letter. " What an old guy she is, mamma! "

" Dick, Dick," said his mother reprovingly, " she is our guest, you know."

"Not if she is at her nephew's," said Dick
triumphantly, turning back to his letter.

Polly at this identical minute was slowly
ascending the stairs, a tray in one hand, the
contents of which she was anxiously regarding
on the way.

"I do hope it is right now," she said,
and presently knocked at Mrs. Chatterton's
door.

"Come in," said that lady's voice fretfully.
And "Do close the door," before Polly and
her tray were well within.

Polly shut the door gently, and approached
the bedside.

"I am so faint I do not know that I can
take any," said Mrs. Chatterton. Whether it
was her white cashmere dressing-robe, and
her delicate lace cap that made her face against
the pillows seem wan and white, Polly did not
know. But it struck her that she looked more
ill than usual, and she said earnestly, "I am
so sorry I wasn't quicker."

"There is no call for an apology from you,"
said Mrs. Chatterton coldly. "Set the tray

down on the table, and get a basin of water; I need to be bathed."

Polly stood quite still, even forgetting to deposit the tray.

" Set the tray down, I told you," repeated Mrs. Chatterton sharply, " and then get the basin of water."

" I will call Hortense," said Polly quietly, placing the tray as desired.

" Hortense has gone to the apothecary's," said Mrs. Chatterton, " and I will not have one of the other maids; they are too insufferable."

And indeed Polly knew that it would be small use to summon one of them, as Martha, the most obliging, had airily tossed her head when asked to do some little service for the sick woman that very morning, declaring, " I will never lift another finger for that Madame Chatterton."

" My neck aches, and my side, and my head," said Mrs. Chatterton irritably; " why do you not do as I bid you?"

For one long istant, Polly hesitated; then she turned to rush from the room, a flood of angry, bitter feelings surging through her heart, more at the insufferable tone and manner, than at what she was bidden to do. Only turned; and she was back by the side of the bed, and looking down into the fretful, dictatorial old face.

"I will bathe you, Mrs. Chatterton," she said gently; "I'll bring the water in a minute."

CHAPTER XI

POOR POLLY!

"YOU are very awkward, child," observed Mrs. Chatterton to Polly on her knees, "and abrupt. Move the sponge more slowly; there, that is better."

Polly shifted her position from one aching knee to another, set her lips closer together, and bent all her young energies to gentler effects. But Mrs. Chatterton cried out irritably:

"Have you never taken care of a sick person, pray tell, or is it all your back-country training, that makes you so heavy-handed?"

"I helped mother take care of Phronsie when she had the measles, and Ben and Joel," said Polly, "five years ago; we haven't been sick lately."

" Humph ! " ejaculated Mrs. Chatterton, not very elegantly. But what was the use of a fine manner when there was nobody but a little back-country maiden to see it?

" I shall have to endure it till Hortense returns," she said with a sigh; " besides, it is my duty to give you something useful to do in this house. You should be thankful that I allow you to bathe me."

Polly's eyes flashed, and the hand holding the sponge trembled. Nothing but the fear of troubling Mamsie, and dear old Mr. King whose forbearance was worn to the finest of threads, kept her at her post.

" Now get the violet water," said Mrs. Chatterton, with an air she would never have dared employ towards Hortense; " it is the bottle in the lower left-hand corner of the case."

Polly got up from her knees, and stiffly stumbled across the room to the case of silver-mounted toilet articles : in her tumult bringing away the upper right-hand corner vial.

" *Stupide!* " exclaimed Mrs. Chatterton among her pillows. " Go back, and do as I bid you, girl; the lower left-hand corner bottle!"

Without a word Polly returned, and bringing the right vial set about its use as directed, in a rapidly growing dismay at the evil feelings surging through her, warning her it would not be safe to stay in the room much longer.

"Do you understand," presently began Mrs. Chatterton, fastening her cold blue eyes upon her, "what your position is in this house? Everybody else appears to be blind and idiotic to the last degree; you seem to have a little quickness to catch an idea."

As Polly did not answer, the question was repeated very sharply: "Do you understand what your position is in this house?"

"Yes," said Polly, in a low voice, and dashing out the violet water with a reckless hand, "I do."

"Take care," impatiently cried Mrs. Chatterton. Then she pushed her pillow into a better position, and returned to the charge.

"What is it, pray, since you understand it so well?"

"I understand that I am here in this house,"

said Polly, quite cold and white, " because dear Mr. King wants me to be here."

"Dear Mr. King!" echoed Mrs. Chatterton, in shrill disdain. "Stuff and nonsense," and she put her head back for an unpleasant cackle; it could hardly be called a laugh. "What an idiot the man is to have the wool pulled over his eyes in this fashion. I'll tell you, Polly"—and she raised herself up on her elbow, the soft lace falling away from the white, and yet shapely arm. This member had been one of her strongest claims to beauty, and even in her rage, Mrs. Chatterton paused a second to glance complacently at it in its new position—"you are, when all is said about your dear Mr. King, and your absurd assumption of equality with refined people who frequent this house, exactly the same underbred country girl as you were in your old brown house, goodness knows wherever that is."

"I'm glad I am," declared Polly. And she actually laughed merrily, while she squared her sturdy shoulders. Nothing could be sweeter than to hear it said she was worthy of the dear little old brown house, and didn't disgrace Mamsie's bringing up.

The laugh was the last feather that overthrew Mrs. Chatterton's restraint. She was actually furious now that she, widow of Algernon Chatterton, who was own cousin to Joseph Horatio King, should be faced by such presumption, and her words put aside with girlish amusement.

"And I'll tell you more," she went on, sitting quite erect now on the bed, "your mother thinks she is doing a fine thing to get all her family wormed in here in this style, but she'll " —

Polly Pepper, the girlish gladness gone from heart and face, waited for no more. "*Our mother!*" she cried stormily, unable to utter another word — "oh-oh!" Her breath came in quick, short gasps, the hot indignant blood mounting to the brown waves of hair on her brow, while she clasped her hands so tightly together, the pain at any other time would have made her scream.

Mrs. Chatterton, aghast at the effect of her words, leaned back once more against her pil-

lows. "Don't try to work up a scene," she
endeavored to say carelessly. But she might
as well has remonstrated with the north wind.
The little country maiden had a temper as well
as her own, and all the more for its long restraint, now on breaking bounds, it rushed at
the one who had provoked it, utterly regardless that it was the great Mrs. Algernon Chatterton.

For two minutes, so breathlessly did Polly
hurl the stinging sentences at the figure on the
bed, Cousin Eunice was obliged to let her
have her own way. Then as suddenly, the tor-
rent ceased. Polly grew quite white. "What
have I done — oh! what have I done?" she
cried, and rushed out of the room.

"Polly — Polly!" called Jasper's voice below. She knew he wanted her to try a new
duet he had gone down town to purchase; but
how could she play with such a storm in her
heart? and, worse than all else, was the con-
sciousness that she had spoken to one whose
gray hairs should have made her forget the
provocation received, words that now plunged
her into a hot shame to recall.

She flew over the stairs — up, away from every one's sight, to a long, dark lumber room, partially filled with trunks, and a few articles of furniture, prized as heirlooms, but no longer admissible in the family apartments. Polly closed the door behind her, and sank down in the shadow of a packing box half filled with old pictures, in a distress that would not even let her think. She covered her face with her hands, too angry with herself to cry; too aghast at the mischief she had done, to even remember the dreadful words Mrs. Chatterton had said to her.

"For of course, now she will complain to Mamsie, and I'm really afraid Mr. King will find it out; and it only needs a little thing to make him send her off. He said yesterday Dr. Valentine told him there was nothing really the matter with her — and — O dear! I don't know what will happen."

To poor Polly, crouching there on the floor in the dim and dusty corner, it seemed as if her wretchedness held no hope. Turn whichever way she might, the dreadful words she had uttered, rang through her heart. They

could not be unsaid; they were never to be
forgotten; but must always stay and rankle
there.

"Oh-oh!" she moaned, clasping her knees
with distressed little palms, and swaying back
and forth, "why didn't I remember what
Mamsie has always told us — that no insult
can do us harm if only we do not say or do
anything in return. Why — why couldn't I
have remembered it?"

How long she stayed there she never knew.
But at last, realizing that every moment there
was only making matters worse, she dragged
herself up from the little heap on the floor,
and trying to put a bit of cheerfulness into a
face she knew must frighten Mamsie, she went
slowly out, and down the stairs.

But no one looked long enough at her face
to notice its change of expression. Polly, the
moment she turned towards the household life
again, could feel that the air was charged with
some intense excitement. Hortense met her on
the lower stairs; the maid was startled out of
her usual nonchalance, and was actually in a
hurry.

"What is the matter?" cried Polly.

"Oh! the Madame is eel," said the maid; "the doctaire says it is not a lie dees time," and she swept past Polly.

Polly clung to the stair-railing, her face whitening, and her gaze fastened upon Mrs. Chatterton's door, where Hortense was now disappearing. Inside, was a sound of voices, and that subdued stir that gives token of a sick room.

"I have killed her!" cried Polly's heart. For one wild moment she was impelled to flight; anywhere, she did not care where, to shake off by motion in the free air, this paralysis of fear. But the next she started and rushing down the stairs, and into Mr. King's room, cried out, "Oh! dear Grandpapa, will Mrs. Chatterton die?"

"No, no, I think not," replied the old gentleman, surprised at her feeling. "Cousin Eunice never did show much self-control; but then, I don't believe this piece of bad news will kill her."

"Bad news?" gasped Polly, hanging to the

table where Mr. King was writing letters.
"Oh Grandpapa! what do you mean?"

"Bless me! where have you been, Polly
Pepper," said Mr. King, settling his eyeglass
to regard her closely, "not to hear the uproar
in this house? Yes, Mrs. Chatterton received
a telegram a half-hour since that her nephew,
the only one that she was very fond of among
her relatives, was drowned at sea, and she has
been perfectly prostrated by it, till she really
is quite ill."

Polly waited to hear no more, but on the
wings of the wind, flew out and up the stairs
once more.

"Where have you been, Polly?" cried Jasper, coming out of a side passage in time to
catch a dissolving view of her flying figure.
"Polly — Polly!" and he took three steps to
her one, and gained her side.

"Oh! don't stop me," begged Polly, flying
on, "don't, Jasper."

He took a good look at her face. "Anything I can help you about?" he asked quickly.

She suddenly stopped, her foot on the stair
above. "Oh, Jasper!" she cried, with clasped

hands, " you don't know — she may die, and I said horribly cruel things to her."

" Who — Mrs. Chatterton? " said the boy, opening his dark eyes; " why, you couldn't have said cruel things to her, Polly. Don't be foolish, child." He spoke as he would to Phronsie's terror, and smiled into her face. But it did not reassure Polly.

" Jasper, you don't know; you can't guess what dreadful things I said," cried poor overwhelmed Polly, clasping her hands tightly together at the mere thought of the words she had uttered.

" Then she must have said dreadful things to you," said the boy.

" She — but, oh, Jasper! that doesn't make it any better for me," said Polly. " Don't stop me; I am going to see if they won't let me do something for her."

" There are ever so many people up there now," said Jasper. " Your mother, and Hortense, and two or three maids. What in the world could you do, Polly? Come down into the library, and tell us all about it."

But Polly broke away from him with an

"Oh! I must do something for her," speeding on until she softly worked her way into the sick room.

Mrs. Pepper was busy with the doctor in the further part of the room, and Polly stood quite still for a moment, wishing she were one of the maids, to whom a bit of active service was given. She could not longer endure her thoughts in silence, and gently going up to her mother's side, with a timorous glance at the bed, as she passed it, she begged, " Mamsie, can't I do something for her? "

Mrs. Pepper glanced up quickly. " No — yes, you can; take this prescription down to Oakley's to be prepared."

Polly seized the bit of paper from Dr. Valentine's hand, and huried out. Again she glanced fearfully at the bed, but the curtain on that side was drawn so that only the outline of the figure could be seen. She was soon out on the street, the movement through the fresh air bringing back a little color to her cheek, and courage to her heart. Things did not seem quite so bad if she only might do something for the poor sick woman that could atone for the wretched work she had done; at least it would be some comfort if the invalid could be helped by her service.

Thus revolving everything in her mind, Polly did not hear her name called, nor rapid footsteps hurrying after.

"Wait!" at last cried a voice; "O dear me! what is the matter, Polly?" Alexia Rhys threw herself up flushed and panting at Polly's side.

"I'm on the way to the apothecary's," said Polly, without looking around.

"So I should suppose," said Alexia; "O dear! I'm so hot and tired. Do go a bit slower, Polly."

"I can't," said Polly. "She's very sick, and I must get this just as soon as I can." She waved the prescription at her, and redoubled her speed.

"Who?" gasped Alexia, stumbling after as best she could.

"Mrs. Chatterton," said Polly, a lump in her throat as she uttered the name.

"O dear me! that old thing," cried Alexia, her enthusiasm over the errand gone.

"Hush!" said Polly hoarsely; "she may die. She has had bad news."

"What?" asked Alexia; the uncomfortable walk might be enlivened by a bit of stray gossip; "what is it, Polly? What news?"

"A telegram," said Polly. "Her favorite nephew was drowned at sea."

"Oh! I didn't know she had any favorite nephew. Doesn't she fight with everybody?"

"Do be quiet," begged Polly. "No; that is, perhaps, other people are not kind to her."

"Oh!" said Alexia, in a surprised voice. "Well, I think she's perfectly and all-through-and-through horrid, so! Don't race like this through the streets, Polly. You'll get there soon enough."

But Polly turned a deaf ear, and at last the prescription was handed over the counter at Oakley's, and after what seemed an endless time to Polly, the medicine was given to her.

"Now as soon as you carry that thing home," observed Alexia, glancing at the white parcel in Polly's hand, "I hope you'll come with us girls. That's what I ran after you for."

"What girls?" asked Polly.

"Why, Philena and the Conwalls; we are going to have a sleighing party to-night, and a supper at Lilly Drexell's. Mrs. Cornwall chaperones the thing."

Polly was surprised to feel her heart bound. It hadn't seemed as if it could ever be moved by any news of girlish frolics, but that its dull ache must go on forever.

"Oh! I can't," she cried the next moment. "I must stay at home, and help take care of Mrs. Chatterton."

"Nonsense!" exclaimed Alexia in a provoked tone; "you are not wanted there, Polly Pepper; the idea, with that great house full of servants."

"Well, I shall not go," declared Polly sharply; "you needn't ask me, Alexia. I shall stay home till she gets well."

"You little idiot!" cried Alexia, thoroughly out of temper. But as this produced no effect on Polly, she began to wheedle and coax. "Now, Polly, do be reasonable. You know we can't go without you; you wouldn't spoil the whole thing; you know you wouldn't. I

shall just tell the Cornwalls that you are coming," and she turned off to the corner of the
avenue.

"Indeed you will not," called Polly after
her. "Don't you dare do that, Alexia Rhys,"
she said, with flashing eyes.

"You are the most uncomfortable girl I
ever saw," cried Alexia, stopping, to come
slowly back. "You spoil every bit of fun
with your absurd notions. I'm quite, quite
put out with you, Polly."

"I'm sorry," said poor Polly, fairly longing
for the snow-revel, and dismayed at disap-
pointing the girls.

"No, you're not," pouted Alexia, "and I
shall tell them all so," and she broke away and
ran off in the opposite direction.

Polly was met at the door by Mrs. Pepper,
who grasped the packet of medicine quickly.

"Isn't there anything else I can do, Mamsie?" begged Polly.

"No; sit down and rest; you're hot and
tired, you've run so."

"I'm not tired," said Polly, not daring to
ask. "Is she better?"

"Well, you must be," said Mrs. Pepper, hurring off, "going all the way down to Oakley's."

So Polly had nothing to do but to sit out in the hall, and listen and watch all the movements in the sick room, every one of which but increased her terror. At last she could bear it no longer, and as Dr. Valentine came out, putting on his gloves, she rushed after him.

"Oh! will she die?" she begged; "please do tell me, sir?"

"Die? no indeed, I hope not," said Dr. Valentine. "She has had a severe shock to her nerves and her age is against her, but she is coming around all right, I trust. Why, Polly, I thought better things of you, my girl." He glanced down into the distressed face with professional disfavor.

"I'm so glad she won't die," breathed Polly, wholly lost to his opinion of her; and her face gleamed with something of her old brightness.

"I didn't know you were so fond of her," observed Dr. Valentine grimly; "indeed, to speak truthfully, I have yet to learn that anybody is fond of her, Polly."

"Now if you really want to help her," he continued thoughtfully, pulling his beard, as Polly did not answer, "I can give you one or two hints that might be of use."

"Oh! I do, I do," cried Polly, with eagerness.

"It will be tiresome work," said Dr. Valentine, "but it will be a piece of real charity, and perhaps, Polly, it's as well for you to begin now as to wait till you can belong to forty charity clubs, and spend your time going to committee meetings." And he laughed not altogether pleasantly. How was Polly to know that Mrs. Valentine was immersed up to her ears in a philanthropic sea with the smallest possible thought for the doctor's home? "Now that maid," said the physician, dropping his tone to a confidential one, "is as well as the average, but she's not the one who is to amuse the old lady. It's that she needs more than medicine, Polly. She actually requires diversion."

Poor Polly stood as if turned to stone.

Diversion! And she had thrown away all chance of that.

" She is suffering for the companionship of some bright young nature," Dr. Valentine proceeded, attributing the dismay written all over the girl's face, to natural unwillingness to do the service. " After she gets over this attack she needs to be read to for one thing; to be told the news; to be made to forget herself. But of course, Polly," he said hastily, buttoning his top coat, and opening the outer door, " it's too much to ask of you; so think no more about it, child."

CHAPTER XII.

NEW WORK FOR POLLY.

IT was Saturday morning, and Polly ran upstairs with a bright face, the morning *Journal* in her hand. " I'm going to stay with Mrs.
Chatterton, Hortense," she announced to that
functionary in the dressing-room.

" And a comfairte may it gif to you," said
Hortense, with a vicious shake of the silk
wrapper in her hand, before hanging it in its
place. " Madame has the *trés diablerie,* cross
as de two steeks, what you call it, dis morning."

Polly went softly into the room, closing the
door gently after her. In the shadow of one
corner of the large apartment, sat Mrs. Chatterton under many wrappings in the depths of
an invalid's chair. Polly went up to her
side.

" Would you like to have me read the news,
Mrs. Chatterton? " she asked gently.

Mrs. Chatterton turned her head and looked
at her. " No," she was about to say shortly,
just as she had repulsed many little offers of
Polly's for the past few days; but somehow
this morning the crackling of the fresh sheet
in the girl's hand, suggestive of crisp bits of
gossip, was too much for her to hear indifferently, especially as she was in a worse state of
mind than usual over Hortense and her bad
temper.

" You may sit down and read a little, if you
like," she said ungraciously. So Polly, happy
as a queen at the permission, slipped into a
convenient chair, and began at once. She happened fortunately on just the right things for
the hungry ears; a description of a large
church wedding, the day before; two or three
bits about society people that Mrs. Chatterton
had lost sight of, and a few other items just
as acceptable.

Polly read on and on, from one thing to
another, not daring to look up to see the effect,

until at last everything in the way of gossip was exhausted.

"Is that all?" asked Mrs. Chatterton hungrily.

Polly, hunting the columns for anything, even a murder account if it was but in high life, turned the paper again disconsolately, obliged to confess it was.

"Well, do put it by, then," said Mrs. Chatterton sharply, "and not whirl it before my face; it gives me a frightful headache."

"I might get the *Town Talk*," suggested Polly, as a bright thought struck her. "It came yesterday. I saw it on the library table."

"So it is Saturday." Mrs. Chatterton looked up quickly. "Yes, you may, Polly," her mouth watering for the revel she would have in its contents.

So Polly ran over the stairs with delighted feet, and into the library, beginning to rummage over the papers and magazines on the reading table.

"Where is it?" she exclaimed, turning them with quick fingers. "O dear! it was right here last evening."

"What is it?" asked Phronsie, from the depths of a big arm-chair, and looking up from her book. Then she saw as soon as she had asked the question, that Polly was in trouble, so she laid down her book, and slid out of the chair. "What is it, Polly? Let me help you, do."

"Why, the *Town Talk* — that hateful old society thing," said Polly, throwing the papers to right and left. "You know, Phronsie; it has a picture of a bottle of ink, and a big quill for a heading. O dear! do help me, child, for she will get nervous if I am gone long."

"Oh! I know where that is," said Phronsie deliberately, laying a cool little hand on Polly's hot one.

"Where?" demanded Polly feverishly. "Oh, Phronsie! where?"

"Jack Rutherford has it."

Polly threw down the papers, and started for the door.

"He has gone," said Phronsie; "he went home almost an hour ago."

Polly turned sharply at her. "What did he want *Town Talk* for?"

"He said it was big, and he asked Grandpapa if he might have it, and Grandpapa said Yes. I don't know what he wanted it for," said Phronsie. "And he took other newspapers, too, Polly; oh! ever so many."

"Well, I don't care how many he took, nor what they were," cried Polly, "only that very identical one. O dear me! Well, I'll ask Jasper."

And rushing from the library, Phronsie following in a small panic over Polly's distress, she knocked at the door of Jasper's den, a little room in the wing, looking out on the east lawn.

"Oh! I am so glad you are here," she exclaimed as "Come in!" greeted her, and both Phronsie and she precipitated themselves with no show of ceremony, in front of his study table. "O, Jasper! could you get me a copy of *Town Talk?* Jack Rutherford has gone off with ours."

"*Town Talk!*" repeated Jasper, raising his head from his hands to stare at her.

"Yes; Jack has taken ours off; Grandpapa gave it to him. Can you, Jasper? Will

it break up your study much?" she poured
out anxiously.

"No — that is — never mind," said Jasper,
pushing the book away and springing from his
chair. "But whatever in the world do you
want that trash for?" He turned, and looked
at her curiously.

"Mrs. Chatterton will let me read it to her;
she said so," cried Polly, clasping her hands
nervously, "but if I don't get the paper soon,
why, I'm afraid she'll change her mind."

Jasper gave a low whistle as he flung himself into his coat. "Inestimable privilege!"
he exclaimed at last, tossing on his cap.

"Oh, Jasper! you are so good," cried Polly
in a small rapture. "I'm so sorry to have to
ask you."

"I'll go for you, Jasper," declared Phronsie; "Mamsie will let me; I almost know she
will."

"No, no, Phronsie," said Jasper, as she was
flying off; "it isn't any place for you to go
to. I shall get one at the hotel — the Allibone.
I'll be back in a trice, Polly."

Polly went out, and sat down in one of the

big oaken chairs in the hall to seize it as it came, and Phronsie deposited herself in an opposite chair, and watched Polly. And presently in came Jasper, waving the desired journal. Polly, with a beaming face, grasped it and rushed off upstairs.

"Polly," called the boy, looking after her, "it isn't too late now for you to go with them. Lucy Bennett met me at the corner and she said they will take the twelve o'clock train, instead of the eleven, and she wanted me to beg you to come."

"No, no," tossed back Polly, rushing on, "I am quite determined to stay at home." Then she went into Mrs. Chatterton's room, and closed the door. But she couldn't so easily shut out the longings that would rise in her heart for the Saturday outing that the other girls were to have. How lovely it would be! the run out to Silvia Horne's charming house some ten miles distant; the elegant luncheon they would have, followed by games, and a dance in the ball-room upstairs, that Silvia's older sisters used for their beautiful parties. Then the merry return before dusk, of the

twelve girls, all capital friends at school.
Oh-oh!"

"You've been an unconscionable time," exclaimed Mrs. Chatterton in a sharp, high key, "just to get a paper. Well, do sit down; I am quite tired waiting for you."

Polly sat down, and resolutely plunged into the column where the news items promised the most plentiful yield, but in between the lines ran the doings of the girls: how they were all assembling by this time at Lucy Bennett's; how they were hurrying off to the train, and all the other delightful movements of the "outing" flashed before her eyes, as she finished item after item of her dreary task. But how Mrs. Chatterton gloated over it!

At last Polly, feeling as if she could not endure another five minutes of it, glanced up to see the old lady's eyes actually sparkling; her mouth had fallen into contented curves, and the jeweled hand resting on the chair-arm was playing with the fringe, while she leaned forward that she might not lose a word.

"Read that again, Polly," she said, "the list of presents exhibited at Arabella Granger's wedding. I didn't hear any mention of the Archibalds. It can't be that they have fallen out; and read more slowly."

So Polly began once more the long lists of gifts that ushered in the matrimonial happiness of Mrs. John Westover *née* Miss Arabella Granger; this time, however, stimulated by the pleasure she was giving, to find it an endurable task.

It seemed to Polly as if Mrs. John Westover had everything on earth given to her that could possibly be presented at a wedding; nevertheless the list was gone through again bravely, Polly retracing her steps two or three times to read the items over for her listener's slow digestion.

"The Archibalds are not mentioned, either as being there or sending a gift, nor the Harlands, nor the Smythes, so I am very glad I didn't remember her," said Mrs. Chatterton, drawing herself up with a relieved sigh. "Those presents sound fine on paper, but it isn't as well as she might have done if she had made a different match. Now something else, Polly," and she dismissed Mrs. Westover with

a careless wave of her hand. Polly flew off
into the fashion hints, and was immediately lost
in the whirl of coming toilets. No one noticed
when the door opened, so of course no one
saw Mrs. Whitney standing smiling behind the
old lady's big chair.

"Well, Polly," said a pleasant voice suddenly.

Down went *Town Talk* to the floor as Polly
sprang up with a glad cry, and Mrs. Chatterton
turned around nervously.

"Oh, Auntie — Auntie!" cried Polly, convulsively clinging to her, "are you really here,
and is Dicky home?"

"Dear child," said Mrs. Whitney, as much a
girl for the moment as Polly herself. And
pressing kisses on the red lips, while she folded
her close — "Yes, Dick is at home. There, go
and find him; he is in Mrs. Pepper's room."

"I am glad to see you so much better, Mrs.
Chatterton," said Mrs. Whitney, leaning over
the invalid's chair to lay the tenderest of palms
on the hand resting on the chair-arm.

"Oh, yes, Marian; I am better," said Mrs.
Chatterton, looking around for Polly, then

down at the delicious *Town Talk* carelessly
thrown on the floor. "Will you send her back
as soon as possible?" she asked with her old
imperativeness.

"Who — Polly?" said Mrs. Whitney, following the glance. "Why, she has gone to see
Dick, you know. Now, why cannot I read a
bit?" and she picked up the paper.

"You don't know what has been read," said
Mrs. Chatterton as Mrs. Whitney drew up a
chair and sat down, running her eye in a prac-
ticed way over the front page. "Dear me,
it makes me quite nervous, Marian, to see you
prowling around all over the sheet that way."

"Oh! I shall find something interesting
quite soon, I fancy," said Mrs. Whitney cheerfully, her heart on her boy and the jolly home-
coming he was having. "Here is the Washing-
ton news; I mean all about the receptions and
teas."

"She has read that," said Mrs. Chatterton.

"Now for the fashion department." Mrs.
Whitney whirled the paper over dexterously.
"Do you know, Mrs. Chatterton, gray stuffs
are to be worn more than ever this spring?"

" I don't care about that," said Mrs. Chatterton quickly, " and besides, quite likely there'll be a complete revolution before spring really sets in, and gray stuffs will go out. Find some description of tea gowns, can't you? I must have one or two more."

" And here are some wonderfully pretty caps, if they are all like the descriptions," said Mrs. Whitney, unluckily dropping on another paragraph.

" Caps! who wants to hear about them?" cried Mrs. Chatterton in a dudgeon. " I hope I'm not at the cap period yet."

" Oh! those lovely little lace arrangements," said Mrs. Whitney hastily; " don't you know how exquisite they are at Pinaud's?" she cried.

" I'm sure I never noticed," said Mrs. Chatterton indifferently. " Hortense always arranges my hair better without lace. if you can't find what I ask you, Marian," raising her voice to a higher key, " you needn't trouble to read at all."

Fortunately the dscription of the gown worn by Lady Hartly Cavendish at a London high tea, stood out in bold relief, as Mrs. Whitney's eyes nervously ran over the columns again, and she seized upon it.

But in just two moments she was interrupted. "Send that girl back again, Marian," cried Mrs. Chatterton. "I had just got her trained so that she suits me. It tires me to death to hear you."

"I do not know whether Polly can come now," said Mrs. Whitney gently; "she"—

"Do not know whether Polly can come!" repeated Mrs. Chatterton sharply, and leaning forward in her chair. "Didn't I say I wanted her?"

"You did." Marian's tone did not lose a note of its ordinary gentleness. "But I shall ask her if she is willing to do it as a favor, Mrs. Chatterton; you quite understand that, of course?" She, too, leaned forward in her chair, and gazed into the cold, hard face.

"Just like your father," cried Mrs. Chatterton, settling herself irascibly back in the chair-depths again. "There is no hope that affairs in this house will mend. I wash my hands of you."

"I am so glad that you consider me like my

father," said Mrs. Whitney gleefully as a child. " We surely are united on this question."

" May I read some more? " cried Polly, coming in softly, and trying to calm the impetuous rush of delight as her eyes met Mrs. Whitney's.

" Yes; I am waiting for you," said Mrs. Chatterton. " Begin where you left off."

Mrs. Whitney bit her pretty lips and slipped out of her chair, just pausing a moment to lay her hand on the young shoulder as she passed, and a world of comfort fell upon Polly, shut in once more to her dreary task.

" How perfectly splendid that I didn't go to Silvia Horne's luncheon party now! " cried Polly's heart over and over between the lines. " If I had, I should have missed dear Auntie's home-coming, and Dicky's." She glanced up with luminous eyes as she whirled the sheet. Mrs. Chatterton, astonishing as it may seem, was actually smiling.

" It's some comfort to hear you read," she observed with a sigh of enjoyment, " because you enjoy it yourself. I wouldn't give a fig for anybody to try to do it."

Polly felt like a guilty little thing to take this quietly, and she eased her conscience by being more glad that she was in that very room doing that very task. And so the moments sped on.

Outside, Dick was holding high revel as every one revolved around him, the hero of the coasting accident, till the boy ran considerable danger from all the attention he was receiving. But one glance and a smile from Mrs. Whitney brought him back to himself.

"Don't talk any more about it," he cried a trifle impatiently. "I was a muff to stick on, when I knew we were going over. Mamma, won't you stop them?"

And she did.

"Do you know, Dicky and I have a secret to tell all of you good people." The color flew into her soft cheek, and her eyes beamed.

"Really, Marian," said her father, whose hand had scarcely ceased patting Dick's brown head since the boy's home-coming, "you've grown young in Badgertown. I never saw you look so well as you do to-day."

Mrs. Whitney laughed and tossed him a gay

little smile, that carried him back to the days when Marian King stood before him looking just so.

" Now listen, father, and all you good people, to my secret — Dicky's and mine; we are allowed to tell it now. Papa Whitney sailed in the *Servia,* and he ought to be in to-day ! "

A shout of joy greeted her announcement. Polly, off in her prison, could hear the merry sounds, and her happy heart echoed them. The misery of the past week when she had been bearing an unatoned fault, seemed to drop away from her as she listened, and to say, " Life holds sunshine yet."

Then a hush dropped upon the gay uproar. She did not know that Dicky was proclaiming " Yes, and he is never, never going back again. That is, unless he takes mamma and me, you know."

Mrs. Chatterton turned suddenly upon the young figure.

" Do go! " She tossed an imperative command with her jeweled fingers. " You have ceased to be amusing since your interest is all in the other room with that boy."

Polly dashed the newspaper to the floor, and rushing impulsively across the room, threw herself, with no thought for the consequences, on her knees at Mrs. Chatterton's chair.

" Oh-oh! " she cried, the color flying up to the brown waves on her temples, " don't send me off; then I shall know you never will forgive me."

" Get up, do! " exclaimed Mrs. Chatterton, in disgust; " you are crushing my gown, and besides I hate scenes."

But Polly held resolutely to the chair-arm, and never took her brown eyes from the cold face.

" I must say, Polly Pepper," cried Mrs. Chatterton with rising anger, " you are the most disagreeable girl that I ever had the misfortune to meet. I, for one, will not put up with your constant ebullitions of temper. Go out of this room! "

Polly rose slowly and drew herself up with something so new in face and manner, that the old lady instinctively put up her eyeglass and gazed curiously through it, as one would look at a strange animal.

"Humph!" she said slowly at last, "well, what do you want to say? Speak out, and then go."

"Nothing," said Polly in a low voice, but quite distinctly, "only I shall not trouble you again, Mrs. Chatterton." And as the last words were spoken, she was out of the room.

"Pretty doings these!" Mr. King, by a dexterous movement, succeeded in slipping back of the portière folds into the little writing-room, as Polly rushed out through the other doorway into the hall. "A fortunate thing it was that I left Dick, to see what had become of Polly. Now, Cousin Eunice, you move from my house!" and descending the stairs, he called determinedly, "Polly, Polly, child!"

Polly, off in her own room now, heard him, and for the first time in her life, wished she need not answer.

"Polly — Polly!" the determined call rang down the passage, causing her to run fast with a "Yes, Grandpapa, I'm coming."

"Now, I should just like to inquire," began Mr. King, taking her by her two young shoulders and looking down into the flushed face, " what she has been saying to you."

" Oh, Grandpapa! " down went Polly's brown head, " don't make me tell. Please don't, Grandpapa."

" I shall! " declared Mr. King; " every blessed word. Now begin! "

" She — she wanted me to go out of the room," said Polly, in a reluctant gasp.

" Indeed! " snorted Mr. King. " Well, she will soon go out of that room. Indeed, I might say, out of the house."

" Oh, Grandpapa! " exclaimed Polly, in great distress, and raising the brown eyes — he was dismayed to find them filling with tears — " don't, don't send her away! It is all my fault; indeed it is, Grandpapa! "

" Your fault," cried Mr. King irately; " you must not say such things, child; that's silly; you don't know the woman."

" Grandpapa," cried Polly, holding back the storm of tears to get the words out, " I never told you — I couldn't — but I said perfectly dreadful words to her a week ago. Oh, Grandpapa! I did, truly."

"That's right," said the old gentleman in a pleased tone. "What were they, pray tell? Let us know."

"Oh, Grandpapa, don't!" begged Polly, with a shiver; "I want to forget them."

"If you would only follow them up with more," said Mr. King meditatively; "when it comes to tears, she must march, you know."

"I won't cry," said Polly, swallowing the lump in her throat, "if you will only let her stay."

She turned to him such a distressed and white face that Mr. King stood perplexedly looking down at her, having nothing to say.

"I'm tired of her," at last he said; "we are all tired of her; she has about worn us out."

"Grandpapa," cried Polly, seeing her advantage in his hesitation, "if you will only let her stay, I will never beg you for anything again."

"Well, then she goes," cried Mr. King shortly. "Goodness me, Polly, if you are going to stop asking favors, Cousin Eunice marches instanter!"

"Oh! I'll beg and tease for ever so many things," cried Polly radiantly, her color coming back. "Will you let her stay, Grandpapa — will you?" She clasped his arm tightly and would not let him go.

"Well," said Mr. King slowly, "I'll think about it, Polly."

"Will you?" cried Polly. "Dear Grandpapa, please say yes."

Mr. King drew a long breath. "Yes," he said at last.

CHAPTER XIII.

A PIECE OF NEWS.

"COLLECT the whole bunch of Peppers and send them into my writing-room, Marian." Old Mr. King mounting the stairs, turned to see that his command was heard.

" You want Mother Pepper too, I presume? " said Mrs. Whitney, pausing at the foot.

" Mother Pepper? No, indeed; the last person in the world I wish to see," cried her father irritably. " The bunch of Pepper children, I want, and at once; see that they all report to me directly." With that he redoubled his efforts and was soon at the top of the long oaken steps.

Polly and Ben closely followed by Joel, David and Phronsie soon rushed over the same ascending thoroughfare, and presented them-

218

selves, flushed and panting, at the writing-room door.

"Come in," called Mr. King from within.

"Here we are, sir," said Ben, spokesman by virtue of being the eldest.

"Yes, yes," said Mr. King nervously, and turning away from some papers he was fumbling to occupy the waiting moments. "Well, do sit down, all of you. I sent for you to have a talk about something that you — that you — well, do sit down."

So all the Peppers deposited themselves in various resting-places; all but Joel. He immediately marched up to the old gentleman's chair.

"If it's good news," he said abruptly, "please let us have it right this minute. But if it's bad, why," a gathering alarm stole over his chubby countenance, as he scanned the face before him, "I'm going out-doors."

"It's good or bad news according as you take it," said the old gentleman. "It ought to be good. But there," pushing back his chair to look at the row of anxious figures the other side of the table, "do sit down with the

rest, Joe, and stop staring me out of coun‧
tenance."

Polly at that, pushed a chair over toward
Joel, who persuading himself into it, sat uncom‧
fortably perched on its edge, where he stared
harder than ever.

"Hum! well, children, now you are all re‧
markably sensible boys and girls. Re-mar‧
kably sensible. I've always said so, and I see
no reason to change my opinion of you now.
And so, although at first my news may not be
quite to your liking, why, you'll quickly make
it so, and be very happy about it in the end.
Hem! well, did you ever think that — that
your mother might possibly marry again?"

The last words were brought out so abruptly,
that to the five pairs of ears strained to catch
their import, it seemed as if the news had shot
by harmlessly. But after a breathing space the
dreadful "marry," and "your mother," came
back to them, bringing the several owners of the
ears out of their chairs at one bound.

"Our mother!" Ben hoarsely exclaimed.

"Oh! how can you?" cried Polly passion‧
ately, a little white line showing around her

mouth, "say such perfectly dreadful things, sir!"

Phronsie clasped her hands in silent terror, and raised big eyes to his face. David began to walk helplessly down the apartment. "See here!" said Joel, turning to the others, "wait a minute, and hold on. Perhaps it's you, sir," whirling back to question with piercing eyes, the old gentleman, "who's going to marry our mother. Then it's all right!"

"Me!" roared the old gentleman. "Oh! bless my soul, what should I want to marry for at my time of life? Oh! my goodness me."

His distress was now so frightful to see, that it brought the Peppers in a measure out of theirs; and they began at once to endeavor to soothe him.

"Don't — oh! don't," they cried, and a common trouble overwhelming them, they rushed around the table, seized his hands, and patted his shoulders and hair. "Oh! this is very dreadful," gasped Polly, "but don't you feel badly, dear, dear Grandpapa."

"I should think it was," said Mr. King. "Phronsie, here, child, get into my lap. I'll come to myself then. There, now, that's something like," as Phronsie, with a low cry, hopped into her usual nest. " Now perhaps I can communicate the rest of my news, when I get my breath."

The Peppers held theirs, and he began once more. " Now, children, it isn't in the course of nature for such a fine bright woman as your mother to remain single the rest of her life; somebody would be sure to come and carry her off. I'm glad it's to be in my lifetime, for now I can be easy in my mind, and feel that you have a protector when I am gone. There, there, we won't talk about that," as the young faces turned dark with sudden pain, while Joel rushed convulsively to the window, " you can see how I feel about it."

" Are you glad? " cried Ben hoarsely. Polly for her life could not speak. The whole world seemed turning round, and sinking beneath her feet.

" Yes, I am," said the old gentleman, " and it won't alter the existing state of things, for he will live here with us, and things will be just the same, if only you children will take

it rightly. But I've no doubt you will in the
end; no doubt at all," he added, brightening
up, " for you are very sensible young people.
I've always said so."

" Who is he? " The dreadful question trembled on all the lips; but no one asked it. Seeing this, Mr. King broke out, " Well, now of
course you want to know who is going to
marry your mother, that is, if you are willing.
For she won't have him unless you are to be
happy about it. Would you like Dr. Fisher for
a father? "

Joel broke away from the window with a
howl, while Polly tumultuously threw herself
within the kind arms encircling Phronsie.

" Next to you," cried the boy, " why, he's a
brick, Dr. Fisher is! "

" Why didn't you tell us before that it was
he? " sobbed Polly, with joyful tears running
over her face. Davie, coming out of his
gloomy walk, turned a happy face towards
the old man's chair, while Ben said something
to himself that sounded like " Thank God! "

Phronsie alone remained unmoved. " What

is Dr. Fisher going to do?" she asked presently, amid the chatter that now broke forth.

"He's going to live here," said old Mr. King, looking down at her, and smoothing her yellow hair. "Won't that be nice, Phronsie?"

"Yes," said Phronsie, "it will. And he'll bring his funny old gig, won't he, and I'll drive sometimes, I suppose?" she added with great satisfaction.

"Yes; you will," said the old gentleman, winking furiously to keep back the excited flow of information that now threatened the child. "Well, Phronsie, you love Dr. Fisher, don't you?"

"Yes, I do," said the child, folding her hands in her lap, "love him very much indeed."

"Well, he's going to be your father," communicated Mr. King, cautiously watching her face at each syllable.

"Oh, no!" cried Phronsie, "he couldn't be; he's Dr. Fisher." She laughed softly at the idea. "Why, Grandpapa, he couldn't be my father."

"Listen, Phronsie," and Mr. King took both her hands in his, "and I'll tell you about it so that you will understand. Dr. Fisher loves your mother; he has loved her for many years — all those years when she was struggling on in the little brown house. But he couldn't tell her so, because he had others depending on him for support. They don't need him now, and as soon as he is free, he comes and tells your mother and me, like a noble good man as he is, all about it. He's a gentleman, children," he declared, turning to the others, " and you will be glad to call him father."

" I don't know what you mean," said Phronsie, with puzzled eyes. " Dear Grandpapa, please tell me."

" Why, he is going to marry your mother, child, and we are all to live here together just the same, and everything is going to be just as happy as possible."

Phronsie gave a sharp and sudden cry of distress. " But Mamsie, my Mamsie will be gone!" and then she hid her face in the old gentleman's breast.

" O dear, dear! get a glass of water, Polly," cried Mr. King. " One of you run and open the window. Phronsie, Phronsie—there. child.

look up and let me tell you." But Phronsie
burrowed yet deeper in the protecting nest,
regardless of his spotless linen.

" Polly, speak to her," he cried in despair;
" where is she? gone for the water? O dear!
Here, Ben, you try. Dear, dear, what a blun-
derer I am."

" Phronsie," said Ben, leaning over the shaking figure, " you are making Grandpapa sick."

Up came Phronsie's yellow head. " Oh,
Grandpapa!" she wailed, putting out an unsteady little hand, " I didn't mean to, dear
Grandpapa, only — only Mamsie will be gone
now."

" Bless your heart, you'll have Mamsie more
than ever," cried Mr. King heartily. " Here,
you children, tell her. Polly, we don't want
the water now, she's come to," as Polly came
rushing in with a glassful. " Make her understand; I can't."

So Polly, setting down her glass, the others
crowding around, took up the task of making
the piece of news as delightful as possible, and
presently Phronsie came out of her despair, to
ask questions.

"Are you really and truly very glad, Polly?" she asked at last, in a lull.

"Really and truly I am so glad I don't know what to do," said Polly, kneeling down by the chair-side. "Don't you see we are so much the richer, Phronsie? We have lost nothing, and we gain Dr. Fisher. Dear splendid Dr. Fisher!"

"You've always wanted to repay Dr. Fisher for his kindness," said Mr. King, "and now's your chance, Polly."

"I guess he'll get his pay back for his stove," cried Joel in a burst; "Polly will wait on him, and kill herself doing things for him."

"And for your new eyes," sang Phronsie in a pleased way. "Oh, Polly!" She jumped out of the old gentleman's lap, and began to dance around the room, softly clapping her hands and exclaiming, "Oh, Polly!"

"Well, now, children," said Mr. King, as the excitement ran low, "you just run and tell your mother, every one of you, how happy she will make you by bringing Dr. Fisher here as your father. Scamper, now!"

No need to urge them. On the wings of

the wind ran the five Peppers up into Mamsie's own room. Mrs. Pepper for once turning aside from the claim of her pressing duties, was standing by the work table. Here stood the mending basket before her, piled to the brim with the weekly installment of stockings big and little, clamoring for attention. But the usually busy needle lay idle, and the busier hands were folded, as the mother-heart went over the words she knew were being rehearsed downstairs by the kind friend who had made a home for them. He was pleading her cause with her children.

"They shall be happy, anyway," she said softly to herself, "bless their hearts!" as they burst in.

"Mother," said Ben — How the boy's cheek glowed! And what a world of joy rang in the usually quiet tones! — "we want to thank you for giving us Dr. Fisher for a father."

"Mamsie," Polly hid her happy face on the dear neck, "I've always loved him, you know; oh! I'm so glad."

Joel whooped out something incoherent, but

his face told the words, while Davie clasped one of the firm, closely folded hands.

"If you'll take me in your lap as much as ever," said Phronsie deliberately, and patting the other hand, "why, I shall be really and truly glad, Mamsie."

"Bless your dear heart!" cried Mother Pepper, clasping her tightly, "and you children, all of you," and she drew them all within her arms. "Now I want you to understand, once for all, that it isn't to be unless you all wish it. You are sure Mr. King hasn't persuaded you to like it?"

"Look at us," cried Ben, throwing back his head to see her eyes. "Do we act as if we had been talked over?"

At that, Polly burst into a merry laugh; and the others joining, Mother Pepper laughing as heartily as the rest, the big room became the jolliest place imaginable.

"No, I don't really think you do," said Mrs. Pepper, wiping her eyes.

"Dear me!" cried Jasper, putting his head in the doorway, "what good fun is going on? I'm not going to be left out."

"Come in, Jasper," they all called.

"And we've a piece of news that will make your hair stand on end," said Joel gayly.

"Joe, don't announce it so," cried Polly in dismay, who dearly enjoyed being elegant. "Ben must tell it; he is the oldest."

"No, no; let Polly," protested Ben.

"Polly shall," said Jasper, hurrying in to stand the picture of patience before the group. "Hurry, do, for I must say my curiosity is hard to keep within bounds."

So Polly was gently pushed into the center of the circle. "Go on," said Joel, "and hurry up, or I shall tell myself."

"Jasper," said Polly, her breath coming fast, "oh! you can't think; we are so glad "— But she got no further, for Phronsie, rushing out of Mother Pepper's arms, piped out suddenly:

"Dr. Fisher is coming here to live always and forever, and I'm going to ride in his gig, and Mamsie likes him, and I'm going to call him father; now, Jasper, I told you!"

"I should think you did," exclaimed Ben.

"Whew!" cried Jasper, "that is a piece of

news all in one breath. Well, Mrs. Pepper,
I'm glad of it, too. I congratulate you." With
that, he marched up to her, Phronsie hanging
to his arm, and shook her hand heartily.

And in two days everybody in the King set
knew that the mother of the five little Peppers
was going to be married.

"I should think you'd want to be condoled
with, Ben," said Pickering Dodge, clapping
him on the shoulder as he rushed down the
aisle of the store occupied by Cabot & Van
Meter.

"Halloo!" said Ben, "can't stop," rushing
past.

"I suppose not," said Pickering carelessly,
and striding after, "so I'll whisper my gentle congratulations in your ear ' on the wing.'
But I'm awfully sorry for you, Ben," he added,
as he came up to him.

"You needn't be," said Ben brightly, "we
are all as glad as can be."

"Sweet innocent, you don't know a step-
father," said Pickering lugubriously.

"I know Dr. Fisher," said Ben, "that's
enough."

"Well, when you want comfort, come to me," said Pickering, "or your uncle!"

"Don't you fill Ben's ears with your foolishness," said the Senior Partner, coming out of the counting-room. "Take yourself off, Pickering; you're hindering Ben."

Pickering laughed. "I'm caught in the very act. Now, Ben, remember I'm your friend when you get into trouble with your dear pa. Good-by, Uncle," with a bright nod, and a lazy shake of his long figure. "Trade always demoralizes me. I'll get back to my books," and he vanished as quickly as he came.

"Back to your books," said his uncle grimly, "hum, I wish you would. See here, Ben," he put a controlling hand on the boy's shoulder, "one word with you," marching him into the private office of the firm. "Don't you follow Pickering too closely, my boy," he said abruptly; "he's a good lad in the main, but if he is my nephew, I must give you warning. He's losing ground."

Ben lifted his head in sudden alarm. "Oh! I hope not, sir," he said.

"It's a fact. Master Nelson says he could

be first scholar in the grammar, but for the last six months he's failed steadily. There's no particular reason, only ambition's gone. And when you say that, you mean there's a general collapse of all my hopes concerning him."

"Oh! no, sir," Ben kept on protesting, his ruddy cheek losing its color. "He'll take hold by and by and give a pull at his books again."

"It isn't a pull now and then that gets a man up hill," observed Mr. Cabot, leaning back in his revolving chair to look into the blue eyes, "that you know as well as I. Now, Ben, I'm not going to see you throw away your prospects, too. Don't let him influence you in the wrong way. He's bright and attractive, but don't pay attention to his ridicule of good things."

"I've a mother," said Ben proudly, "and I don't believe any boy could say much to me, that I'd think of twice, if she didn't like it."

"You always tell her everything, do you, Ben?" asked Mr. Cabot with a curious glance.

"I should think so, sir," said Ben, with a short laugh.

" You'll do, then," said Mr. Cabot, bringing his palm down on a pile of unread letters awaiting him. " Go ahead. I don't promise anything, but I will say this. If you work on as you have done these two years since you came in here as errand boy, Ben, I'll make you a power in the house. Understand I don't expect you to do brilliant things; that isn't in your line. You will be a success only as a steady, faithful worker. But keep at it, and hang on to Cabot & Van Meter, and we'll hang on to you."

CHAPTER XIV.

MAMSIE'S WEDDING.

"POLLY," said Dr. Fisher, coming suddenly out of a corner of the library as she ran around the portière folds, "you are sure you are willing — are willing it should go on?"

The little man peered at her anxiously through his big glasses, and he looked so exactly as he did on that morning so long ago when Polly's eyes were at their worst, that she could do nothing but gaze speechlessly into his face.

"I see you don't consider it quite best, child," said the little doctor brokenly, "but you are trying with your good heart, to make it so. Don't be afraid; it is not too late to end it all."

"I was thinking," cried Polly with a gasp,

235

" how good you were to me, when you saved
my eyes, and how you kept Joel from dying
of the measles. Oh! I couldn't speak — but
I love you so."

She threw her young arms around him.
" Papa Fisher — for you are almost my father
now — I am the very, very happiest girl because you are going to live here, and now I
can show you just how much I really and
truly love you."

The little man beamed at her. Then he took
off his spectacles, wiped them, and clapped
them into place again. " You see, Polly,"
he said deliberately, " it was impossible to see
your mother and not love her. She has had
— well, there, child, I cannot bear to talk about
it," and he walked to the window, blew his
nose violently on an immense pocket-hand-
kerchief, leaving the words poised in mid-air.

" It was the greatest trial of my life that I
couldn't show her then when she was strug-
ling so bravely to keep the wolf from the
door, how I felt. But my hands were tied,
child," he added, coming back, his usual self
again. " Now I can make her, she says, happy,

that is, if you children like it. Just think, Polly, she said happy! It's stupendous, but she said so, Polly, she really did!"

He folded his hands and looked at her in astonishment, behind which shone an intense gratification, that lighted up his plain little face till he seemed to grow young every instant.

"Indeed she did!" repeated Polly like a bird, and laughing merrily. "Oh, Papa Fisher! you ought to hear Mamsie sing. She doesn't know I'm hearing her, but she sings at her work now."

"Does she?" cried the doctor radiantly. "Well, Polly, we must see that she sings every day, after this."

"Yes, let us," cried Polly, clasping his hand; "we will."

"And," proceeded the doctor, "after the wedding is over — I really dread the wedding, Polly — but after that is over, I do believe we shall all be comfortable together!"

Polly gave a little cry of delight. Then she said, "You needn't dread the wedding one bit, Papa Fisher. There will be only the people that we love, and who love us — Grandpapa promised that."

"But that will make it very big," said Dr. Fisher, with round eyes and a small shiver he could not suppress.

"Oh, no!" said Polly cheerily, "sixty-five friends; that's all we are going to ask; Mamsie and I made out the list last night."

"Sixty-five people!" exclaimed Dr. Fisher in dismay. "Oh! isn't it possible to be married without sixty-five friends to stare at you?"

"Oh! that's not many," said Polly; "sixty-five is the very smallest number that we could manage. We've been over the list ever so many times, and struck out quantities of names. You see, everybody loves Mamsie, and they'll want to see her married."

"I know — I know," assented the doctor, "but that makes one hundred and thirty eyes. Did you ever think of that, Polly?"

Polly burst into such a laugh that Jasper popped in, and after him, Phronsie, and a general hilarity now reigning, the dreaded wedding preparations soon sank away from the doctor's perturbed vision.

But they went on merrily nevertheless. All over the old stone mansion there were hints of the on-coming festivities; and though all signs of it were tucked away from the little doctor on his occasional visits, the smothered excitement flamed afresh immediately his departure became an assured thing. Everybody had the wildest plans for the occasion; it appearing impossible to do enough for the one who had stood at the helm for five long years, and who was to be reigning housekeeper for as much longer as her services were needed.

And Dr. Fisher never knew how perilously near he had been to the verge of brilliant evening festivities, in the midst of which he was to be ushered into matrimony.

For Polly had suddenly waked one morning, to find herself, not " famous," but alive with the sense of being — as her mother had so often expressed it — " Mamsie's little right-hand woman."

" It will be much better to have everything plain," said Polly, communing with herself, as she turned on her pillow. " Mamsie has always been without show, of any kind, and so," but here Polly's heart stood still. Dearly she loved the bright, conspicuous accompaniments to the wedding whereby Mr. King was determined to show his respect for the family under his care. And her soul secretly longed for the five hundred guests named on a list of the old gentleman's drawing up. And the feast and the lights, and the pretty dresses, and the dancing party for the young people to follow. For Mr. King had announced himself as about to usher in the brightest of days for the young Peppers to remember.

"Beside it brings our new physician into notice," he would answer when any faint protest was made. "And we shall all have reason to be immensely proud of him, I tell you!"

"Oh, dear!" cried Polly, burrowing deeper within the pillow folds, "why aren't pleasant things best to do? Why, I wonder!"

Cherry, twittering in the window, chirped something vague and unsatisfactory. Polly brought up her brown head suddenly and laughed.

"Nonsense! our happiness doesn't depend upon a lot of people coming together to help it along. Mamsie's face whenever Grandpapa plans all this magnificence, is enough to make me feel wretched at the thought of it. Dear Mamsie! she's afraid of ingratitude if she doesn't try to like it. She shall have the little morning wedding with a few people around, and the gray silk gown instead of the lavender one Grandpapa wants her to wear, for Mamsie always knows just what is right."

With that, Polly sprang out of bed, and rushed at her toilet, and after breakfast she quietly captured Mr. King on the edge of some other extravagant plan, and led him into the library.

" Everything is going on finely, Polly," he cried in elation. " Ring for Thomas, child; stay, I'll do it myself. I shall go in an hour to give my orders for the wedding supper."

" Grandpapa," cried Polly, turning quite pale, and laying a quick, detaining hand on his arm, " oh! do wait, dear Grandpapa, I have something to say."

" Well, child," but he still retained his hand on the cord.

" Oh, Grandpapa!" how could she say it?

But she must. " Mamsie will be ever so much happier if the wedding might be a quiet one. She really would, Grandpapa."

" No doubt Mrs. Pepper finds it a little hard to adjust her ideas to the large affair," said the old gentleman, considerably disturbed, and by no means relinquishing the bell-cord, " but it is due to you children to have a bright time, and I must see that you all have it. That is my affair," and this time the cord was pulled, and the bell rang a loud, insistent message.

Polly stood still in despair. " Grandpapa," she said distinctly, finding it hard to proceed, with his face before her, " we children do not want the large party; that is I do not."

It was all out at last.

" Stuff and nonsense! " exclaimed Mr. King sharply, for his surprise was too great to allow of composure, " who has been putting this idea into your head? Your mother couldn't have done it, for she promised it should all be as you young people wanted."

" Mamsie never said a word," cried Polly, recovering herself as she saw a chance to make things right for Mother Pepper; " it all came

to me, Grandpapa, all alone by myself. Oh! I
hate the big display!" she declared with sudden vehemence, astonishing herself with the
repulsion that now seized her.

"Hoity toity!" exclaimed Mr. King, "it's
not quite the thing, Polly, my child, to express
yourself so decidedly, considering your years."

"Grandpapa," cried Polly, with a sudden
rush of tears, "forgive me, do; I did not mean
to be so naughty. I did not, dear Grandpapa."
She looked like Phronsie now, and the old
gentleman's heart melted. "But I am quite
sure that none of us children would be a bit
happy not to have it as Mamsie would like."

"Well, but I am not sure that the others
wouldn't like it," said Mr. King persistently.

"Ben wouldn't," said Polly triumphantly,
"I know, for he all along shrank from the big
party."

"Oh! well, Ben, I suppose, would object
somewhat," conceded the old gentleman slowly.

"And Davie," cried Polly, flushing eagerly;
"Oh, Grandpapa! David would much prefer
the morning wedding and the plain things."

"But how about Joel and Phronsie?" interrupted Mr. King, utterly ignoring Davie's claims to be heard. " Ah! Polly, my dear, until you tell me that they will prefer to give up the fine party, you mustn't expect me to pay any attention to what you say. It's due to Phronsie that your mother's wedding is a thing worthy to remember as a fine affair."

" Perhaps Joel and Phronsie will think as we do," said Polly. But her heart said No.

"All right if they do," said Mr. King easily, " but unless you come and tell me it is their own choice, why, I shall just go on with my plans as mapped out," he added obstinately. " Thomas," as that functionary appeared in the doorway, " take the letters to the post at once; you will find them on my writing table."

" All right, sir."

" I'll give you till to-morrow to find out," said Mr. King. " Now come and kiss me, Polly dear. You'll see it's all right after it's over, and be glad I had the sense to keep my mind about it."

Polly put up her lips obediently. But it was a sad little kiss that was set upon his mouth, and it left him feeling like a criminal.

And running out, she met her difficult task without a moment of preparation.

"Halloo, Polly!" whooped Joel, rushing around an angle in the hall, "Grandpapa promised me that I might go out with him, to give the supper orders, and all that kind of nonsense."

Polly's heart stood still.

"Joel," she began, seizing his jacket with trembling fingers, "come up into my room a minute."

"What's up?" cried Joel with curiosity; "some more mysteries? There's nothing but whisperings, and secrets, and no end of jolly understandings, ever since Mamsie commenced to marry Dr. Fisher. Go ahead, I'll come."

"And Phronsie, too,,' said Polly, seeing the yellow head emerge from the breakfast-room doorway.

"Come on, Phron," sang out Joel, "up in Polly's room — she wants you," and the three hurried off.

"Now, Joel," said Polly, closing the door and facing him desperately, " you are Mamsie's own boy."

" I should think so, " said Joel, " I'm not anybody's else. Is that all you brought me up here to say? " thrusting his hands in his pockets and looking at her.

" And you can make her happy, or just as miserable as I can't say what," went on Polly incoherently.

" What in the world are you firing at? " demanded the boy, visions of certain pranks at school unpleasantly before him. " Don't shoot over my head, Polly, but keep somewhere near your mark," he advised irritably.

Phronsie surveyed the two with wide eyes, and a not wholly pleased manner.

" Mamsie does not want a big wedding," declared Polly, going to the heart of the matter, " but dear kind Grandpapa thinks it will please us children, and so he wants to give her one."

" And so it will," cried Joel, " please us children. Whoop la! give us your hand, Phronsie, this is the way we'll dance afterwards at the party."

" I don't want to dance," said Phronsie, standing quite still in the middle of the room. The morning sun shone across her yellow hair.

but no light came into the large eyes. " Polly wants something, first; what is it, Joel? "

" I'm sure I don't know," said Joel, poised on a careless foot, and executing a remarkable *pas seul*. " I don't believe she knows herself. Polly is often queer, you know, Phronsie," he added cheerfully.

" Tell me, Polly, do," whispered Phronsie, going over to her.

" Phronsie," said Polly very slowly, " Mamsie doesn't want a big party in the evening to see her married, but to have a cunning little company of friends come in the morning, and " —

" Ugh! " cried Joel in disgust, coming down suddenly to both feet.

" It will please Mamsie best," went on Polly, with a cold shoulder to Joel. " And I never should be happy in all this world to remember that I helped to make my Mamsie unhappy on her wedding day."

Phronsie shivered, and her voice held a miserable little thrill as she begged, " Oh! make her be married just as she wants to be, Polly, do."

" Now that's what I call mean," cried Joel in a loud, vindictive tone back of Polly, " to work on Phronsie's feelings. You can't make me say I don't want Mamsie to have a wedding splurge, so there, Polly Pepper! "

Polly preserved a dignified silence, and presented her shoulder again to his view.

" You can't make me say it, Polly Pepper! " shouted Joel shrilly.

" Oh, Phronsie! " exclaimed Polly in a rapture, throwing her arms around the child, " Mamsie will be so pleased — you can't think. Let us go and tell her; come! "

" See here! " called Joel, edging up, " why don't you talk to me? "

" I haven't anything to say," Polly condescended to give him, without turning her head. " Come, Phronsie," holding out her hand.

" Wait a minute."

" Well, what is it? " Polly's hand now held Phronsie's, but she paused on the way to the door.

" I guess I can give up things as well as she can, if I know Mamsie wants me to," said Joel, with a deeply injured manner.

"Mamsie doesn't want any of us to give up anything unless we do it as if we were glad to," said Polly. For her life, she couldn't conceal a little scornful note in her voice, and Joel winced miserably.

"I — I wish she wouldn't have the big party," he whined.

"I thought you wanted it," said Polly, turning to him.

"I — I don't. I'd rather Mamsie would be happy. O dear! don't look at me so."

"I'm not looking at you so," said Polly. "You acted just as if you had your heart set on the party."

"Well, it isn't. I'll — I'll — if you say party to me again!" and he faced her vindictively.

"Joel Pepper!" cried Polly, holding him with her brown eyes, "do you really mean that you are glad to give up that big evening party, and have the little teeny one in the morning?"

"Yes," said Joel, "as true as I live and breathe, I do!"

"Oh! oh! oh!" cried Polly, and seizing

his arm, she led off in a dance, so much surpassing his efforts, that Phronsie screamed with delight to see them go. When they could dance no more, Polly, flushed and panting, ran out of the room, leaving the two to find out as best they might, the cause of the strange demeanor.

"Grandpapa," Polly rushing over the stairs, met him coming up to Mrs. Whitney's room, "Joel says it's the little morning wedding — please; and Phronsie too!"

The old gentleman gave no sign of his defeat, beyond a "Humph! and so I'm beaten, after all!"

And Dr. Fisher never knew all this.

Mamsie's wedding-day! At last it came! Was any other ever so bright and beautiful? Phronsie thought not, and thereupon she impeded the preparations by running up to kiss her mother every few moments, until such time as Félicie carried her off to induct her into a white muslin gown. Polly, here, there, and everywhere, was in such a rapture that she seemed to float on wings, while the boys of the household, with the exception of Jasper, lost

their heads early in the day, and helplessly suc-
cumbed to all demands upon them.

Every flower had to be put in place by the
young people. Old Turner for once stood one
side. And Polly must put the white satin boxes
filled with wedding cake on the little table
where one of the waiters would hand them to
departing guests. And Phronsie must fasten
Mamsie's pearl broach — the gift of the five
little Peppers — in her lace collar the very last
thing. And Jasper collected the rice and set
the basket holding it safely away from Joel's
eager fingers till such time as they could shower
the bride's carriage. And all the boys were
ushers, even little Dick coming up grandly to
offer his arm to the tallest guest as it happened.

And old Mr. King gave the bride away!
And Dr. Fisher at the last forgot all the one
hundred and thirty eyes, and his " I will," rang
out like a man's who has secured what he has
long wanted. And ever so many of the guests
said " What a good father he will make the
children," and several attempted to tell the

Peppers so. " As if we didn't know it before,"
said Joel indignantly.

And Alexia and all the other girls of Polly's
set were there, and Joel's little blue and white
creature, came to his great satisfaction, with
her aunt, who was quite intimate in the family;
and Pickering Dodge was there of course, and
the Alstynes, and hosts of others.

And Mother Pepper in her silver-gray gown
and bonnet, by the side of her husband, with
Phronsie clinging to one hand, heard nothing
but heart-felt wishes for her happiness and that
of the five little Peppers.

And there was not so much as the shadow of
a skeleton at the wedding breakfast. And
Cousin Mason Whitney took charge of the
toasts — and everybody felt that just the right
things had been said. And then there was a
flutter of departure of the bridal party, and in
the rattle of the wheels Phronsie piped out
bravely as she threw the slipper after the departing coach :

" Mamsie has been taking care of us all these
years; now we're going to be good and let her
be happy."

CHAPTER XV.

"POLLY is learning to play beautifully," mused Phronsie, nursing one foot contemplatively, as she curled up on the floor. "And Ben is to be a capital business man, so Papa Fisher says, and Joel is going to buy up this whole town sometime, and Davie knows ever so many books from beginning to end, but what can I do?"

Down went the little foot to the floor, and the yellow head drooped over the white apron.

"Nothing," mourned Phronsie, "just nothing at all; not even the wee-est teeniest bit of anything do I know how to do. O dear!"

Outside, Jasper was calling to Prince. Phronsie could hear the big dog rushing over the lawn in response, barking furiously as he went. But she did not move.

"And Mamsie will never be glad for me, unless I learn how to do things too. If I don't hurry, I shall never be grown up."

"Tweet — tweet — ch-r-r-r" — Cherry in his cage over her head, chirped vigorously by way of consolation, but Phronsie did not lift her head. Cherry seeing all his efforts in vain, stopped his song and rolled one black eye down at her in astonishment, and soon became quite still.

Presently the rustle of a stiff black satin gown became the chief intruder upon the silence. It was so asserting, that Phronsie lifted her head to look into the face of Mrs. Chatterton, standing before her, playing with the rings on her long white hands, and regarding her as if she would soon require an explanation of such strange conduct.

"What are you doing, Phronsie?" at last demanded the lady.

"Thinking," said Phronsie; and she laid her chin in her hand, and slowly turned her gaze upon the thin, disagreeable face before her, but not as if in the slightest degree given up to a study of its lines and expression.

"So I perceive," said Mrs. Chatterton harshly. "Well, and what are you thinking of, pray tell?"

Still Phronsie looked beyond her, and it was not until the question had been repeated, that an answer came.

"Of many things," said Phronsie, "but I do not think I ought to tell you."

"And why not, pray?" cried the lady, with a short and most unpleasant laugh.

"Because I do not think you would understand them," said Phronsie. And now she looked at the face she had before overlooked, with a deliberate scrutiny as if she would not need to repeat the attention.

"Indeed!" exclaimed Mrs. Chatterton angrily, "and pray how long since your thoughts have been so valuable?"

"My thoughts are nice ones," said Phronsie, slowly, "because they are about nice people."

"Ah!"

"And they won't tell themselves. And I ought not to make them. They would fly away then, and I should never find them again, when I wanted to think them."

"Your mother brought you up well, I must say," observed Mrs. Chatterton, deliberately drawing up a chair and putting her long figure within it, "to talk in this style to a lady as old as I am."

Phronsie allowed one foot to gently trace the pattern on the carpet before she answered. "I know you are very old,' she said at last, "but I cannot tell my thoughts to you."

"Very old!" cried Mrs. Chatterton, her chin in the air. "Indeed! well, I am not, I would have you know, Miss Phronsie," and she played with the silk cord of her satin wrapper. "I hate a child that is made a prig!" she added explosively under her breath.

Phronsie made no reply, being already deep in her own calculations once more.

"Now, Phronsie," said Mrs. Chatterton, suddenly drawing herself out of her angry fit, and clearing her brow, "I want you to give your attention to me a moment, for I have something I must say to you. That's why I came in here, to find you alone. Come, look at me, child. It isn't polite to be staring at the carpet all the time."

Phronsie thus admonished, took her gaze from the floor, to bestow it on the face above her.

"It's something that nobody is to know but just you and me," began Mrs. Chatterton, with a cautious glance at the door. Then she got out of her chair, and going across the room, closed it carefully. "There, that's better; Polly is always around. Now we are quite alone," coming back to her seat.

"You see, Phronsie," she proceeded, not caring that the brown eyes were slowly adding to their astonshment an expression that augured ill for any plans she might be hoping to carry out toward propitiation. "It is necessary to be careful not to be overheard, for what I am going to say to you, must be kept quite secret."

"I must tell Mamsie," said Phronsie distinctly.

"Indeed you will not," declared Mrs. Chatterton. "She is the very one of all others who ought not to know. You can help her, Phronsie, if you only keep quiet."

Phronsie's eyes now became so very large, that Mrs. Chatterton hastened to add:

" You know Polly is learning to be a music
teacher when she grows up."

Phronsie made no reply.

" And a very creditable one she will be, from
all accounts I can gather," contributed Mrs.
Chatterton carelessly.   " Well, Ben is doing
well in Cabot & Van Meter's, so he's no trouble
to your mother. As for the two boys, I know
nothing about them, one way or the other. But
you, as you are a girl, and the only one not
provided for, why, I shall show a little kindness in your direction. It's wholly disinter-
ested and quixotic, I know," added Mrs. Chatterton, with a sweeping gaze at the walls and
ceilings, " for me to give myself a thought
about you or your future. And I shall never
receive so much as a thank you for it. But I've
passed all my life in thinking of others, Phronsie," here she brought down her attention to the
absorbed little countenance, " and I cannot
change now," she finished pensively.

A silence fell upon them, so great that Mrs.
Chatterton broke it nervously. " Goodness me,
Phronsie, you are not like a child; you are too

uncanny for anything. Why don't you ask questions about my secret?"

"Because I ought not to know it," said Phronsie, finding her tongue.

"Haven't I told you that you will help your mother only by not telling her?" said Mrs. Chatterton. "How would you like to learn how to take care of yourself when you are a big girl?"

A light slowly gathered in the brown eyes, becoming at last so joyous and assured, that Mrs. Chatterton's face dropped its hard lines, to lose itself in a gratified smile.

"Now you make me see some real hope that my scheme won't be wholly a wild piece of philanthropy," she exclaimed. "Only look like that, Phronsie, and I'll do anything for you."

"If I can do anything for Mamsie," cried Phronsie, clasping her hands in rapture. "Oh! do tell me, dear Mrs. Chatterton," she pleaded.

"Oh! now I am dear Mrs. Chatterton," cried that lady, with a hard, ill-favored smile. But she lowered her tone to a gentler one, and extending one jeweled hand, took the little folded ones in her clasp.

"I will be a good friend to you, and show you how you can learn to do something so that when you grow up, you can take care of yourself, just as Polly will. Just think, Phronsie, just as Polly will," cried Mrs. Chatterton artfully.

"How — how?" demanded Phronsie, scarcely breathing.

"Listen, Phronsie. Now you know I haven't any little girl."

Phronsie drew a long breath.

"Well, I have been looking for one for a long time. I want one who will be a daughter to me; who will grow up under my direction, and who will appreciate what I sacrifice in taking her. She must be nice-looking, for I couldn't stand an ill-favored child. I have found several who were much better looking than you, Phronsie; in fact, they were beauties; but I don't like the attitude of their families. The poor things actually thought they were doing me a favor by accepting my proposition for the children."

As this statement required no remark on the part of the hearer, Phronsie was silent, not removing her eyes from Mrs. Chatterton's face.

"Now, although you haven't as much to recommend you as many other children that I have fancied, I hope to make you serve my purpose. I am going to try you, at least. Every day, Phronsie, you can come to my room. It's lucky that you don't go to school, but do pretty much as you like in this house, so no questions will be asked."

"I go to Grandpapa's room every day," said Phronsie, in a distressed tone, "to my lessons."

"Of course. I know that; a very silly thing it is too. There's no use in trying to break it up now, I suppose, or I'd put my hand to the attempt. But you can come to me after you've got through toadying Mr. King."

"What is toding?" asked Phronsie.

"Never mind; that hasn't anything to do with the business in hand," replied Mrs. Chatterton impatiently. "Now if you come to me every day, and give me as much time as you can, why, I'll show you what I want of you, and teach you many things. Then after a while, Phronsie, when you learn to appreciate

it, I shall tell you what I am going to do.
The adoption will be an easy matter, I fancy,
when the child is interested," she added, taking the precaution to mutter it.

"You must do everything as I tell you,"
Mrs. Chatterton leaned forward, and said with
great deliberateness, "else you will lose this
chance to help your mother. And you will
never have another like it, but will grow up to
be a good-for-nothing little thing when Polly
and all the rest are earning money for your
Mamsie, as you call her."

"I shall earn money too," declared Phronsie
on a high note, and nodding her yellow head
with great decision.

"Never!" Mrs. Chatterton brought her
foot, incased in its black satin slipper, down
with force on the carpet. "You will never
earn a cent of money in all this world, unless
you do exactly as I say; for you are a child
who hasn't it in her to learn anything. But
you can help me, and I shall teach you many
things, and do well by you."

"When I grow a big girl, will anybody want
me to do those things that you are going to

teach me?" asked Phronsie, drawing near to
lay her hand on the stiff black gown, and
speaking earnestly. "Then if they will, I'll
try to do them just exactly as you tell me."

"Of course they will," declared Mrs. Chatterton carefully, edging off from the little fingers; "ever so many people will want you,
Phronsie. And I shall give you a great deal
of money."

"I shall give it all to Mamsie," interrupted
Phronsie, her brown eyes dilating quickly,
"every single twenty-five cents you give me.
Then I guess she will be glad, don't you?"
she cried, clasping her hands in sudden rapture,
while she began to dance up and down.

"I shall give you so many twenty-five cents,"
cried Mrs. Chatterton, beginning to feel her
old heart beat with more enthusiasm than she
had known for many a day, "that you will be
very rich, Phronsie."

"Oh-oh!" cried Phronsie, coming to an
abrupt pause in the middle of the floor, her
cheek paling in excitement. And then she
could say no more.

"But you must do exactly as I tell you."

Mrs. Chatterton leaned forward suddenly, and seized the little hands, now so still in their delight. " Remember, it is only when you follow my commands in every single thing, that you will have any chance of earning all this money for your mother, and helping her just as Polly is going to do. Remember now, Phronsie! "

" I will remember," said Phronsie slowly, as her hands were released.

"Very good. We will begin now then." Mrs. Chatterton threw herself back in her chair, and drew a long breath. " Lucky I found the child alone, and so tractable. It's singularly good fortune," she muttered. " Well," aloud, with a light laugh, " now, Phronsie, if you are going to be your mother's helper, why, this is your first duty. Let us see how well you perform it. Run upstairs to the closet out of the lumber-room, and open the little black box on the shelf in front of the door — the box isn't locked — and bring me the roll of black velvet ribbon you will find there."

Phronsie was about to ask, " Why does not Hortense go up for it ? " but Mrs. Chatterton forestalled the question by saying with a frown, " Hortense has gone down to the dressmaker's. No child who calls me to account for anything I ask of her, can be helped by me. Do as you like, Phronsie. No one will compel you to learn how to do things so that you can be a comfort to your mother. Only remember, if you don't obey me, you will lose your only chance." After this speech, Mrs. Chatterton sat back and played with her rings, looking with oblique glances of cold consideration at the child.

" I'll go," said Phronsie with a long sigh, " and do every thing you say."

" I do really believe I can bend one of those dreadful Pepper children to my will," thought Mrs. Chatterton exultingly. " She is my only hope. Polly does better than she did, but she is too old to be tractable, and she has a shrewd head on her practical body, and the others are just horrible! " She gave a shiver. " But Phronsie will grow up to fit my purpose, I think. Three purposes, I may say — to get the Peppers gradually out from under Horatio King's influence, and to train up a girl to wait

on me so that I can get away from these
French villains of maids, and to spite Alex-
ander's daughter by finally adopting this Phronsie if she suits me. But I must move carefully. The first thing is to get the child fastened to me by her own will."

Phronsie, ascending the stairs to the lumber-
room, with careful deliberateness, found no
hint of joy at the prospect before her, reaching into the dim distance to that enchanted
time when she should be grown up. But there
was a strangely new sense of responsibility,
born in an hour; and an acceptance of life's
burdens, that made her feel very old and wise.

" I shall be a comfort to my mother," she
said confidently, and mounted on.

CHAPTER XVI

WHERE IS PHRONSIE?

PHRONSIE shut the door of the lumber-room, and with a great sigh realized that she had with her own hand cut herself off from the gay life below stairs.

"But they are not so very far off," she said, "and I shall soon be down again," as she made her way across the room and opened the closet door.

A little mouse scurried along the shelf and dropped to the floor. Phronsie peered into the darkness within, her small heart beating fearfully as she held the knob in her hand.

"There may be more," she said irresolutely. "I suppose he wouldn't live up here all alone. Please go away, mousie, and let me get the box."

For **answer there was a scratching** and

nibbling down in the corner that held more
terrors for the anxious ears than an invading
army.

"I must go in," said Phronsie, "and bring
out the box. Please, good mouse, go away for
one moment; then you may come back and
stay all day."

But the shadowy corner only gave back the
renewed efforts of the sharp little teeth; so
at last, Phronsie, plucking up courage, stepped
in. The door swung to after her, giving out
a little click, unnoticed in her trepidation as
she picked her way carefully along, holding
her red gown away from any chance nibbles.
It was a low narrow closet, unlighted save
by a narrow latticed window, in the ceiling,
for the most part filled with two lines of shelves
running along the side and one end. Phronsie
caught her breath as she went in, the air was
so confined; and stumbling over in the dim
light, put her hand on the box desired, a small
black affair, easily found, as it was the only
one there.

"I will take it out into the lumber-room;
then I can get the velvet roll," and gathering

it up within her arms, she speedily made her way back to the door.

"Why "— another pull at the knob; but with the same result, and Phronsie, setting the box on the floor, still with thoughts only of the mouse, put both hands to the task of opening the door.

"It sticks, I suppose, because no one comes up here only once in a great while," she said in a puzzled way. "I ought to be able to pull it open, I'm sure, for I am so big and strong." She exerted all her strength till her face was like a rose. The door was fast. Phronsie turned a despairing look upon the shadowy corner.

"Please don't bite me," she said, the large tears gathering in her brown eyes. "I am locked in here in your house; but I didn't want to come, and I won't do anything to hurt you if you'll let me sit down and wait till somebody comes to let me out."

Meanwhile Mrs. Chatterton shook out her black satin gown complacently, and with a satisfied backward glance at the mirror, sailed off to her own apartments.

"Madame," exclaimed Hortense breathlessly, meeting her within the door, "de modiste will not send de gown; you must " —

"Will not send it?" repeated her mistress
in a passion. "A pretty message to deliver.
Go back and get it at once."

"She say de drapery — de tournure all
wrong, and she must try it on again," said
the maid, glad to be defiant, since the dressmaker supported her.

"What utter nonsense! Yet I suppose I
must go, or the silly creature will have it
ruined. Take off this gown, Hortense, and
bring my walking suit, then ring and say I'd
like to have Thomas take me down there at
once," and throwing off her bracelets, and the
various buckles and pins that confined her laces,
she rapidly disrobed and was expeditiously in-
ducted by Hortense into her walking apparel,
and a parlor maid announcing that Thomas
with the coupé was at the door, she hurried
downstairs, with no thought for anything beyond a hasty last charge to her maid.

"Where's Phronsie?" cried Polly, rushing
into Mother Fisher's room; "O dear me, my

hair won't stay straight," pushing the rebellious waves out of her eyes.

"It looks as if a brush wouldn't do it any harm," observed Mother Fisher critically.

"O dear, dear! well, I've brushed and brushed, but it does no good," said Polly, running over to the mirror; "some days, Mamsie, no matter what I do, it flies all ways."

"Good work tells generally," said her mother, pausing on her way to the closet for a closer inspection of her and her head; "you haven't taken as much pains, Polly, lately with your hair; that is the trouble."

"Well, I'm always in such a hurry," mourned Polly, brushing furiously on the refractory locks. "There, will you stay down?" to a particularly rebellious wave.

"One at a time is the best way to take things," said Mrs. Fisher dryly. "When you dress yourself, Polly, I'd put my mind on that, if I were you."

With that, she disappeared within the closet.

"O dear, I suppose so," sighed Polly, left to her own reflections and brushing away. "Well, that's the best I can make it look now, for I can't do the braid over. Where is Phronsie, I wonder! Mamsie," she threw down the brush and ran over to put her head in the closet, " where did she go? "

" I told her she might run over to Helen Fargo's, right after breakfast," said Mrs. Fisher, her head over a trunk, from which she was taking summer dresses. " Polly, I think you'll get one more season's wear out of this pink cambric."

" Oh! I am so glad," cried Polly, " for I had such splendidly good times in it," with a fond glance at the pink folds and ruffles. " Well, if Phronsie is over at Helen's, there's no use in asking her to go down town with us."

" Where are you going? " asked Mrs. Fisher, extricating one of Phronsie's white gowns from its winter imprisonment.

" Down to Candace's," said Polly. " Jasper wants some more pins for his cabinet. No, I don't suppose Phronsie would tear herself away from Helen for all the down-towns in the world."

" You would better let her stay where she is," advised Mother Fisher: " she hasn't been

over to Helen's for quite a while, so its a pity
to call her away," and she turned to her un-
packing again, while Polly ran off on the wings
of the wind, in a tremor at having kept Jasper waiting so long.

"Candace" was the widow of an old col-
ered servant of Mr. King's; she called herself a "relict;" that, and the pride in her
little shop, made her hold her turbaned head
high in the air, while a perennial smile en-
wreathed her ,round face.

The shop was on Temple Place, a narrow
extension thrown out from one of the city's
thoroughfares. She was known for a few
specialties; such as big sugary doughnuts that
appealed alike to old and young. They were
always fresh and sweet; with just the proper
amount of spice to make them toothsome; and
she made holders of various descriptions, with
the most elaborate patterns wrought always in
yellow worsted; with several other things that
the ladies protested could never be found else-
where. Jasper had been accustomed to run
down to Candace's little shop, since pinafore
days, when he had been taken there by his

nurse, and set upon a high stool before the small counter, and plied with dainties by the delighted Candace.

" The first thing I can remember," he had often told Polly, " is Candace taking out huge red and white peppermint drops, from the big glass jar in the window, and telling me to hold out both hands."

And after the " pinafore days " were over, Candace was the boy's helper in all his sports where a woman's needle could stitch him out of any difficulty. She it was who made the sails to his boats, and marvelous skate bags. She embroidered the most intricate of straps for his school-books, and once she horrified him completely by working in red cotton, large " J's " on two handkerchiefs. He stifled the horror when he saw her delight in presenting the gift, and afterwards was careful to remember to carry a handkerchief occasionally when on an errand to the shop.

Latterly Candace was occupied in preparing pins for Jasper's cabinet, out of old needles that had lost their eyes. She cleverly put on red and black sealing wax heads, turning them out as round as the skillful manipulation of deft fingers could make them. In this new employment, the boy kept her well occupied, many half-dollars thereby finding their way into her little till.

"I wish Phronsie had come," said Polly, as she and Jasper sorted the pins in the little wooden tray Candace kept for the purpose. "How many red ones you will have, Jasper — see — fifteen; well, they're prettier than the others."

"Ef little Miss had come wid you," said Candace, emerging from the folds of a chintz curtain that divided the shop from the bedroom, "she'd 'a' seen my doll I made for her. Land! but it's a beauty."

"Oh, Candace!" exclaimed Polly, dropping the big pin she held, and allowing it to roll off the counter to the floor. "What a pity we didn't bring her! Do let us see the doll."

"She's a perfec' beauty!" repeated Candace in satisfaction, "an' I done made her all myself fer de little Miss," and she dodged behind the curtain again, this time bringing out a large rag doll with surprising black bead eyes, a generous crop of wool on its head, and a red worsted mouth.

"Dat's my own hair," said Candace, pointing to the doll's head with pride, "so I know it's good; an' ain't dat mouf pretty?"

"Oh, Candace!" exclaimed Polly, seizing the doll, and skillfully evading the question, "what a lovely dress — and the apron is a dear" —

"Ain't it?" said Candace, her black face aglow with delight. "Ole Miss gimme dat yeller satin long ago, w'en I belonged to her befo' de war. An' dat yere apun was a piece of ole Miss's night-cap. She used to have sights of 'em, and dey was all ruffled like to kill, an' made o' tambour work."

Polly had already heard many times the story of Madame Carroll's night-caps, so she returned to the subject of the doll's beauty as a desirable change.

"Do you want us to take this to Phronsie?" she asked. "Jasper, won't she be delighted?"

"Land, no!" cried Candace, recovering the doll in alarm; "I'd never sleep a week c'

nights ef I didn't put dat yere doll into dat
bressed child's arms."

"Then I'll tell Phronsie to come over to-
morrow," said Polly. "Shall I, Candace?"

"Yes," said Candace, "you tell her I got
somefin' fer her; don't you tell her what, an'
send her along."

"All right," said Jasper. "Just imagine
Phronsie's eyes when she sees that production.
Candace, you've surpassed yourself."

"You go 'long!" exclaimed Candace, in
delight, and bestowing a gentle pat of depreca-
tion on his shoulder, "'tain't like what I could
do; but la! well, you send de bressed chile
along, and mabbe she'll like it."

"Jasper, we'll stop at Helen's now," said
Polly as the two hurried by the tall iron fence,
that, lined with its thick hedge, shut out the
Fargo estate from vulgar eyes, "and get
Phronsie; she'll be ready to come home now;
it's nearly luncheon time."

"All right," said Jasper; so the two ran
over the carriage drive to a side door by which
the King family always had entrée.

"Is Phronsie ready to come home?" asked

Polly of the maid. "Tell her to hurry and get her things on; we'll wait here. Oh, Jasper!" turning to him, "why couldn't we have the club next week, Wednesday night?"

"Miss Mary," said the maid, interrupting, "what do you mean? I haven't seen Miss Phronsie to-day."

Polly whirled around on the step and looked at her.

"Oh! she's upstairs in the nursery, playing with Helen, I suppose. Please ask her to hurry, Hannah."

"No, she isn't, Miss Mary," said Hannah. "I've been sweeping the nursery this morning; just got through." She pointed to her broom and dustpan that she had set in a convenient corner, as proof of her statement.

"Well, she's with Helen somewhere," said Polly, a little impatiently.

"Yes; find Helen, and you have the two," broke in Jasper. "Just have the goodness, Hannah, to produce Helen."

"Miss Helen isn't home," said Hannah. "She went to Greenpoint yesterday with Mrs. Fargo to spend Sunday."

"Why," exclaimed Polly in bewilderment, "Mamsie said she told Phronsie right after breakfast that she could come over here."

"She hasn't been here," said the maid positively. "I know for certain sure, Miss Mary. Has she, Jane?" appealing to another maid coming down the hall.

"No," said Jane. "She hasn't been here for ever so many days."

"Phronsie played around outside probably," said Jasper quickly; "anyway, she's home now. Come on, Polly. She'll run out to meet us."

"Oh, Jasper! do you suppose she will?" cried Polly, unable to stifle an undefinable dread. She was running now on frightened feet, Jasper having hard work to keep up with her, and the two dashed through the little gate in the hedge where Phronsie was accustomed to let herself through on the only walk she was ever allowed to take alone, and into the house where Polly cried to the first person she met, "Where's Phronsie?" to be met with what she dreaded, "**Gone over to Helen Fargo's.**"

And now there was indeed alarm through the big house. Not knowing where to look, each fell in the other's way, quite as much concerned for Mr. King's well-being; for the old gentleman was reduced to such a state by the fright, that the entire household had all they could do to keep him in bounds.

"Madame is not to come home to luncheon," announced Hortense to Mrs. Whitney in the midst of the excitement. "She told me to tell you that de Mees Taylor met her at de modiste, and took her home with her."

Mrs. Whitney made no reply, but raised her eyes swollen with much crying, to the maid's face.

"Hortense, run as quickly as possible down to Dr. Fisher's office, and tell him to come home."

"Thomas should be sent," said Hortense, with a toss of her head. "It's not de work for me. Beside I am Madame's maid."

"Do you go at once," commanded Mrs. Whitney, with a light in her blue eyes that the maid never remembered seeing. She was even guilty of stamping her pretty foot in the exigency, and Hortense slowly gathered herself up.

" I will go, Madame," with the air of conferring a great favor, " only I do not such t'ings again."

CHAPTER XVII.

PHRONSIE IS FOUND.

"I AM glad that you agree with me." Mrs.
Chatterton bestowed a complacent smile
upon the company.

"But we don't in the least agree with you,"
said Madame Dyce, her stiff brocade rustling
impatiently in the effort to put her declaration
before the others, "not in the least."

"Ah? Well, you must allow that I have
good opportunities to judge. The Pepper en-
tanglement can be explained only by saying
that my cousin's mental faculties are im-
paired."

"The rest of the family are afflicted in the
same way, aren't they?" remarked Hamilton
Dyce nonchalantly.

"Humph! yes." Mrs. Chatterton's still
shapely shoulders allowed themselves a shrug

intended to reveal volumes. "What Jasper Horatio King believes, the rest of the household accept as law and gospel. But it's no less infatuation."

"I'll not hear one word involving those dear Peppers," cried Madam Dyce. "If I could, I'd have them in my house. And it's a most unrighteous piece of work, in my opinion, to endeavor to arouse prejudice against them. It goes quite to my heart to remember their struggles all those years."

Mrs. Chatterton turned on her with venom. Was all the world arrayed against her, to take up with those hateful interlopers in her cousin's home? She made another effort. "I should have credited you with more penetration into motives than to allow yourself to be deceived by such a woman as Mrs. Pepper."

"Do give her the name that belongs to her. I believe she's Mrs. Dr. Fisher, isn't she?" drawled Livingston Bayley, a budding youth, with a moustache that occasioned him much thought, and a solitary eyeglass.

"Stuff and nonsense! Yes, what an absurd thing that wedding was. Did anybody ever

hear or see the like!" Mrs. Chatterton lifted
her long jeweled hands in derision, but as no
one joined in the laugh, she dropped them
slowly into her lap.

"I don't see any food for scorn in that
episode," said the youth with the moustache.
"Possibly there will be another marriage there
before many years. I'm sweet on Polly."

Mrs. Chatterton's face held nothing but
blank dismay. The rest shouted.

"You needn't laugh, you people," said the
youth, setting his eyeglass straight, "that girl
is going to make a sensation, I tell you, when
she comes out. I'm going to secure her
early."

"Not a word, mind you, about Miss Polly's
preferences," laughed Hamilton Dyce aside to
Miss Mary.

"'Tisn't possible that she could be anything
but fascinated, of course," Mary laughed back.

"Of course not. The callow youth knows
his power. Anybody else in favor of the Peppers?" aloud, and looking at the company.

"Don't ask us if we like the Peppers," cried
two young ladies simultaneously. "They are

our especial and particular pets, every one of them."

"The Peppers win," said Hamilton Dyce, looking full into Mrs. Chatterton's contemptuous face. "I'm glad to record my humble self as their admirer. Now " —

"Well, pa!" Mary could not refrain from interrupting as her father suddenly appeared in the doorway.

"I can't sit down," he said, as the company made way for him to join them. "I came home for some important papers. I suppose you have heard the trouble at the Kings? I happened to drop in there. Well, Dyce," laying his hand on that gentleman's chair, "I scarcely expected to see you here to-day. Why aren't you at the club spread?"

"Cousin Horatio! I suppose he's had a paralytic attack," interrupted Mrs. Chatterton, with her most sagacious air.

"What's the trouble up there?" queried Mr. Dyce, ignoring the question thrust at him.

"It's the little beauty — Phronsie," said Mr. Taylor.

"Nothing's happened to that child I hope!" cried Madame Dyce, paling.

"Now, Mr. Taylor, you are not going to harrow our feelings by telling us anything has harmed that lovely creature," exclaimed the two young ladies excitedly.

"Phronsie can't be found," said Mr. Taylor.

"Can't be found!" echoed all the voices, except Mrs. Chatterton's. She ejaculated "Ridiculous!"

Hamilton Dyce sprang to his feet and threw down his napkin. "Excuse me, Miss Taylor. Come, Bayley, now is the time to show our devotion to the family. Let us go and help them out of this."

Young Baylay jumped lightly up and stroked his moustache like a man of affairs. "All right, Dyce. *Bon jour*, ladies."

"How easily a scene is gotten up," said Mrs. Chatterton, "over a naughty little runaway. I wish some of the poor people in this town could have a tithe of the attention that is wasted on these Peppers," she added virtuously.

Madam Dyce turned uneasily in her seat,

and played with the almonds on her plate. "I think we do best to reserve our judgments," she said coolly. "I don't believe Phronsie has run away."

"Of course she has," asserted Mrs. Chatterton, in that positive way that made everybody hate her to begin with. "She was all right this morning when I left home. Where else is she, if she hasn't run away, pray tell?"

Not being able to answer this, no one attempted it, and the meal ended in an uncomfortable silence.

Driving home a half-hour later, in a cab summoned for that purpose, Mrs. Chatterton threw off her things, angry not to find Hortense at her post in the dressing-room, where she had been told to finish a piece of sewing, and not caring to encounter any of the family in their present excitement, she determined to take herself off upstairs, where "I can kill two birds with one stone; get rid of everybody, and find my box myself, because of course that child ran away before she got it."

So she mounted the stairs laboriously, counting herself lucky indeed in finding the upper part of the house quite deserted, and shutting the lumber-room door when she was well within it, she proceeded to open the door of the closet.

" Hortense didn't tell me there was a spring lock on this door," she exclaimed, with an impatient pull. " Oh! good heavens." She had nearly stumbled over Phronsie Pepper's little body, lying just where it fell when hope was lost.

" I have had nothing to do with it," repeated Mrs. Chatterton to herself, following Mr. King and Jasper as they bore Phronsie downstairs, her yellow hair floating from the pallid little face. " Goodness! I haven't had such a shock in years. My heart is going quite wildly. The child probably went up there for something else; I am not supposed to know anything about it."

" Is she dead? " cried Dick, summoned with the rest of the household by Mrs. Chatterton's loud screams, and quite beside himself, he clambered up the stairs to get in every one's way.

Mrs. Chatterton, with an aimless thrust of

her long jeweled hands, pushed him one side.
And Dick boiled over at that.

"What are you here for?" he cried savagely. "You don't love her. You would better get out of the way." And no one thought
to reprove him.

Polly was clinging to the post at the foot
of the stairs. "I shall die if Phronsie is dead,"
she said. Then she looked at Mother Fisher,
waiting for her baby.

"Give her to me!" said Phronsie's mother,
holding out imperative arms.

"You would better let us carry her; we'll
put her in your bed. Only get the doctor."
Mr. King was almost harsh as he endeavored
to pass her. But before the words were over
his lips, the mother held her baby.

"Mamsie," cried Polly, creeping over to her
like a hurt little thing, "I don't believe but
that she'll be all right. God won't let anything
happen to our Phronsie. He couldn't, Mamsie."

Dr. Fisher met them at the door. Polly
never forgot the long, slow terror that clutched
at her heart as she scanned his face while he

took the child out of the arms that now yielded
up their burden. And everything turned dark
before her eyes — Was Phronsie dead?

But there was Mamsie. And Polly caught
her breath, beat back the faintness and helped
to lay Phronsie on the big bed.

" Clearly I have had nothing to do with it,"
said Mrs. Chatterton to herself, stumbling into
a room at the other end of the hall. But her
face was gray, and she found herself picking
nervously at the folds of lace at her throat.
" The child went up there, as all children will,
to explore. I shall say nothing about it —
nothing whatever. Oh! how is she? " grasping blindly at Jasper as he rushed by the door.

" Still unconscious " —

" Stuff and — oh! well," muttering on.
" She'll probably come to. Children can bear
a little confinement; an hour or two doesn't
matter with them — Hortense! " aloud, " bring
me my sal volatile. Dear me! this is telling
on my nerves." She caught sight of her face
in the long mirror opposite, and shivered to see
how ghastly it was. " Where is the girl?
Hortense, I say, come here this instant! "

A maid, summoned by her cries, put her head in the door. " Hadn't you better go into your own room, Mrs. Chatterton? " she said, in pity at the shaking figure and blanched face.

" No — no," she sharply repulsed her. " Bring Hortense — where is that girl? " she demanded passionately.

" She's crying," said the maid, her own eyes filling with tears. " I'll help you to your room."

" Crying? " Madam Chatterton shrieked. " She's paid to take care of me; what right has she to think of anything else? "

" She says she was cross to Phronsie once — though I don't see how she could be, and — and — now that she's going to die, she " — and the maid burst into tears and threw her apron over her face.

" Die — she sha'n't! What utter nonsense everybody does talk in this house! " Madam Chatterton seized her arm, the slender fingers tightening around the young muscles, and shook her fiercely.

The maid roused by her pain out of her tears looked in affright into the gray face above her. "Let me go," she cried. "Oh! madam, you hurt me."

"Give me air," said Madam Chatterton, her fingers relaxing, and making a great effort not to fall. "Help me over to the window, and open it, girl" — and leaning heavily on the slight figure, she managed to get across the room.

"There — now," drawing a heavy breath as she sank into a chair and thrust her ashen face out over the sill, "do you go and find out how the child is. And come back and tell me at once."

"Madam, I'm afraid to leave you alone," said the girl, looking at her.

"Afraid? I'm not so old but that I can take care of myself," said Mrs. Chatterton with a short laugh. "Go and do as I tell you," stamping her foot.

"Still unconscious" —

Would no one ever come near her but this detestable maid, with her still more detestable news? Mrs. Chatterton clutched the window casing in her extremity, not feeling the soft springy air as she gasped for breath. The maid, too frightened to leave her, crept into a corner where she watched and cried softly.

There was a stir in the household that they might have heard, betokening the arrival of two other doctors, but no word came. And darkness settled upon the room. Still the figure in the window niche held to its support, and still the maid cried at her post.

As the gray of the twilight settled over the old stone mansion, Phronsie moved on her pillow.

" Dear mouse," — the circle of watchers around the bed moved closer, — " I'll go away when some one comes to open the door."

" Hush!" Dr. Fisher put his hand over the mother's lips.

" Don't please bite me very hard. I won't come up again to your house. Oh! where's Grandpapa? "

Old Mr. King put his head on his hands, and sobbed aloud.

The little white face moved uneasily.

" Grandpapa always comes when I want him," in piteous tones.

" Father," said Jasper, laying a hand on the

bowed shoulders, "you would better come out. We'll call you when she comes to herself."

But Mr. King gave no sign of hearing.

A half-hour ticked slowly away, and Phronsie spoke again. "It's growing dark, and I suppose they will never come. Dear mouse" — the words died away and she seemed to sleep.

"I shall not tell," Mrs. Chatterton was saying to herself in the other room; "what good could it do? Oh! this vile air is stifling. Will no one come to say she is better?" And so the night wore on.

As morning broke, Phronsie opened her eyes, and gave a weak little cry. Polly sprang from her knees at the foot of t e bed, and staggered toward the child.

"Don't!" cried Jasper, with a hand on her arm.

"Let her alone," said Dr. Fisher quickly.

"Oh, Polly!" Phronsie raised herself convulsively on the bed. "You did come — you did!" winding her little arms around Polly's neck. "Has the mouse gone?"

"Yes, yes," said Polly as convulsively; "he's

all gone, Phronsie, and I have you fast; just
see. And I'll never let you go again."

"Never?" cried Phronsie, straining to get
up further into Polly's arms.

"No, dear; I'll hold you close just as long
as you need me."

"And he won't come again?"

"He can't Phronsie; because, you see, I
have you now."

"And the door will open, and I'll have
Mamsie and dear Grandpapa?"

"Yes, yes, my precious one," began Mr.
King, getting out of the large arm-chair into
which they had persuaded him.

"Don't do it. Stay where you are," said
Dr. Fisher, stopping him half-way across the
room.

"But Phronsie wants me; she said so," exclaimed old Mr. King hoarsely, and trying to
push his way past the doctor. "Why, man,
don't stop me."

Dr. Fisher planted his small body firmly in
front of the old gentleman. You must obey
me."

Obey? When had Mr. King heard that

word addressed to himself. He drew a long breath, looked full into the spectacled eyes, then said, "All right, Fisher; I suppose you know best," and went back to his arm-chair.

"I'm so tired, Polly," Phronsie was saying, and the arms, Polly could feel, were dropping slowly from her neck.

"Are you, Pet? Well, now, I'll tell you what we'll do. Let us both go to sleep. There, Phronsie, now you put your arms down, so" — Polly gave them a swift little tuck under the bedclothes — "and I'll get up beside you, so" — and she crept on to the bed — "and we'll both go right to 'nid-nid-nodland,' don't you know?"

"You're sure you won't let me go?" whispered Phronsie, cuddling close, and feeling for Polly's neck again.

"Oh! just as sure as I can be," declared Polly cheerfully, while the tears rained down her cheek in the darkness.

"I feel something wet," said Phronsie, drawing back one hand. "What is it, Polly?"

"Oh! that," said Polly with a start. "Oh — well, it's — well, I'm crying, Phronsie; but

I'm so glad — oh! you don't know how glad I am, sweet," and she leaned over and kissed her.

"If you're glad," said Phronsie weakly, "I don't care. But please don't cry if you are not glad, Polly."

"Well, now we're fixed," said Polly as gayly as she could. "Give me your hand, Pet. There, now, good-night."

"Good-night," said Phronsie. Polly could feel her tucking the other hand under her cheek on the pillow, and then, blessed sound — the long quiet breathing that told of rest.

"Oh! better, is she?" Mrs. Chatterton looked up quickly to see Mrs. Whitney's pale face. "Well, I supposed she would be. I thought I'd sit here and wait to know, since you were all so frightened. But I knew it wouldn't amount to much. Now, girl," nodding over to the maid still in the corner, "you may get me to bed." And she stretched her stiff limbs, and held out her hand imperatively.

"It was very fortunate that I did not tell," she said, when the slow passage to her own apartments had been achieved. "Now if the child will only keep still all will be well."

CHAPTER XVIII.

THE GIRLS HAVE POLLY AGAIN.

"PHRONSIE shall have a baked apple this morning," said Mother Fisher, coming into the sunny room where Phronsie lay propped up against the pillows.

"Did Papa-Doctor say so?" asked Phronsie, a smile of supreme content spreading over her wan little face.

"Yes, he did," said her mother; "as nice an apple, red and shiny as we could find, is down-stairs baking for you, Phronsie. When it's done, Sarah is to bring it up."

"That will be very nice," breathed Phronsie slowly. "And I want my little tea-set — just the two cups and saucers — and my own little pot and sugar-bowl. Do let me, Mamsie, and you shall have a cup of milk

298

with me," she cried, a little pink color stealing
into either cheek.

"Yes, yes, child," said Mother Fisher.
"There, you mustn't try to lean forward. I'll
bring the little table Grandpapa bought, so;"
she hurried over across the room and wheeled
it into place. "Now isn't that fine, Phronsie?" as the long wing swung over the bed.
"Did you ever see such a tea-party as you
and I'll have?"

"Breakfast party, Mamsie!" hummed
Phronsie; "isn't that just lovely?" wriggling
her toes under the bed-clothes. "Do you think
Sarah'll ever bring that apple?"

"Yes, indeed — why, here she is now!"
announced Mrs. Fisher cheerily. "Come in,
Sarah," as a rap sounded on the door. "Our
little girl is all ready for that good apple. My!
what a fine one."

"Bless honey's heart!" ejaculated Sarah,
her black face shining with delight. "Ain't
he a beauty, though?" setting down on the
table-wing a pink plate in the midst of which
reposed an apple whose crackling skin dis-
closed a toothsome interior. "I bring a pink

sasser so's to match his insides. But ain't he rich, though!"

"Sarah," said Phronsie, with hungry eyes on the apple, "I think he is very nice indeed, and I do thank you for bringing him."

"Bless her precious heart!" cried Sarah, her hands on her ample hips, and her mouth extended in the broadest of smiles.

"Do get me a spoon, Mamsie," begged Phronsie, unable to take her gaze from the apple. "I'm so glad he has a stem on, Sarah," carefully picking at it.

"Well, there," said Sarah, "I had the greatest work to save that stem. But, la! I wouldn't 'a' brung one without a stem. I know'd you'd want it to hold it up by, when you'd eat the most off."

"Yes, I do," said Phronsie, in great satisfaction fondling the stem.

"And here's your spoon," said her mother, bringing it. "Now, child, enjoy it to your heart's content."

Phronsie set the spoon within the cracked skin, and drew it out half-full. "Oh, Mamsie!" she cried, as her teeth closed over it, "do just taste; it's so good!"

"Hee-hee!" laughed Sarah, "I guess 'tis. Such works as I had to bake dat apple just right. But he's a beauty, ain't he, though?"

Phronsie did not reply, being just at that moment engaged in conveying a morsel as much like her own as possible, to her mother's mouth.

"Seems to me I never tasted such an apple," said Mother Fisher, slowly swallowing the bit.

"Did you, now?" cried Sarah.

Down-stairs Polly was dancing around the music-room with three or four girls who had dropped in on their way from school.

"Give me a waltz now, Polly," begged Philena. "Dear me, I haven't had a sight of you hardly, for so long, I am positively starved for you. I don't care for you other girls now," she cried, as the two went whirling down the long room together.

"Thank you, Miss Philena," cried the others, seizing their partners and whirling off too.

"I feel as if I could dance forever," cried

Polly, when Amy Garrett turned away from the piano and declared she would play no more — and she still pirouetted on one foot, to come up red as a rose to the group.

"Look at Polly's cheeks!" cried Amy.

"You've been a white little minx so long," said Alexia, putting a fond arm around Polly; "I went home and cried every day, after I would steal around the back way to see how Phronsie was" —

"Won't Phronsie be down-stairs soon?" asked Amy.

"I don't know," said Polly. "Papa-Doctor is going to be dreadfully careful of her, that she doesn't get up too soon."

"Say, Polly," cried another girl, "don't you have to take a lot of pills and stuff, now that Dr. Fisher is your father?"

Polly threw back her head and laughed merrily. It sounded so strangely to her to hear the sound echoing through the room so long silent, that she stopped suddenly.

"Oh, girls! I can't hardly believe even yet that Phronsie is almost well," she cried.

"Well, you'd better," advised Alexia philosophically, " because she is, you know. Do laugh again, Polly; it's good to hear you."

" I can't help it," said Polly, " Cathie asks such a funny question."

" Cathie's generally a goose," said Alexia coolly.

" Thank you," said Cathie, a tall girl, with such light hair and sallow face that she looked ten years older than her fourteen summers. " I sometimes know quite as much as a few other people of my acquaintance," she said pointedly.

" I didn't say but that you did," said Alexia composedly. " I said you were generally a goose. And so you are. Why, everybody knows that, Cath."

" Come, come, girls, don't fight," said Polly. " How can you when Phronsie is getting better? Alexia didn't mean anything, Cathie."

" Yes, she did," declared Cathie with a pout; " she's always meaning something. She's the hatefulliest thing I ever saw — so there! "

" Nonsense! " said Polly, with a gay little laugh. " She says perfectly dreadful things to me, and so I do to her, but we don't either of us mind them."

"Well, those are in fun," said Cathie; "that's a very different matter"—

"So you must make these in fun," said Polly. "I would if I were you." But she drew away from Alexia's arm.

"Polly, don't be an idiot and fight with me," whispered Alexia in her ear.

"Go away," said Polly, shaking her off.

"Polly, Polly, I'll say anything if you won't look like that. See here, Cathie, let's make up," and she ran over seized the tall girl by the waist and spun her around till she begged to stop.

"Is that your way of making up?" cried Cathie, when she had the breath to speak.

"Yes; it is as good as any other way. It spins the nonsense out of you. There!" with a last pat on the thin shoulder, she left her, and ran back to Polly.

"It's all done," she cried. "I'm at peace with the whole world. Now don't look like an ogre any longer."

"Phronsie's actually hungry now all the

time," confided Polly in a glow, " and we can't get enough to satisfy her."

" Good — good ! " cried the girls.

" I'm going to send her some of my orange jelly," declared Alexia. " I'll make it just as soon as I go home. Do you think she will like it, Polly? " she asked anxiously.

" Yes, I do believe she will," said Polly, " because she loves oranges so."

" Well, I sha'n't make any old orange jelly," cried Cathie, her nose in the air. " Faugh ! it's insipid enough ! "

" But 'tisn't when it's made the way Alexia makes it," said Polly, viewing in alarm the widening of the breach between the two. " I've eaten some of hers, and it's too splendid for anything."

" I don't know anything about hers, but all orange jelly I have tasted is just horrid. I hate it ! I'm going to make almond macaroons. They're lovely, Polly."

" Oh ! don't, Cathie," begged Polly in distress.

" Why not, pray tell," whirling on one set of

toes. " You needn't be afraid they won't be
good. I've made them thousands of times."

" But she couldn't eat them," said Polly.
" Just think, almond macaroons! Why, Papa-
Doctor would " —

" Now I know the doctor makes you take
perfectly terrible things, and won't let you eat
anything. And macaroons are the only things
I can make. It's a shame! " and down sat
Cathie in despair on an ottoman.

" What's the matter? " Dr. Fisher put his
head in at the doorway, his spectacled eyes
sending a swift glance of inquiry around.

" O dear me! " exclaimed Cathie in a fright,
jumping up and clutching the arm of the girl
next to her. " Don't let Polly tell him what I
said — don't."

" Polly won't tell," said the girl, with a
superb air; " don't you know any better, Cathie
Harrison, you goose, you! "

To be called a goose by two persons in the
course of an hour was too much for Cathie's en-
durance, and flinging off the girl's arm, she
cried out passionately, " I won't stay; I'm
going home! " and rushed out the door.

Dr. Fisher turned from a deliberate look at the girl's white cheeks, as she ran past, to the flushed ones before him.

" I'm very sorry that anything unpleasant has happened. I dropped in to tell you of a little surprise, but I see it's no time now."

" Oh, Papa-Doctor! " cried Polly, flying up to him from the center of the group, " it was nothing — only " —

" A girl's quarrel is not a slight thing, Polly," said little Dr. Fisher gravely, " and one of your friends has gone away very unhappy."

" Oh! I know it," said Polly, " and I'm so sorry."

" We can't any of us help it," said Alexia quickly. " Cathie Harrison has the temper of a gorilla — so there, Doctor Fisher."

Dr. Fisher set his spectacles straight, and looked at Alexia, but he did not even smile, as she hoped he would do. " I can't help it," she said, tracing the pattern of the carpet with the toe of her boot, " she makes us all so uncomfortable, oh! you can't think. And I wish she'd stay home forever."

Still no answer from the doctor. He didn't

act as if he heard, but bowing gravely, he withᐧ drew his head and shut the door.

"O dear, dear!" cried Alexia, when they had all looked at each other a breathing space. "Why didn't he speak? I'd much rather he'd scold like everything than to look like that. Polly, why don't you say something?"

"Because there isn't anything to say." Polly got no further, and turned away, suspiciously near to tears. Was this the first meeting with the girls to which she had looked forward so long?

"To think of that Cathie Harrison making such a breeze," cried Alexia angrily; "a girl who's just come among us, as it were, and we only let her in our set because Miss Salisbury asked us to make things pleasant for her. If it had been any one else who raised such a fuss!"

Meantime Dr. Fisher strode out to the west porch, intending to walk down to his office, and buttoning up his coat as he went along. As he turned the angle in the drive, he came suddenly upon a girl who had thrown herself down on a rustic seat under a tree, and whose shoulders were shaking so violently that he knew she was sobbing, though he heard no sound.

"Don't cry," said the little doctor, "and what's the matter?" all in the same breath, and sitting down beside her.

Cathie looked up with a gasp, and then crushed her handkerchief over her eyes. "Those girls in there are perfectly horrid."

"Softly, softly," said Dr. Fisher.

"I can't — help it. No matter what I say, they call me names, and I'm tired of it. O dear, dear!"

"Now see here," said the doctor, getting up on his feet and drawing a long breath. "I'm on my way to my office; suppose you walk along with me a bit and tell me all about it."

Cathie opened her mouth, intending to say, "Oh! I can't" — instead she found herself silent, and not knowing how, she was presently pacing down the drive by the doctor's side.

"Polly Pepper!" exclaimed Alexia, as a turn in the drive brought the two figures in view of the music-room windows, "did you ever see such a sight in your life? Cathie is walking off with Dr. Fisher! There isn't any-thing her tongue won't say!"

"Did you tell Polly?" cried Jasper, a half-hour later, putting his head into Dr. Fisher's office. "Oh! beg pardon; I didn't know you were busy, sir."

"Come in, said the doctor, folding up some powders methodically. "No, I didn't tell Polly."

"Oh!" said Jasper, in a disappointed tone.

"I hadn't a fair chance" —

"But she ought to know it just as soon as it's talked of," said Jasper, fidgeting at a case of little vials on the table. "Oh! beg pardon again. I'm afraid I've smashed that chap," as one rolled off to the floor. "I'm no end sorry," picking up the bits ruefully.

"I have several like it," said the doctor kindly, and settling another powder in it's little paper.

"There were a lot of girls with Polly when I looked in upon her on my way out. But we'll catch a chance to tell her soon, my boy."

"Oh! I suppose so. A lot of giggling crea-

tures. How Polly can stand their chatter, I
don't see," cried Jasper impatiently.

"They've been shut off from Polly for some
time, you know," said Dr. Fisher quietly. "We
must remember that."

"Polly doesn't like some of them a bit better
than I do," said Jasper explosively, "only she
puts up with their nonsense."

"It's rather a difficult matter to pick and
choose girls who are in the same classes," said
the doctor, "and Polly sees that."

"Don't I know it?" exclaimed Jasper, in an
astonished tone. "Dear me, Dr. Fisher, I've
watched Polly for years now. And she's always done so." He stopped whirling the
articles on the office table, and bestowed a half-
offended look on the little physician.

"Softly, softly, Jasper," said Dr. Fisher
composedly. "Of course you've used your
eyes. Now don't spoil things by saying anything, but let Polly 'go her own gait,' I beg of
you." Then he turned to his powders once more.

"She will, any way," declared Jasper.
"Whatever she makes up her mind to do, Polly
does that very thing."

"Not a bad characteristic," laughed the doctor.

"I should say not."

"Now when I come up home for dinner, you and I will find Polly, and tell her the good news. If she's with a lot of those silly girls, I'll — I'll tear her off this time." Dr. Fisher glared so fiercely as he declared this determination, that Jasper laughed outright.

"I thought no one was to disturb Polly's good intentions in that line," he cried.

"Well, there's an end to all things, and patience ceases to be a virtue sometimes."

"So I've thought a good many times, but I've borne it like a man." Jasper drew himself up, and laughed again at the doctor's face.

"Oh! you go along," cried Dr. Fisher, his eyes twinkling. "I'll meet you just before dinner."

"All right," as Jasper rushed off.

Dr. Fisher jumped to his feet, pushing aside the litter of powder papers, and bottles, and ran his fingers through the shock of gray hair standing straight on his head.

"Yes, yes," he muttered, walking to the win-

dow, " it will be a good thing for Polly, now I
tell you, Adoniram." He always preferred to
address himself by his first name; then he was
sure of a listener. " A vastly good thing. It's
quite time that some of the intimacies with
these silly creatures are broken up a bit, while
the child gains immensely in other ways." He
rubbed his palms gleefully. " Oh! good-morning, good-morning! "

A patient walking in, looked up at the jolly
little doctor. " I wish I could laugh like that,"
he ejaculated, his long face working in the
unusual effort to achieve a smile.

" You would if you had a gay crowd of
children such as I have," cried the little doctor
proudly. " Why, man, that's better than all
my doses."

" But I haven't the children," said the patient
sourly, and sitting down with a sigh.

" I pity you, then," said Dr. Fisher, with the
air of having been a family man for years.
" Well, besides owning the Peppers, I'm going
off with them to " — there he stopped, for before he knew it, the secret was well-nigh out.

CHAPTER XIX.

PHRONSIE IS WELL AGAIN.

BUT Polly was not to be told yet. When Papa Fisher walked in to dinner, the merry party around the oak table were waiting over the ices and coffee for his appearance.

"Oh, Papa Fisher!" cried Polly in dismay, turning from one of Alexia's sallies, and dropping her spoon. "Now you're all tired out — too bad!"

Mother Fisher flushed up, and set her lips closely together. Ben looked disapproval across the board, and Polly knew that the wrong thing had been said.

"Oh! I didn't mean — of course you must take care of the sick people," she said impulsively.

"Yes, I must," said Dr. Fisher wearily, and pushing up the shock of gray hair to a stiffer brush over his brow. "That's what I set out to do, I believe."

"But that's no reason why you should tire yourself to death, and break down the first year," said Mr. King, eying him sharply. "Zounds, man, that isn't what I brought you up from the country for."

Dr. Fisher looked into his wife's eyes and smiled. "I believe you brought me," the smile said. But he kept his tongue still.

"And you must get accustomed to seeing suffering that you can't help. Why, man alive, the town's full of it; you can't expect to stop it alone."

"I'll do what I can to help," said the little doctor between his teeth, and taking a long draught of the coffee his wife put by his plate. "I suppose there's no objection to that. Now, that's good," smaking his lips in a pleased way.

"Of course not, if you help in the right way," said old Mr. King stoutly, "but I'll wager anything that you're picking up all sorts of odd jobs among the poor, that belong to the young doctors. Your place is considerably higher, where you can pick and choose your patients."

Dr. Fisher laughed — an odd little laugh, that along with its pleasant note, carried the ring of a strong will.

"Oh! well, you know, I'm too old to learn new ways," he said. "Better let me wag on at the old ones."

Mr. King gave an exclamation of disapproval. "It's lucky your time is short," he said grimly, and the secret was nearly out!

"Phronsie is coming downstairs to-morrow, isn't she?" asked Jasper quickly, over to the doctor.

"Oh! no, indeed, I think not," answered Mr. King before Dr. Fisher had time to reply. "She would better wait a day or two longer. Isn't that so, Doctor?" at last appealing to him.

"I don't agree with you," the little doctor drew off his attention from his plate. "You see she has regained her strength remarkably. Now the quicker she is in the family life again, the better for her."

"Oh, good! good!" cried Polly, delighted

at the safe withdrawal from the precipice of dangerous argument. "Alexia, now you must help us think up something to celebrate her coming downstairs."

"Not so fast, Polly." The little doctor beamed at her in a way surprising to see after the morning's affair. "Phronsie won't be ready for any celebration before next week. Then I think you may venture."

Alexia pouted and played with her spoon.

"O dear!" cried Dick dolefully, "what's the reason we must wait a whole week, pray tell?"

"Because Father Fisher says so," replied Ben across the table; "that's the principal reason — and it doesn't need any more to support it" —

"Well, I tell you," broke in Polly in her brightest way, "let us think up perfectly splendid things. It's best as it is, for it will take us a week to get ready."

"I shall get her a new doll," declared Mr. King. The rest shouted. "Her others must be quite worn out."

"What could you get her," cried Mr. Whitney, "in the way of a doll? Do tell us, for I really do not see."

"Why, one of those phonograph dolls, to be sure," cried Mr. King promptly.

"Are they on sale yet?" asked Jasper. "I thought they had not perfected them enough for the market."

"I think I know where one can be bought," said his father. "They must be perfected — it's all nonsense that I can't find one if Phronsie wants it! Yes, she shall have a phonograph doll."

"That will be perfectly elegant," exclaimed Polly, with sparkling eyes. "Won't Phronsie be delighted when she hears it talk?"

"She ought to have a Punch and Judy show," said Mrs. Whitney, "she's always so pleased with them, father."

Mr. King pushed away his coffee-cup, and pulled out his note-book.

"'Punch and Judy,' down that goes," he said, noting it after "phonograph doll." "What else?"

"Can't we have some of those boys up from the Orphan Asylum?" asked Polly, after a minute in which everybody had done a bit of hard thinking. " Phronsie loves to hear them sing when she goes there. Oh! they are so cunning."

" She'll want to give them her best toys and load them down with all her possessions. You see if she doesn't," warned Jasper.

" Well, she won't give away her new doll, anyway," cried Polly.

" No, she never gives away one of the dolls you've given her, father," said Mrs. Whitney slowly, "not a single one. I tried her one day, asking her to give me one to bestow on a poor child, and she quite reproached me by the look in her brown eyes. I haven't asked her since."

" What did she say?" asked Mr. King abruptly.

" ' I can't, Aunty; dear Grandpapa gave them to me himself.' Then she ran for her savings bank, and poured out the money in my lap. ' Let's go out and buy the poor child a doll,' she begged, and I really had to do it. And there must be at least two hundred dolls in this house."

"Two hundred dolls!" cried Alexia in astonishment, and raising her hands.

"Why, yes; father has been bringing Phrosie dolls for the last five years, with the greatest faithfulness, till her family has increased to a painful extent."

"O dear me!" cried Alexia, with great emphasis. "I should think they'd be under foot in every room."

"Well, indeed they're not," said Polly; "she keeps them up in her playroom."

"And the playroom closet," said Mrs. Whitney, "that is full. I peeped in there yesterday, and the dolls are ranged according to the times when father gave them to her."

"And the baby-house is just crowded," laughed Jasper. "I know, because I saw her moving out her chairs and tables to make room."

"O dear me!" exclaimed Alexia again, for want of something else to say.

"I just hate dolls," exploded Dick. "Faugh! how can girls play with them; they're so silly. And Phronsie always has something to do for hers, so she can't come when I want her to. I wish they were burnt up," he added vindictively.

Mr. King rubbed his forehead in a puzzled way. "Perhaps she has enough," he said at last. "Yet what shall I give her if I don't buy a doll?"

"I'd give her the phonograph one, father," said Mrs. Whitney, "anyway."

"Yes, of course; but after that, what shall I do?"

He looked so troubled that Mrs. Whitney hastened to say, "Oh, well, father! you know when you are abr" — and the secret was nearly out for the second time!

But they were saved by the appearance of Alexia's father, who often dropped in on the edge of the dinner hour, for a second cup of coffee.

The next morning Phronsie was waiting for Grandpapa King, who insisted that no one else should carry her down stairs, the remainder of the household in various stages of delight and expectation, revolving around her, and curbing their impatience as best they might, in hall and on staircase.

"Oh, Grandpapa! do hurry," begged Dick, kicking his heels on the stairs.

"Hush, Dicky boy," said mamma. "Grandpapa can't come till his agent is gone. Don't you hear them talking in the library?"

"Well I wish Mr. Frazer would take himself off; he's a nuisance," declared the boy. "He's been here a whole hour."

"Here comes Grandpapa!" announced Polly gleefully, from a station nearer the library. "Hush, now, Mr. Frazer's going!"

The library door opening at this announcement, and a few sentences charged with business floating up the staircase, the bustle around Phronsie became joyfully intense.

"Mamsie, don't you think she ought to have a shawl on?" cried Polly anxiously, running over the stairs. "She's been shut up so long!"

"No," said Mother Fisher. "Doctor told me particularly not to bundle her up. It was the last thing he said before he went to his office."

"Well," said Polly with a sigh, "then there isn't absolutely anything more to do for her. Why doesn't Grandpapa come?"

"You are worse than Dicky," said Mrs. Fisher with a little laugh. "Dear me, Polly, just think how old you are."

Phronsie stood quite still in the middle of the floor and folded her hands. "I want to see Grandpapa all alone when he comes up," she said.

"What for?" cried Polly, pausing in astonishment.

"Do you want us all to go out, Phronsie?" asked her mother slowly.

"Yes," said Phronsie, shaking her yellow head with great decision, "please every single one go out, Mamsie. I want to see Grandpapa quite alone."

"All right, child," said Mrs. Fisher, with a look at Polly. So after a little demur and consequent delay on the part of the others, the door was closed and she was left standing alone.

Phronsie drew a long breath. "I wish Grandpapa would come," she said to herself.

"And so you wanted me, did you, dear?" cried Mr. King joyfully, as he hurried in and closed the door carefully. "Well, now, see if I can guess what you want to tell me."

" Grandpapa," said Phronsie, standing quite still and turning a puzzled face toward him, " I don't want to tell you anything; I want to ask you something."

" Well, well, dear, what is it? " Old Mr. King, not stopping for a chair, leaned over her and stroked her yellow head. " Now, then, look up, and ask me right off, Phronsie."

" Must a person keep a promise? " asked Phronsie, " a really and truly promise, Grandpapa? "

" Yes, yes," said the old gentleman with great abruptness, " to be sure one must, Phronsie. To be sure. So now if any one has promised you anything, do you make him stick to it. It's mean enough to break your word, child."

Phronsie drew a long breath.

" That's all, Grandpapa," she said, and lifting up her arms; " now take me downstairs, please." She laid a cool little cheek against his, as he raised her to his shoulder.

" Remember what I say, Phronsie," laughed Mr. King, his mind more intent on the delightful fact that he was carrying down the longed-for burden to the family life, than on what he was saying, " and if any one has promised you anything, keep him up sharp to pay you. I verily believe it is that scamp Dick. Here goes!" and reaching the door he threw it wide. " Forward, march!"

" Well, is the important conference over?" asked Polly, with a keen look at them both.

Mrs. Fisher's eyes did their duty, but she said nothing.

" Yes, indeed," declared Mr. King, marching on gaily. " Now clear the way there, all you good people. Here, you Dick, drumming your heels, go ahead, sir."

" I'm glad enough to," shouted Dick, racing down the remainder of the stairs. " Halloo, Phronsie," waving his hand at her, " three cheers and a tiger! Bother! Here comes Mrs. Chatterton."

Which was quite true. To every one's astonishment the door of that lady's apartment opened slowly, disclosing her in new morning wrapper, preparing to join the cavalcade.

" Good morning, Cousin Eunice," cried Mr. King gaily. He could be merry with any one this day. " Come on, this is a festal occasion, you see; Phronsie's going down-stairs for the first time. Fall into line!"

" I'm not able to go down," said Mrs. Chatterton, coming slowly out into the hall, " but I'll stand here and see the parade."

" Bully!" exploded Dick softly, peering up from the foot of the stairs.

Phronsie looked over Mr. King's shoulder at her as she was borne down the stairs, and, putting out her hand, " I'm all well now," she said.

" Yes, I see," said Mrs. Chatterton. Then she pulled up her white shawl with a shiver. " It's rather cold here," she said; " after all, I believe I must get back to my room."

Nobody noticed when she crept back, the hilarity now being so great below stairs.

" I certainly am losing ground," she muttered, " every little thing affects me so. I'll step into Bartram's office next time I go down town and set that little matter straight, since I've made up my mind to do it. It never would do to let him come to the house. Horatio would suspect something to see my lawyer here, and the whole household imagine I was going to die right off. No, no; I must go there, that's clear. Then if it's attended to, I'll live all the longer, with nothing on my mind."

Phronsie, meanwhile, was going around from room to room in a pleased way, and touching different objects gently. "Everything's new, isn't it, Polly," she said at last, "when you stay upstairs? Oh! there's my kittens in the basket," pointing to a bisque vase on the table.

"Yes," said Polly; "Mamsie brought it in here. And we've some flowers; Alexia sent them over. They're out in the back hall; we saved them for you to put in yourself."

"Oh!" exclaimed Phronsie, "that's so good in you, Polly."

"Don't stop now," cried Dick in disgust. "Faugh! you can fix flowers any time. Come out into the dining-room — and you'll see something like."

Phronsie smothered a sigh, and turned slowly away from the kittens waiting in their basket for Alexia's flowers. "Come on!" shouted Dick, seizing her hand. "You never can guess what it is, in all this world."

"Is it a new dog?" asked Phronsie fearfully, whose memory of Dick's latest purchase was not altogether happy.

"No," said Dick, pulling her on, "better than that."

"Don't hurry her so," said Polly. "What have you got, Dick?"

"Now, do you mind, sir," cried Jasper, "else we'll stop your pretty plan."

"I won't hurry her," said Dick, slackening his gait. "Well, here we are," opening the dining-room door. "Why, Jane has let it out!"

Phronsie fell back a step at this and tried to cover her feet with her gown, searching the floor for the "it."

"Lookout!" cried Dick suddenly. "There he goes!" And something whirred over Phronsie's head.

"Oh! what is it?" she cried, tumbling into Jasper's arms and clasping his neck. "Oh! oh!"

"Why, it's a swallow," cried Dick, in the babel that ensued, "a beautiful one, too. I've just caught him, and I made Jane let me bring it in here to surprise you," he added proudly.

"Well, you've succeeded," cried Jasper, holding Phronsie close. "There, there, child, it's all right. It's a bird, Phronsie, and he's gone upstairs."

"He'll frighten my dolls," cried Phronsie in new alarm, hanging to Jasper's neck. "Oh! do let us go upstairs, and tell them he's only a bird."

"Run along, Dick, and catch your old bird," cried Jasper, "and clear out with him — quick now!"

"He's the best thing there is in this house," cried Dick, going over the back stairs two at a time. "Girls are so silly."

"Bring him down," said Polly, moving along to the foot, "and I'll show him to Phronsie, and tell her about him. Then she'll like him, Dick."

"I'll like him, Dick," echoed Phronsie, "if he doesn't frighten my dolls."

This episode taking the family life to the rear of the house, no one noticed that soft footsteps were passing through the open front door, that Jane, who was sweeping the vestibule, had left ajar to run and tell Dick that she had not let the bird out of the dining-room. So the uninvited guest to the household let himself up easily to the scene of his hopes — the location of the ladies' jewel-boxes.

CHAPTER XX.

THE SECRET.

MRS. CHATTERTON standing by her toilet table, carefully examining her wealth of gray hair to note the changes in its tint, was suddenly surprised in the very act of picking out an obnoxious white hair, by a slight noise in the further corner of the apartment. And dropping her fingers quickly and .urning away from the glass, she exclaimed, " How dare you, Hortense, come in without knocking? "

" If you make a noise I'll kill you," declared a man, standing in the shadow of a portière and watching her underneath a slouched black hat. There was a slight click that caused the listener's nerves to thrill. But her varied life had brought her nothing if not self-control, and she coolly answered, " If you want my money, say so."

" Not exactly money, ma'am," said the man, " for I don't suppose you have much here. But I'll thank you to hand over that there box of diamonds." He extended the other hand with its dingy fingers toward a large ebony jewel-case elaborate with its brass hinges, and suggestive of double locks, o i a corner of the table.

" If you are determined to take it, I suppose I must give it to you," said Mrs. Chatterton, with evident reluctance handing the box designated, very glad to think she had but a few days before changed the jewels to another repository to escape Hortense's prying eyes. In making the movement she gave a sweeping glance out the window. Should she dare to scream? Michael was busy on the lawn, she knew; she could hear his voice talking to one of the under gardeners.

" See here, old lady," warned the man, " you keep your eyes in the room. Now then," his greedy glance fastened on the glittering gems on her fingers, " I'll thank you to rip them things off." Dick, racing along the further end of the hall after his bird with a " Whoop, la — I've almost caught you," startling him, he proceeded to perform the service for himself.

" There he goes! " cried Dick, " in her room. Bother! Well, I must catch him." So without the preamble of knocking, the boy dashed into the dressing-room. The bird whizzing ahead of him, flashed between the drawn folds of the portière.

" Excuse me," cried Dick, rushing in, " but my swallow — oh! "

" Go back! " cried Mrs. Chatterton hoarsely, " you'll be killed."

The bird flying over his head, and the appearance of the boy, disconcerted the robber for one instant. He held the long white hand in his, tearing off the rings. There was no chance for her to escape, she knew, but she could save Dick.

" Go back! " she screamed again. There was only a moment to think, but Dick dashed in, and with a mighty spirit, but small fists, he flung himself against the stalwart arms and shoulders.

"O heavens!" screamed Mrs. Chatterton. "He's but a boy, let him go. You shall have the rings. Help — help!"

Dick, clutching and tearing blindly at whatever in the line of hair or ragged garment he could lay hold of, was waging an unequal warfare. But what he did, was accomplished finely. And the bird, rushing blindly into the midst of the contention, with whirrings and flappings indescribable, helped more than an army of servants, to confuse the man. Notwithstanding, it was soon over, but not before Mrs. Chatterton had wrenched her fingers free, and grasped the pistol from its loose hold in his other hand. The box under his arm fell to the floor, and Dick was just being tossed to the other side of the room; she could hear him strike the cheval-glass with a dull thud.

"I can shoot as well as you," said Mrs. Chatterton, handling the pistol deftly. "Make a noise, and I will."

He knew it, by her eyes, and that she had taken good aim.

"Where are you, Dick?" cried Polly's voice outside, and rapping at the door. "Mrs. Chatterton, have you seen him?"

"Come in," called Mrs. Chatterton, with firmest of fingers on the trigger and her flashing eyes fastened upon the seamed, dirty face before her.

Polly threw wide the door.

"We have a man here that we don't want," said Mrs. Chatterton. "I'll take care of him till you get help. Hurry!"

"Oh, Dick!" cried Polly in a breath, with a fearful glance at the boy lying there.

"I think he's all right, Polly." She dared say no more, for Dick had not stirred.

Polly clasped her hands, and rushed out almost into Jasper's face. "A burglar — a burglar!" and he dashed into Mrs. Chatterton's room.

"Don't interfere," said Mrs. Chatterton, "I'm a splendid markswoman."

"You needn't shoot," said the man sullenly, "I won't stir."

"No, I don't think you will," said the gray

haired woman, her eyes alight, and hand firm as a rock. "Well, here are the men."

Jasper had seized a table-spread, and as Michael and the undergardeners advanced, he went back of the robber, and cleverly threw it over his head. It was easy to secure and bind him then. Polly rushed over to Dick.

"Turn the creature over and let us see how he looks," said Mr. King, hurrying in as the last knot of the rope was made fast. The old slouched hat had fallen off in the struggle, and the man's features came plainly to view. "He's no beauty, and that's a fact."

"I've seen that fellow round here for mony a day," said Michael, giving the recumbent legs a small kick. "Oncet he axed me ef we wanted ony wourk done. I mind yees, yer see," with another attention from his gardening boot.

"I want to tie one rope," cried a voice. Dick opened his eyes, rubbed them, and felt of his head. "I'm all right, Polly. I saw stars, but I've got over it, I guess. Let me give him the last knot." He staggered blindly to his feet.

"I'll tie for you," said Jasper, "trust me. Dick's all right, only stunned," he telegraphed to the rapidly increasing group.

"Tell his mother so, do, somebody," said old Mr. King.

"Well, Cousin Eunice, you've covered yourself with glory," he turned on her warmly. She had thrown aside the pistol, and now sank into a chair.

"Never mind," she waved it off carelessly, "I'll imagine the compliments. Just now I want a glass of wine. Call Hortense, will you?"

The man on the floor tried to raise his head. But he couldn't, so was obliged to content himself with an ugly grin.

"That bird has flown," he said. "I'll peep. She put me up to it; we was goin' shares on the old lady's stuff."

With that Mrs. Chatterton's spirit returned. She sprang from her chair, and rushed around from bureau to closet to see the extent of her maid's dishonesty. But beyond a few minor deficiencies of her wardrobe, there was no robbery to speak of. Evidently Hortense had considered it unwise to be burdened with much *impedimenta*. So the robber was hauled off to justice, and Phronsie, coming wonderingly up the stairs, came softly in upon them, in time to see Dick rush up to Mrs. Chatterton with a " You're a brick! " before them all.

After that, there was no more hope of keeping things quiet in the house for Phronsie's sake. Meanwhile the bird, who had played no mean part in the engagement, now asserted himself, and blindly rushed into capture.

" Isn't he lovely! " cried Phronsie, tearing her gaze off from the wonderful wings, as the swallow fluttered under the mosquito netting speedily brought in.

" Yes, his wings are," said Polly. " Oh, Dick! do tell over again how it all happened."

So Dick rehearsed once more as far as he knew the story, tossing off lightly his part of it.

" Your poor head, does it ache? " cried Polly, feeling of the big bump on the crown.

" No, not a bit," declared Dick, shaking his brown poll. " I'm glad I didn't crack the glass."

"That heavy plate?" cried Polly, looking over at the cheval-glass with a shiver.

Phronsie deserted the fascinating bird, and began to smooth Dick's head with both hands.

"Do let me bathe it," she begged. "I'll get the Pond's Extract."

"No, I won't," said Dick. "It smells awfully, and I've had so much of it for my leg. I'm all right, Phronsie. See his wings now — he's stretching."

But Phronsie was not to be diverted from her purpose.

"I'll get Bay Rum," she said. "May I?"

Dick made a wry face. "Worse and worse."

"Cologne, then."

"No, I hate it."

"He doesn't want it bathed, Phronsie dear," said Polly. "Boys like to get hurt, you know. 'Tisn't manly to be fixed up."

Phronsie gave a sigh, which so went to Dick's heart, that he said, "All right, bring on some water if you want to. But don't you get any brown paper; I had enough of that when I was a boy."

And at the end of that exciting day, the

secret came out, after all, in rather a tame fashion. Dr. Fisher and Jasper met Polly in an angle of the hall, as she was running upstairs after dinner for her schoolbooks.

"Polly," asked the little doctor, putting both hands on her shoulders, and looking into the brown eyes, "should you be willing to go abroad with your mother and Phronsie, Mr. King and Jasper?"

"Oh!" Polly gasped. "But you?" came in a later breath, "we couldn't leave you," she cried loyally.

"Well, I suppose I should go along too," said the little doctor, enjoying her face.

"Why, Jasper Elyot King!" cried Polly, slipping out from under the doctor's palms, and seizing the two hands extended, she began to spin around as in the olden days, "did you ever, ever hear of anything so perfectly magnificent! But Ben and Joel and Davie!" and she paused on the edge of another pirouette.

Dr. Fisher made haste to answer, "Polly, Mrs. Whitney will take care of them." And Jasper led her off into the dance again.

"How can we ever leave the boys! Oh! I

don't see," cried Polly, a bit reproachfully,
her hair blown over her rosy cheeks. As they
danced lightly down the long hall, Dr. Fisher
leaned against a pillar, and watched them.

"Have to," said Jasper, guiding his partner
deftly in the intricacies of the chairs and stat-
uary. "That's a good spin, Polly," he said,
as they brought up by the little doctor's side.

"Lovely!" said Polly, pushing back her
locks from the sparkling eyes.

"I'm almost tempted to dance myself," said
Dr. Fisher. "If I wasn't such an old fellow,
I'd try; that is, if anybody asked me."

"I will," said Polly, laughing. "Come,
Papa Fisher," holding out her hand, "do give
me the honor."

"All right," said Dr. Fisher bravely. So
Jasper took the deserted post by the pillar, and
whistled a Strauss waltz. Thereupon a most
extraordinary hopping up and down the hall
was commenced, the two figures bobbing like
a pair of corks on a quivering water-surface.

The doors opened, and several faces appeared, amongst the number Mrs. Fisher's.

"I couldn't help it," said the little doctor,

coming up red and animated, and wiping his forehead. His spectacles had fallen off long since, and he had let them go. "It looked so nice to see Jasper and Polly, I thought I'd try it. I didn't suppose I'd get on so well; I really believe I can dance."

"Humph!" laughed Mr. King, "it looks like it. Just see Polly."

"Oh, Papa Fisher!" cried Polly with a merry peal in which Jasper, unpuckering his lips from the Strauss effort, had joined, "we must have looked" — Here she went off again.

"Yes," said Jasper, "you did. That's just it, Polly, you did. Lucky you two caperers didn't break anything."

"Well, if you've got through laughing," observed Dr. Fisher, "I'll remark that the secret is out."

"Do you like it, Polly?" asked Mr. King, holding out his hand. "Say, my girl?" And then before she could answer, he went on, "You see, we can't do anything without a doctor on our travels. Now Providence has given us one, though rather an obstinate speci-

men," he pointed to Father Fisher. "And he
wants to see the hospitals, and you want to
study a bit of music, and your mother wants
rest, and Jasper and Phronsie and I want fun,
so we're going, that's all."

"When?" demanded Polly breathlessly.

"In a month."

CHAPTER XXI.

THE WHITNEYS' LITTLE PLAN.

" I THINK it's a mean shame," cried Joel, on a high vindictive key. " You've had burglars here twice, and I haven't been home."

" You speak as if we appointed the meeting, Joe," said Ben with a laugh.

" Well, it's mean, anyway," cried Joel, with a flash of his black eyes. " Now there won't any come again in an age."

" Goodness, I hope not," ejaculated Mr. King, lowering his newspaper to peer over its top.

" I'd have floored him," declared Joel, striking out splendidly from the shoulder, " if I'd only have been here."

" All very well," said Percy negligently, " but you weren't here," and he laughed softly.

344

"Do you mean to say that I couldn't have handled the burglar?" demanded Joel belligerently, and advancing on Percy, "say? Because if you do, why, I'll try a bout with you."

"I didn't say anything what you could or couldn't do. I said you weren't here, and you weren't. That's enough," and Percy turned his back on him, thrust his hands in the pockets of his morning jacket and stalked to the window.

Van opened his mouth to speak, then thought better of it, and gave a low whistle. Joel finding no enthusiasm for tales of his fighting prowess, ran off to interview Dick on the old topic of the burglary and to obtain another close account of its details.

"To think Phronsie saw the other burglar five years ago, and now Dick was on hand for this one — those two babies," he fumed, "and none of us men around."

"Percy," said Van, "come out in the hall, will you?"

"What do you want?" asked Percy lazily.

"Oh! you come along," cried Van, laying hold of his jacket. "See here," dropping his voice cautiously, as he towed him successfully out, "let's give Joe a chance to see a burglar; he wants to so terribly."

"What do you mean?" asked Percy, with astonished eyes, his hands still in his pockets.

Van burst into a loud laugh, then stopped short. "It'll take two of us," he whispered.

"Oh, Van!" exclaimed Percy, and pulling his hands from their resting places, he clapped them smartly together.

"But we ought not, I really suppose," he said at last, letting them fall to his sides. "Mamma mightn't like it, you know."

"She wouldn't mind," said Van, yet he looked uneasy. "It would be a great comfort to every one, to take Joe down. He does yarn so."

"It's an old grudge with you," said Percy pleasantly. "You know he beat you when you were a little fellow, and he'd just come."

"As if I cared for that," cried Van in a dudgeon, "that was nothing. I didn't half try; and he went at me like a country sledge-hammer."

"Yes, I remember," Percy nodded placidly,

"and you got all worsted and knocked into a heap. Everybody knew it."

"Do you suppose I'd pound a visitor?" cried Van wrathfully, his cheeks aflame. "Say, Percy Whitney?"

"No, I don't," said Percy, "not when 'twas Joe."

"That's just it. He was Polly's brother."

At mention of Polly, Percy's color rose, and he put out his hand. "Beg pardon, Van," he said. "Here, shake, and make up. I forgot all about our promise," he added penitently.

"I forgot it, too," declared Van, quieting down, and thrusting out his brown palm to meet his brother's. "Well, I don't care what you say if you'll only go halves in this lark," he finished, brightening up.

"Well, I will," said Percy, to make atonement.

"Come up to our room, then, and think it out," cried Van gleefully, flying over the stairs three at a bound. "Sh-sh! and hurry up!"

Just then the door-bell gave a loud peal, and Jencks the butler opened it to receive a box about two feet long and one broad.

" For Miss Phronsie Pepper," said the footman on the steps, holding it out, " but it's not to be given to her till to-morrow."

" All right," said Jencks, taking it. " That's the sixth box for Miss Phronsie that I've took in this morning," he soliloquized, going down the hall and reading the address carefully. " And all the same size."

" Ding-a-ling," Jencks laid the parcel quickly on one of the oaken chairs in the hall, and hurried to the door, to be met by another parcel for " Miss Phronsie Pepper: not to be given to her till to-morrow."

" And the i-dentical size," he ejaculated, squinting at it as he went back to pick up the first parcel, " as like as two peas, they are."

Upstairs Polly was at work with happy fingers, Alexia across the room, asking every third minute, " Polly, how does it go? O dear! I can't do anything unless you look and see if it's right."

And Polly would turn her back on a certain cloud of white muslin and floating lace, and flying off to Alexia to give the necessary criticism, with a pull here and a pat there, would set matters straight, presently running back to her own work again.

"You see," she said, "everything must be just right, for next to Mamsie's wedding, this is to be the most important occasion, Alexia Rhys, that we've ever known. We can't have anything too nice for Phronsie's getting-well party."

"That's so," said Alexia, twitching a pink satin bow on the handle of a flower-basket. "O dear me! this bow looks like everything! I've tried six different times to make it hang down quite careless and refined. And just to provoke me, it pokes up like a stiff old thing in my face. Do come and tie it, Polly."

So Polly jumped up again, and laying determined fingers on the refractory bow, sent it into a shape that Alexia protested was "too lovely for anything."

"Are you going to have a good-by party?" asked Alexia after a minute.

"I suppose so," said Polly. "Grandpapa said I would better, but O dear me, I don't believe I can ever get through with it in all this world," and Polly hid her face behind a cloud of muslin that was slowly coming into shape as a dress for one of Phronsie's biggest dolls.

"It will be dreadful," said Alexia, with a pathetic little sniff, and beginning on a second pink bow, "but then, you know, it's your duty to go off nicely, and I'm sure you can't do it, Polly, without a farewell party."

"Yes," said Polly slowly, "but then I'd really rather write little notes to all the girls. But I suppose they'll all enjoy the party," she added.

"Indeed they will," declared Alexia quickly. "O dear me, I wish I was going with you. You'll have a perfectly royal time."

"I'm going to work hard at my music, you know," declared Polly, raising her head suddenly, a glow on her round cheek.

"Oh! well, you'll only peg away at it when you've a mind," said Alexia carelessly, and setting lazy stitches. "Most of the time you'll be jaunting around, seeing things, and having fun generally. Oh! don't I wish I was going with you."

"Alexia Rhys!" cried Polly in astonish-

ment, and casting her needle from her, she
deserted the muslin cloud summarily. " Only
peg away when I have the mind?" she repeated indignantly. " Well, I shall have the
mind most of the time, I can tell you. Why,
that's what I am going abroad for, to study
music. How can I ever teach it, if I don't go,
pray tell?" she demanded, and now her eyes
flashed, and her hands worked nervously.

" Oh! nonsense," cried Alexia, not looking
at the face before her, and going on recklessly,
" as if that meant anything, all that talk about
your being a music-teacher, Polly," and she
gave a little incredulous laugh.

Polly got out of her chair somehow, and
stood very close to the fussing fingers over
the pink satin bow. " Do you never dare say
that to me again," she commanded; " it's the
whole of my life to be a music-teacher — the
very whole."

" Oh, Polly!" down went the satin bow
dragging with it Alexia's spool of silk and the
dainty scissors. " Don't — don't — I didn't
mean anything; but you really know that Mr.
King will never let you be a music-teacher

in all this world. Never; you know it, Polly.
Oh! don't look like that; please don't."

"He will," said Polly, in a low but perfectly distinct voice, "for he has promised
me."

"Well, he'll get out of it somehow," said
Alexia, her evil genius urging her on, "for
you know, Polly, it would be too queer for
any of his family, and — and a girl of our
set, to turn out a music-teacher. You know,
Polly, that it would."

And Alexia smiled in the most convincing
way and jumped up to throw her arms around
her friend.

"If any of the girls in our set," said Polly
grandly, and stepping off from Alexia, "wish
to draw away from me, they can do so now.
I am to be a music-teacher; I'm perfectly
happy to be one, I want you all to understand. Just as happy as I can possibly be in
all this world. Why, it's what I've been studying and working for, and how else do you
suppose I can ever repay dear Grandpapa for
helping me?" Her voice broke, and she

stopped a minute, clasping her hands tightly to keep back the rush of words.

"Oh, Polly!" cried Alexia in dismay, and beginning to whimper, she tried again to put her arm around her.

"Don't touch me," said Polly, waving her off with an imperative hand.

"Oh, Polly! Polly!"

"And the rest of our set may feel as you do; then I don't want them to keep on liking me," said Polly, with her most superb air, and drawing off further yet.

"Polly, if you don't stop, you'll — you'll kill me," gasped Alexia. "Oh, Polly! I don't care what you are. You may teach all day if you want to, and I'll help get you scholars. I'll do anything, and so will all the girls; I know they will. Polly, do let me be your friend just as I was. O, dear, dear! I wish I hadn't said anything — I wish I had bitten my tongue off; I didn't think you'd mind it so much," and now Alexia broke down, and sobbed outright.

"You've got to say it's glorious to teach," said Polly, unmoved, and with her highest air on, "and that you're glad I'm going to do it."

"It's glo-glorious to teach," mumbled poor Alexia behind her wet handkerchief.

"And I'm glad you're going to do it," dictated Polly inflexibly.

"I'm glad you're going to do it," echoed Alexia in a dismal tone.

"Then I'll be your friend once more," consented Polly with a slow step toward Alexia, "that is, if you never in all this world say such a dreadful thing again, Alexia Rhys."

"Don't ask me. You know I won't," promised Alexia, her spirits rising. So Polly went over to her and set a kiss on her wet cheek, comforting her as only Polly could, and before long the pink satin bow with the spool of silk hanging to it, and the scissors, were found under the table, and Polly attacked the muslin cloud with redoubled vigor, and the girls' voices carried merry laughter and scraps of happy talk, and Mrs. Chatterton stole out of the little reading-room next to them and shut herself up in her own apartment.

"Dear me, how fine that doll's gown is to

be, Polly," exclaimed Alexia after a bit. "Is the lace going on all around the bottom?"

"Yes," said Polly, biting off her thread, and giving the muslin breadths a little shake; "Félicie is tucking the flounce; then I shall have to sew on the lace."

"How many dolls are there to refurbish before to-morrow?" asked Alexia suddenly.

"Four — no, five," said Polly, rapidly counting; "for the one that Grandpapa gave her Christmas before last, Celestine, you know, does need a new waist. I forgot her. But that doesn't count the new sashes, and the hair ribbons and the lace ruffles around the necks; I guess there are almost fifty of them. Dear me, I must hurry," and she began to sew faster yet.

"What a nuisance all those dolls are," said Alexia, "they take up every bit of your spare time."

"That isn't the worst of it," said Polly. "Alexia, I don't know what we shall do, for Phronsie works over them till she's quite tired out. You ought to see her this morning."

"She's up in the play-house at it now, I

suppose," said Alexia, " dressing every one of them for the party to-morrow."

" Yes," said Polly, " she is."

" Well, I hope no one will give her a doll to-morrow," said Alexia, " at least no one but Mr. King. Of course he will."

" Oh! no one else will," declared Polly cheerfully. " Of course not, Alexia."

And then Jencks walked in with his seven boxes exactly alike as to size, and deposited them solemnly in a row on the blue and white lounge. " For Miss Phronsie Pepper, and not to be opened till to-morrow, Miss Mary."

" Polly," said Alexia in a stage whisper, and jumping up as Jencks disappeared, to run over to the row, " do you suppose they are dolls?"

" I shall die if they are," declared Polly desperately, and sitting quite still.

" They surely look like dolls on the very covers," said Alexia, fingering the cords. " Would it be so very wrong to open one box, and just relieve our suspense? Just one, Polly?"

" No, no, don't," cried Polly sharply. " They belong to Phronsie. But O dear me!"

"And just think," said Alexia, like a Job's comforter, and looking over at the clock, "it's only half-past eleven. Polly Pepper, there's time for oceans more to come in yet."

"It's perfectly horrid to get such a scrap of an outing," said Joel that night, sprawling on the rug before the library fire, "only four days! Why couldn't Mr. Marks be sick longer than that, if he was going to be sick at all, pray?"

"These four days will give you strength for your 'exams,' won't they, Joe?" asked Van.

Joel turned his black eyes on him and coolly said "Yes," then made a wry face, doubled up a bit of paper, and aimed it at Van.

Davie sighed, and looked up anxiously. "I hope Mr. Marks will come out all right so that we can go back Monday."

"I only hope he'll stay ill," said Joel affectionately. "'Tisn't safe anyway for us to go back Monday. It may be typhoid fever, you know, Mamsie," looking over at her.

"They'll let us know soon enough if that's the case," said Mother Fisher in the lamplight over by the center-table. "No, I expect your letter to-morrow will say ' Come Monday.' "

" Well, it's a downright shame for us to be pulled off so soon," cried Joel indignantly, sitting straight.

" Think how soon the term ends, Joe," cried Polly, " then you have such a long outing." She sighed as she thought of the separation to come, and the sea between them.

" That's nothing; only a dreadful little time — soon will be gone," grunted Joel, turning his face to look at the brightly-leaping flames the cool evening had made necessary.

Ben glanced over at Polly. " Don't talk of the summer," he was going to say, but stopped in time. Phronsie set her doll carefully in the corner of the sofa, and went over to Joel.

" Does your head ache often at school, Joel?" she asked, softly laying her cool little palm on his stubby hair.

" Yes," said Joel, " it does, awfully, Phronsie; and nobody cares, and says ' Stop studying.' "

A shout greeted this.

" That's too bad," said Phronsie pityingly.

"I shall just write and ask Mr. Marks if he won't let you stop and rest when it aches."

"'Twouldn't do any good, Phronsie," said Joel, "nothing would. He's a regular old grinder, Marks is."

"Mr. Marks," said Phronsie slowly, "I don't know who you mean by Marks, Joel. And what is a grinder, please?" getting down on her knees to look in his face.

"And he works us boys so, Phronsie — you can't think," said Joel, ignoring the question.

"What is a grinder, Joel, please tell me," repeated Phronsie with gentle persistence.

"Oh! a grinder is a horrid buffer," began Joel impatiently.

"Joel," said Mrs. Fisher, reprovingly. The fire in her black eyes was not pleasant to look at, and after one glance, he turned back to the blazing logs once more.

"I can't help it," he muttered, picking up the tongs to poke the fire.

"Don't ever let me hear that excuse from a son of mine," said Mother Fisher scornfully. "Can't help it. I'd be master of myself, that's one thing."

Joel set the tongs back with an unsteady hand. They slipped and fell to the hearth with a clang.

"Mamsie, I didn't mean," he began, finding his feet. And before any one could draw a long breath, he rushed out of the room.

There was a dreadful pause. Polly clasped her hands tightly together, and looked at her mother. Mrs. Fisher quietly put her sewing into the big basket and got out of her chair.

"Oh! what is the matter with Joey?" cried Phronsie, standing quite still by the deserted hearth-rug. "Mamsie, do you suppose his head aches?"

"I think it must," said Mrs. Fisher gravely. Then she went out very quietly and they could hear her going up the stairs.

With a firm step she went into her own room, and turned up the gas. The flash revealed Joel, face downward on the broad, comfortable sofa. Mrs. Fisher went over and closed the door, then came to his side.

"I thought, my boy," she said, "that I should find you here. Now then, tell mother all about it," and lifting his head, she sat down and took it into her lap.

"O dear!" cried Joel, burrowing deep in the comfortable lap, "O dear — O dear!"

"Now, that is silly, Josey," said Mother Fisher, "tell me at once what all this trouble is about," passing her firm hands over his hot forehead, and trying to look in his face.   But he struggled to turn it away from her.

"In the first place I just hate school!" he exploded.

CHAPTER XXII.

JOEL.

"HATE school?" cried Mother Fisher. "Oh, Josey! think how Ben wanted more schooling, only he wouldn't take the chance when Mr. King offered it to him because he felt that he must be earning money as soon as possible. Oh, Josey!"

That "Oh, Josey!" cut deeply. Joel winced and burrowed deeper under his mother's fingers.

"That's just it," he cried. "Ben wanted it, and I don't. I hate it, and I don't want to go back."

"Don't want to go back?" repeated Mrs. Fisher in dismay.

"No, I don't. The fellows are always twitting me, and every one gets ahead of me, and I'm everlastingly staying in from ball-games

362

to make up lessons, and I'd like to fire the books, I would," cried Joel with venom.

Mrs. Fisher said nothing, but the hands still stroked the brown stubby head in her lap.

"And nobody cares for me because I won't be smart like the others, but I can't help it, I just hate school!" finished Joel in the same strain.

"Joel," said Mrs. Fisher slowly, "if that is the case, I shall go down to Mr. King and tell him that we, Father Fisher and I, Polly and Phronsie, will not go abroad with him."

Joel bolted upright and putting down his two hands, brought his black eyes to bear on her.

"What?"

"I shall go directly downstairs and tell Mr. King that Father Fisher and I, Polly and Phronsie, will not go abroad with him," repeated his mother slowly and distinctly while she looked him fully in the face.

"You can't do that," said Joel in amazement. "He's engaged the state-rooms."

"That makes no difference," said Mrs. Fisher, "when a woman has a boy who needs

her, nothing should stand in the way. And
I must stay at home and take care of you,
Joel."

Joel sprang to his feet and began to prance
up and down the floor. "I'm big enough to
take care of myself, mother," he declared, coming up to her, to prance off again.

"So I thought," said Mrs. Fisher composedly, "or I shouldn't have placed you at
Mr. Marks's school."

"The idea, Mamsie, of your staying at home
to take care of me," said Joel excitedly. "Why,
feel of that." He bared his arm, and coming
up, thrust it out for inspection. "Isn't that
splendid? I do verily believe I could whip
any fellow in school, I do," he cried, regarding his muscles affectionately. "If you don't
believe it, just pinch them hard. You don't
mean it really, Mamsie, what you said, of
course. The idea of staying at home to
take care of me," and he began to prance
again.

"I don't care how many boys you can whip,"
observed Mother Fisher coolly, "as long as
you can't whip your own self when you're

naughty, you're too weak to go alone, and I must stay at home."

Joel stopped suddenly and looked at her.

" And before I'd give up, a boy of thirteen, and beg to be taken away from school because the lessons were hard, and I didn't like to study, I'd work myself to skin and bone but I'd go through creditably." Mrs. Fisher sat straight now as an arrow in her corner of the sofa. " I've said my say, Joel," she finished after a pause, " and now I shall go down and tell Mr. King."

" Mother," howled Joel, dashing across the room to her, " don't go! I'll stay, I will. Don't say that again, about my having to be taken care of like a baby. I'll be good, mother, and study."

" Study doesn't amount to much unless you are glad of the chance," said Mrs. Fisher sharply. " I wouldn't give a fig for it, being driven to it," and her lips curled scornfully.

Joel wilted miserably. " I do care for the chance," he cried; " just try me, and see."

Mrs. Fisher took his sunburnt face between her two hands. " Do you really wish to go back to school, and put your mind on your books? Be honest, now."

" Yes, I do," said Joel, without winking.

" Well, you never told me a lie, and I know you won't begin now," said Mother Fisher, slowly releasing him. " You may go back, Joe; I'll trust you."

" Phronsie," said Jasper, as the sound of the two voices could be heard in Mother Fisher's room, " don't you want to come into my den? I've some new bugs in the cabinet — found a regular beauty to-day."

Phronsie stood quite still just where Joel had left her; her hands were clasped and tears were rolling slowly down her cheeks. " No," she said, without looking at him, " Jasper, I don't."

" Do come, Phronsie," he begged, going over to her, and holding out his hand. " You can't think how nice the new one is, with yellow stripes and two long horns. Come and see it, Phronsie."

" No, Jasper," said the child quietly. Then in the next breath, " I think Joey must be very sick."

"Oh! Mamsie is taking care of him, and he'll soon be all right," broke in Polly cheerily. "Do go with Jasper, Phronsie, do, dear." She took hold of the clasped hands, and smiled up into the drooping face.

But Phronsie shook her head and said "No."

"If Grandpapa should come in and find her so 'twould be very dreadful!" exclaimed Polly, looking over at the five boys, who in this sudden emergency were knocked speechless. "Do let us all play some game. Can't some one think of one?"

"Let us play 'Twenty Questions,'" proposed Jasper brightly. "I'll begin it, I've thought of something."

"That's horrid," cried Van, finding his tongue, "none of us want to play that, I'm sure."

"I do," said David. "I think 'Twenty Questions' is always nice. Is it animal, vegetable or mineral, Jasper?"

"I'm sick of it. Do play something not quite as old as the hills, I beg."

"Well, you think of something yourself,

old man," said Jasper, nodding furiously at him. "Hurry up."

"I'd rather have Polly tell a story than any game you could possibly think of," said Van, going over to her, where she sat on the rug at Phronsie's feet. "Polly, will you?" he asked wheedlingly.

"Don't ask her to-night," interposed Jasper.

"Yes, I shall. It's the only time we shall have," said Van, "before we go back to school. Do, Polly, will you?" he begged again.

"I can't think of the first thing," declared Polly, pushing back little rings of brown hair from her forehead.

"Don't try to think; just spin it off," said Van. "Now begin."

"You're a regular nuisance, Van!" exclaimed Jasper indignantly. "Polly, I wouldn't indulge him."

"I know Phronsie wants a story; don't you, Phronsie?" asked Van artfully, and running over to peer into her face.

But to his astonishment, Phronsie stood perfectly still. "No," she said again, "I don't want a story; Joey must be sick."

"Jasper," cried Polly in despair, and springing up, "something must be done. Grandpapa's coming; I hear him."

"Phronsie," said Jasper, bending to speak into her ear, "do you know you are making Polly feel very unhappy? Just think; the next thing I don't know but what she'll cry."

Phronsie unfolded her hands. "Give me your handkerchief, Polly," she said, winking back the rest of the tears.

"Now, there's a dear," cried Polly, pulling out her handkerchief and wiping the wet, little face. None too soon; the door opened and Mr. King came in.

"Well — well — well!" he exclaimed, looking over his spectacles at them all. "Playing games, hey?"

"We're going to," said Ben and Jasper together.

"No, Polly is going to tell a story," said Van loudly, "that is, if you want to hear it, Grandpapa. Do say you do," he begged, going over to whisper in his ear.

"I want immensely to hear it!" declared the old gentleman, pulling up an easy-chair to the fireside. "There now," sitting down, "I'm fixed. Now proceed, my dear."

Van softly clapped his hands. "Phronsie," Mr. King beckoned to her, and then suggestively touched his knee, "here, dear."

Phronsie scurried across the room to his side. "Yes, Grandpapa."

"There, up she goes!" sang Mr. King, swinging her into position on his lap. "Now then, Polly, my child, we are all ready for the wonderful tale. Stay, where is Joel?"

"Joel went upstairs a little while ago," said Jasper quickly. "Well, now, Polly, do begin."

"I'll tell how we went to buy Phronsie's shoes," said Polly, drawing up an ottoman to Mr. King's side. "Now, boys, bring your chairs up."

"Joel ought to know that you are going to tell a story, Polly," said Mr. King. "One of you boys run out and call him at the foot of the stairs."

"He's in Mamsie's room," said Ben. "I suppose when she gets through with him, he'll come down."

"Oh! ah!" said the old gentleman. "Well,

Polly, then perhaps you would better proceed."

So Polly began on the never tiresome recital, how Phronsie fell down the stairs leading from the kitchen to the "provision room" in the little brown house, with the bread-knife in her hand; and how, because she cut her thumb so that it bled dreadfully, mother decided that she could at last have a pair of shoes bought especially for her very own self; and how Deacon Brown's old horse and wagon were procured, and they all set forth, except mother, and how they rode to town, and how the Beebes were just as good as gold, and how the red-topped shoes fitted as if they were made for Phronsie's feet, and how they all went home, and how Phronsie danced around the kitchen till she was all tired out, and then went to bed carrying the new shoes with her, and how she fell asleep with —

"Why, I declare," exclaimed Polly, reaching this *dénouement* in a delightfully roundabout way, "if she isn't asleep now!"

And indeed she was. So she had to be carried up to bed in the same old way; only this time it was Jasper instead of Polly, who held her.

"Don't you believe we'd better put it off till some other night?" whispered Percy to Van on the way upstairs to bed, the library party having broken up early. "A fellow doesn't want to see a burglar on top of the time Joel has had."

"No, no," said Van; "it'll be good for him, and knock the other thing out of his head, don't you see, Percy? I should want something else to think of if I were Joel. You can't back out; you promised, you know."

"Well, and I'll do it," said Percy testily.

"It's no use trying to sleep," declared Joel, in the middle of the night, and kicking the bedclothes for the dozenth time into a roll at the foot, "as long as I can see Mamsie's eyes. I'll just get up and tackle that Latin grammar now. Whew! haven't I got to work, though! Might as well begin at it," and he jumped out of bed.

Stepping softly over to the door that led into David's little room, he closed it carefully, and with a sigh, lighted the gas. Then he

went over to the table where his school books
ought to have been. But instead, the space
was piled with a great variety of things — one
or two balls, a tennis racket, and a confusion
of fishing tackle, while in front, the last thing
that had occupied him that day, lay a book of
artificial flies.

Joel set his teeth together hard, and looked
at them. "Suppose I sha'n't get much of this
sort of thing this summer," he muttered.
"Here goes!" and without trusting himself
to take another look, he swept them all off
down to the floor and into a corner.

"There," he said, standing up straight, "lie
there, will you?" But they loomed up in a
suggestive heap, and his fingers trembled to
just touch them once.

"I must cover up the things, or else I know
I'll be at them," he said, and hurrying over to
the bed, he dragged off the coverlid. "Now,"
and he threw it over the fascinating mass,
"I've *got* to study. Dear me, where are my
books?"

For the next five minutes Joel had enough
to do to collect his working instruments, and

when at last he unearthed them from the corner of his closet where he had thrown them under a pile of boots, he was tired enough to sit down.

"I don't know which to go at first," he groaned, whirling the leaves of the upper book. "It ought to be Latin — but then it ought to be algebra just as much, and as for history — well there — here goes, I'll take them as they come."

With a very red face Joel plunged into the first one under his hand. It proved to be the Latin grammar, and with a grimace, he found the page, and resting his elbows on the table, he seized each side of his stubby head with his hands. "I'll hang on to my hair," he said, and plunged into his task.

And now there was no sound in the room but his hard breathing, and the noise he made turning the leaves, for he very soon found he was obliged to go back many lessons to understand how to approach the one before him; and with cheeks growing every instant more scarlet with shame and confusion, the drops of perspiration ran down his forehead and fell on his book.

" Whew ! " he exclaimed, " it's horribly hot," and pushing back his book, he tiptoed over to the other window and softly raised it. The cool air blew into his face, and leaning far out into the dark night, he drew in deep breaths.

" I've skinned through and saved my neck a thousand times," he reflected, " and now I've got to dig like sixty to make up. There's Dave now, sleeping in there like a cat; he doesn't have anything to do, but to run ahead of the class like lightning — just because he " —

" Loves it," something seemed to sting the words into him. Joel drew in his head and turned abruptly away from the window.

" Pshaw ! well, here goes," he exclaimed again, throwing himself into his chair. " She said ' I'd work myself to skin and bone but I'd get through creditably.' " Joel bared his brown arm and regarded it critically. " I wonder how 'twould look all skin and bone." and he gave a short laugh.

"But this isn't studying." He pulled down his sleeve, and his head went over the book again.

Outside, a bright blue eye applied to the keyhole, gave place to a bright brown one, till such time as the persons to whom the eyes belonged, were satisfied as to the condition of the interior they were surveying.

"What do you suppose he's doing?" whispered the taller figure, putting his face concealed under a black mask, closely to the ear of the other person, whose countenance was similarly adorned.

"Don't know," whispered the second black mask. "He acts dreadfully queer, but I suppose he's got a novel. So you see it's our duty to break it up," he added virtuously.

The taller figure shook his head, but as it was very dark on their side of Joel's door, the movement was unobserved.

"Well, come on," whispered the second black mask. "Are you ready?"

"Yes."

"Come then."

"O, dear, dear!" grunted Joel. "I'd rather

chop wood as I used to, years ago, to help the little brown house out," swinging his arms up over his head. " Why " —

And he was left in darkness, his arms falling nervously to his side, while a cautious step across the room made his black eyes stand out in fright.

" A burglar — a burglar! " flashed through his mind. He held his breath hard and his knees knocked together. But Mamsie's eyes seemed to look with scorn on him again. Joel straightened up, clenched his fist, and every minute expecting to be knocked on the head, he crept like a cat to the further corner, even in this extremity, grumbling inwardly because Mr. King would not allow firearms. " If I only had them now! " he thought. " Well, I must get my club."

But there was no time to get it. Joel creeping along, feeling his way cautiously, soon knew that there were two burglars instead of one in the room, and his mind was made up.

" They'll be after Grandpapa's money, sure,"

he thought. " I have got to get out, and warm him."

But how? that was the question.

Getting down on all - fours, holding his breath, yet with never a thought of danger to himself, he crept along toward the door leading into the hall, then stopped and rested under cover of the heavy window drapery. But as quick as a flash, two dark figures, that now, his eyes becoming more accustomed to the darkness, he could dimly distinguish, reached there before him, and the key clicking in the lock, Joel knew that all hope from escape by that quarter was gone.

Like a cat, he sprang to his feet, swung the drapery out suddenly toward the figures, and in the next second hurled himself over the window-sill, hanging to the edge, grasping the blind, crawling to the next window, and so on and over, and down, down, by any friendly thing he could grasp, to the ground.

Two black masks hung over the deserted window-edge.

" Joe — Joe! it's only we boys — Percy and Van. Joe — Joe! "

"He'll be killed!" gasped Van, his face as white as Joel's robe fluttering below them in his wild descent. "Stop him, Percy. Oh! do stop him."

Percy clung to the window-sill, and danced in distress. "Stop him!" he was beyond uttering anything more.

"Yes, oh, Joe! don't you see it's only Percy and Van?" cried Van persuasively, and hanging out of the window to the imminent danger of adding himself to Joel's company.

Percy shoved him back. "He's 'most down," he said, finding his breath. "Now we'll run downstairs and let him in."

Van flew off from the window. "I'll go; it's my scrape," and he was unlocking the door.

"I'm the oldest," said Percy, hurrying to get there first. "I ought to have known better."

This made Van furious, and pushing Percy with all his might, he wriggled out first as the door flew open, and not forgetting to tiptoe down the hall, he hurried along, Percy behind him, to hear the noise of men's feet coming over the stairs.

Van tried to rush forward shouting, "Thomas, it's we boys — Percy and Van." Instead, he only succeeded in the darkness, in stumbling over a chair, and falling flat with it amid a frightful racket that drowned his voice.

Old Mr. King who had been awakened by the previous noise, and had rung his burglar alarm that connected with Thomas's and Jencks's rooms in the stable, now cried out from his doorway. "Make quick work, Thomas," and Percy saw the gleam of a pistol held high in Thomas's hand.

Up with a rush came bare feet over the back stairs; a flutter of something white, and Joel sprang in between them. "It's Percy — it's Percy!" he screamed, "don't you see, Thomas?"

"I'm Percy — don't shoot!" the taller burglar kept saying without intermission, while the flaring of candles and frightened voices, told of the aroused household.

"Make quick work, Jencks!" shouted Mr. King from his doorway, to add to the general din.

Thomas, whose blood was up, determined

once for all to put an end to the profession of burglary as far as his master's house was concerned, now drew nearer, steadying his pistol and trying to sight the nearest fellow. This proved to be Van, now struggling to his feet.

Joel took one wild step forward. " Thomas — don't shoot! It's Van!"

" Make quick work, Thomas!" called Mr. King.

There was but a moment in which to decide. It was either Van or he; and in an instant Joel had stepped in front of the pistol.

CHAPTER XXIII.

OF MANY THINGS.

VAN threw his arms around Joel.

"Make quick work, Thomas," called Mr. King from his doorway. The pistol fell from Thomas's hand. "I've shot one of the boys. Och, murther!" he screamed.

And everybody rushing up, supposed it was Van, who was writhing and screaming unintelligibly in the corner.

"Oh! I've killed him," they finally made out.

"Who — who? Oh, Van! who?"

"Joey," screamed Van, bending over a white heap in the floor. "Oh! make him get up. Oh! I've killed him."

The mask was hanging by one end from his white face, and his eyes protruded wildly. Up

382

flew another figure adorned with a second black mask.

"No, no, it was I," and Percy rushed forward with an "Oh, Joel, Joel!"

Somebody lighted the gas, that flashed suddenly over the terrified group, and somebody else lifted the heap from the corner. And as they did so, Joel stirred and opened his eyes.

"Don't make such a fuss," he said crossly. One hand had gripped the sleeve of his night-dress, trying to hold it up in a little wad on the shoulder, the blood pouring down the arm. At sight of this, Van collapsed and slid to the floor.

"Don't frighten Mamsie," said Joel, his head drooping, despite his efforts to hold it up. "I'm all right; nothing but a scratch. Ugh! let me be, will you?" to Mr. Whitney and Jasper, who were trying to support him.

And Mother Fisher, for the first time since the children had known her, lost her self-control.

"Oh, Joey! and mother was cross to you," she could only sob as she reached him.

Polly, at a nod from the little doctor's night-cap and a few hurried words, ran as in a dream, for the case of instruments in his bedroom.

"All right, Mamsie!" exclaimed Joel in surprise, and trying to stagger to his feet.

"Good heavens and earth!" cried old Mr. King, approaching. "What? oh! it's monstrous — Joel!"

"Och, murther!" Thomas sidled along the edge of the group, rolling fearful eyes at them, and repeating over and over, "I've shot that boy — that boy!"

All this occupied but an instant, and Joel was laid on his bed, and the wound which proved to be only a flesh one, the ball cutting a little furrow as it grazed the shoulder, was dressed, and everybody drew a long breath. "Tell Van that I'm all right," Joel kept saying all the time.

Polly undertook to do this.

"Van — Van!" she cried, running out into the hall to lay a shaking hand on his arm, where he lay on the floor. "Joel sent me to say that he is all right."

"Polly, I've killed him!" Van thrust his head up suddenly and looked at her, with wild eyes. "I have — don't speak to me, or look at me. I've killed Joel!"

"Take off this dreadful thing," said Polly with a shiver, and kneeling down, she seized the strings that tied the mask. "O dear! it's all in a knot. Wait, I'll get the scissors," and she found her feet, and ran off to her room.

"Now you are all right;" he gave a little sob as the mask tumbled off. "Oh! how could you?" she wanted to say, but Van's distress was too dreadful for anything but comfort.

"Don't you see," said Polly, sitting down on the floor and cuddling up his head in her lap, "that Joel is really all right now? Suppose we hadn't a Father Fisher who was a doctor, what should we do then?" and she even managed a faint laugh.

"O dear ! but I've killed Joel." Van covered his face with the folds of her flannel dress and wailed on.

"Now, just see here, Van Whitney," said Polly, with the air of authority, "I tell you that Joel is all right now. Don't you say that again — not once more, Vanny."

"But I have ki — I mean I saw Thomas

shoot, and I couldn't stop him," and Van writhed fearfully, ending with a scream "I've ki"—but Polly, clapping her hand over his mouth, kept the words back.

Meanwhile Percy had rushed out of the house.

"Oh!" cried Polly, when this new alarm sprang up, and everybody was running hither and thither to comfort him by the assurance that Joel was not much hurt, "do, Uncle Mason and Jasper, let me go with you."

"No, no, you stay here, Polly," cried Jasper, throwing wide the heavy front door. "Brother Mason and I will find him. Don't worry, Polly."

"I know I could help," said Polly, hanging over the stair-railing. "Oh! do let me," she begged.

"No, no, child," said Mr. Whitney, quickly. "Stay where you are, and take care of the others. Now, then, Jasper, is Jencks ready with the lantern?"

"All right," said Jasper. "Come on."

Polly, longing to fly to the window to watch at least, the lantern's twinkling light across the lawn, hurried off to comfort Aunt Whitney, who at this new stage in the affairs, was walking her room, biting her lips to keep from screaming the terror that clutched at her heart.

"Oh, Polly!" she cried, "I'm so glad you've come. I should die if left alone here much longer;" her soft hair floated down the white robe, and the blue eyes were filled with tears. "Do tell me, don't you think they will find Percy?"

"Yes, indeed!" declared Polly, cuddling up to the little woman. "Oh, Aunty! remember when Dicky's leg was broken."

"But this is much worse," said Mrs. Whitney, sobbing, and holding close to Polly's warm hand.

"But we thought he was dead," and Polly gave a little shiver.

"Don't — don't," begged Mrs. Whitney, clasping her hands; "Oh, Polly! don't."

"But he wasn't, you see, Aunty," Polly hurried on, "and so now you know it will come out all right about Per — There! Oh! they've found him!" as a shout from the lawn rang out.

"Do you suppose it, Polly?" cried Mrs. Whitney, breathlessly. "Oh! do run to the window and see!"

So Polly ran to the window in the next room that overlooked that part of the lawn where Mr. Whitney and Jasper were searching, and strained her gaze up and down, and in every direction.

"Have they? oh! have they?" cried Mrs. Whitney. "Oh, Polly! do tell me."

"I don't see any of them," said Polly, listening eagerly for another cry, "but I do believe they've found him."

"Do come back," implored Mrs. Whitney; "there, now, don't go again, Polly," as Polly hurried to her side, "but just hold my hand."

"I will," said Polly, "just as tight as I can, Aunty."

"Oh — oh! Percy is so much worse off than Joel," wailed Mrs. Whitney. "Oh! to do such a thing, Polly!" she groaned.

"They only meant it in fun," said Polly, swallowing hard the lump in her throat, "don't let us talk about it, Aunty."

"And Van," cried Mrs. Whitney, running

on. "Oh! my poor, poor boys. Will your mother ever forgive me, Polly?"

"Oh, Aunty! don't talk so," said Polly tenderly; "and we both ought to be out helping. There's Van, Aunty; just think how he feels."

"I can't go near him," cried Mrs. Whitney in distress, "as long as he is in Joel's room, for I can't see your mother's eyes, Polly. It would kill me to have her look at me."

The door opened at this, and the trail of a long silken wrapper was heard on the floor.

"Mrs. Chatterton," said Mrs. Whitney, raising her head and looking at the new-comer with as much anger as her gentle face could contain, "I really cannot see you in my room to-night. Excuse me, but I am unstrung by all that has occurred. Will you please not come in" —

"I thought I might sit with you," said Mrs. Chatterton. In the brief interval since the arousing of the household, she had contrived to make a perfect breakfast toilet, and she folded her hands over her handsome gown. "Polly might then be with her mother. But if you don't wish me to remain, I will go."

"I do not need you," said Mrs. Whitney, decidedly, and she turned to Polly again.

Mrs. Chatterton moved away, and closed the door after her.

"Aunty," said Polly, "she really wants to help you."

"Polly, you needn't say anything about it," exclaimed Mrs. Whitney, like many other gentle creatures, when roused, becoming unreasonably prejudiced; "I cannot bear the sight of that woman. She has been here so long, and is so intensely disagreeable to us all."

Polly's eyes became very round, and she held her breath in astonishment.

"Don't look so, child," said Mrs. Whitney at length, "you don't understand, my dear. But you would if you were in my place" —

"She's sorry for it," said Polly, finding her tongue at last.

"And father is nearly worn out with her," continued Mrs. Whitney. "And now to come parading her attentions upon me, it" —

"Who — who?" Dicky, now that the excitement in Joel's room had died down, had lost his relish for it, and he now pranced into Mrs. Whitney's room. "Who, mamma?"

"Mrs. Chatterton," said Mrs. Whitney unguardedly. "She has disagreeably intruded herself upon me."

"Has she been in here?" asked Dick in astonishment.

"Yes; asking if she can sit with me," and Polly started at the look in the usually soft blue eyes.

"And you wouldn't let her?" asked Dick, stopping short and regarding his mother curiously.

"Of course not, Dicky," she made haste to say.

"Then I think you did very wrong," declared Dick flatly.

"Oh, Dick!" exclaimed Polly in consternation.

"And you don't act like my mother at all," said Dick, standing quite stiffly on his sturdy legs, and gazing at her with disapprobation. "Didn't Mrs. Chatterton save my life," he exploded, "when the real burglar was going for me? Say, didn't she?" he cried.

"I have yet to find out that is the truth," said Mrs. Whitney, finding her voice. "Oh, Dicky," she added, hurt that he should defend another, worst of all, Mrs. Chatterton, "don't talk about her."

"But I ought to talk about her," persisted Dick. "She saved me as much as she could. Because she won't let anybody thank her, I like her more myself. I'm going to stay with her."

With that, he held his head high, and marched to the door.

"Dick, Dick!" called his mother, "come back, dear."

Dick slowly turned and made his way to her side, but he still regarded her with disapproval.

"Dick, I want you to go to Mrs. Chatterton's room, and say that I am sorry I refused her offer to help, and that I would like to have her sit with me. Remember, say I am sorry I refused her offer to help, Dicky." She leaned forward and kissed her boy, her long, soft hair falling like a veil around the two faces.

Dick threw his arms around her neck.

"Now, you're a brick!" he declared impulsively. "I'll bring the old lady, and we'll both sit with you."

So Polly was free to run back to Mamsie. On the way there she opened the door of Phronsie's little room, just out of Father and Mother Fisher's.

"How good it is that she sleeps through it all," said Polly, listening to the regular breathing. Then she stole across the room and stood beside the small bed.

"She looks just as she did the night she took her new shoes to bed," thought Polly; "one hand is over her head, exactly as it was then. Oh, Phronsie! to think that you're to have no party to-morrow," and she turned off with a sigh, went out, and closed the door.

"Percy's here — all right!" cried Jasper, running over the stairs to meet her at the top.

His eyes were gleaming with excitement, and his face was torn and bleeding.

"Are you hurt?" cried Polly, feeling as if the whole family were bound to destruction. "Oh, Jasper! did you fall?"

"Nothing but a scratch. I was fool enough to forget the ledge, and walked off for my pains" —

"Oh, Jasper!" cried Polly, with paling cheeks, "let me bathe it for you, do;" her strength began to return at the thought of action, and she sprang for a basin of water.

"Nonsense. No, Polly!" cried Jasper, with a quick hand detaining her, "it's nothing but a mere scratch, I tell you, but I suppose it looks terribly. I'll go and wash it off. Run and tell his mother that Percy is found."

"Is he all right?" asked Polly fearfully, holding her breath, for the answer.

"Sound as a nut," declared Jasper; "we found him streaking it down the locust path; he said he was going to run off to sea."

"Run off to sea!" repeated Polly. "Oh, Jasper!"

"Well, he was so frightened, of course he didn't know what to say," replied Jasper. "And ashamed, too, he didn't care to show his head at home. I don't know as I blame him, Polly. Well, it's too bad about Phronsie's party, isn't it?" added Jasper, mopping up his face as the two went down the hall.

"Yes," said Polly with a sigh, stopping at Mrs. Whitney's door, "but, oh! think how happy we are now that Percy is safe, Jasper."

"Still, it's too bad for Phronsie," repeated Jasper, looking back.

But Joel flatly declared that the first one that even so much as hinted that a single item of the arrangements for Phronsie's getting-well party should be changed, he'd make it disagreeable as only he knew how, for that one when he got up from his bed. "Yes, sir!" and he scolded, and fretted, and fussed, and laid down the law so generally to all, not excepting the doctor, that at last it was decided to let the party go on. Then he lay back against the pillows quite exhausted, but with a beatific face.

"I should think you would be tired, Joe," exclaimed Jasper, "you've bullied us so. Dear me! people ought to be angelic when they're sick, at least."

"If you'd had him to take care of as I did,"

observed Dr. Fisher, " you'd know better, goodness me! the little brown house scarcely held him when he was getting over the measles."

" What's the use of being sick," said Joel reflectively, turning on his pillow, " if you can't make people stand round, I'd like to know. Now that point's settled about Phronsie's party, won't you all go out? I'd like to speak to Father Fisher a moment."

" You don't mean me, Joey? " said Mother Fisher at the head of the bed, holding her boy's hand.

" Yes; you, too, Mamsie," said Joel, giving her an affectionate glance, " it's something that only the doctor and I are to know."

" You're not hurt anywhere else, are you, Joey? " asked his mother, a sudden alarm leaping to her black eyes.

" Not a scratch," said Joel promptly. " I want to see Father Fisher about something. Some time you shall know, Mamsie." He gave her hand a sudden pressure, then let it go.

" Perhaps you would better step out, my dear," said the little doctor, nodding to his wife. So Mrs. Fisher, smothering a sigh, went out reluctantly.

" All out ? " asked Joel, trying to raise his head to see for himself.

" Every soul," said Dr. Fisher.

" Well, see here, will you," said Joel, pointing to the table, the schoolbooks scattered as he had left them, " pack those things all away in the closet on the shelf, you know, and put the rubbish on the floor there, back on the table ? "

Dr. Fisher could not for his life, refrain from asking curiously, as he did as requested, " Been having a pull at the books, eh, Joe ? "

" Um — um — maybe," said Joel, twisting uneasily. " Well, now, come here, please, Father Fisher."

The little man turned away from the table, with its sprawling array of delightful things, to stand by the bedside.

" You must get me well as soon as you can," said Joel confidentially.

" All right; I understand," Dr. Fisher nodded professionally.

" And whatever you say, don't let it be that I must be careful of my eyes," said Joel.

" All right; that is, if you get up quickly," agreed the doctor.

" That's all," said Joel in great satisfaction. " Now, call Mamsie in and the others."

And in the morning, no one told Phronsie what had happened the night before. She only knew that Joel was not very well, and was going to keep his room; all her pleadings to do something for him being set one side by Grandpapa's demands upon her instant attention whenever the idea suggested itself to her. And so the time wore along till the party began.

Alexia was the first to arrive, her bowl of orange jelly in her hand, and after her, a tall slight figure jumped from the carriage, her flaxen hair streaming out in two pale braids.

" I thought I'd pick Cathie up," said Alexia carelessly; " had to pass her door, you know. O dear me, what perfectly dreadful times you had last night, Polly Pepper."

" I didn't bring macaroons," said Cathie, " as I really think that they wouldn't be good for Phronsie. Besides, I've forgotten how to make them, and our cook was cross and said I shouldn't come into her kitchen. But I bought a doll for Phronsie; my mother said it would be a great deal more sensible present," and she hugged the long box under her arm with great satisfaction.

" O dear! dear! " groaned Alexia, falling back with Polly as the three raced along the hall, " she showed it to me in the carriage, and it's a perfect guy, besides counting one more."

But afflictions like this were small to Polly now, and although for the next hour it rained dolls into Phronsie's puzzled hands, Polly helped her to thank the givers and to dispose them safely on neighboring chairs and tables and sofas.

Mrs. Chatterton's was the pattern of old Mr. King's phonograph doll, at which discovery he turned upon her with venom in his eye.

" My gift to my little granddaughter," taking especial care to emphasize the relationship, " has always been a doll, I suppose you knew that, Cousin Eunice; and to try to procure one exactly like the one I have purchased, is very presuming in you, to say the least."

"And why may I not present a doll to Phronsie Pepper, if I care to, pray tell?" demanded Mrs. Chatterton in a high, cold tone.

"Why? because you have always showed a marked dislike for the child," cried old Mr. King angrily, "that's why, Cousin Eunice."

"Grandpapa — Grandpapa," said Phronsie, laying her hand on his arm.

"And to parade any special affection, such as the presentation of a gift indicates, is a piece of presumption on your part, I say it again, Cousin Eunice."

"Grandpapa!" said Phronsie again at his elbow.

"Now Phronsie," turning to her, "you are to take that doll," pointing to a gorgeous affair reposing on the sofa, with Mrs. Algernon Chatterton's card attached to it, "and go over to Mrs. Chatterton, and say, very distinctly, 'I cannot accept this gift;' mind you say it distinctly, Phronsie, that there may be no mistake in the future."

"Oh, Grandpapa!" cried Phronsie in dismay.

"Yes, child; I know what is best for you. Take that doll, and do exactly as I bid you."

A dreadful pause fell upon the room. Polly clasped her hands, while Alexia and the other girls huddled into a corner saying softly, "Oh! how perfectly dreadful!"

"No use to say anything to father when he looks like that," groaned Jasper, when Polly besought him to try his influence, "his blood is up now; he's borne a good deal, you know, Polly."

"O dear, dear!" whispered Polly, back again, "just look at Mrs. Chatterton's face, and at poor Phronsie's; can't you do something, Jasper?"

"I'm afraid not," said Jasper gloomily. "No; he's making her give it back; see, Polly."

"You'll know it's for the best," Mr. King was repeating as he led the child to Mrs. Chatterton standing cold and silent at the end of the room, "some time, child, and then you'll thank me that I saved you from further annoyance of this sort. There, Cousin Eunice, is your gift," taking the doll from Phronsie's hand, and placing it in the long, jeweled one. " My little granddaughter receives presents only from those who love her. All others are unwarranted, and must be returned."

Phronsie burst out tearfully, " She's sorry, Grandpapa, I know she is, and she loves me now. Please let me keep the doll."

But Mrs. Chatterton had left the room, the doll in her hand.

CHAPTER XXIV.

AWAY.

AND after that everybody had to be as gay as possible, to keep Phronsie's sad little face from being flooded with tears.

"Dear me!" exclaimed Jasper, "here comes Candace! Now what do you suppose she has for you, Phronsie?"

Candace sailed through the doorway with ample satisfaction with everything and herself in particular.

"Whar's little Miss?" she demanded, her turban nodding in all directions, and her black eyes rolling from side to side.

"There, Candace," said some one, "over in the corner with Jasper."

"Oh! I see her," said Candace, waddling over to them. "Well, now, Phronsie, seein' you couldn't come to me for somethin' I made 'xpressly fer you, w'y, Candace has to come to you. See dat now, chile!"

She unrolled the parcel, disclosing the wonderful doll adorned with Candace's own hair, and "Ole Missus' ruffles," then stood erect, her bosom swelling with pride and delight.

"O my goodness me!" exclaimed Alexia, tumbling back after the first and only glance, and nearly overturning Cathie who was looking over her shoulder. "Polly Pepper, oh dear me!" Then she sat down on the floor and laughed till she cried.

"Hush — hush!" cried Polly, running over to her, "do stop, Alexia, and get up. She'll hear you, and we wouldn't hurt her feelings for the world. Do stop, Alexia."

"O dear me!" cried Alexia gustily, and holding her sides while she waved back and forth; "if it had been — a — respectable doll, but that — horror! O dear me!"

"Stop — stop!" commanded Polly, shaking her arm.

But Alexia was beyond stopping herself. And in between Candace's delighted recital,

how she combed " de ha'r to take de curl out,"
and how " ole Missus' ruffles was made into de
clothes," came the peals of laughter that finally
made every one in the room stop and look at
the girls.

"Candace, come into my 'den' and get a
pattern for some new pins I want you to make
for me," cried Jasper, desperately dragging
her off.

"It's no use to lecture me," said Alexia, sitting straight as Candace's feet shuffled down
the hall, and wiping her face exhaustedly. "I
know it was dreadful — O dear me! Don't
anybody speak to me, or I shall disgrace myself again!"

"Now, Phronsie, what do you suppose we
are to do next?"

Phronsie looked up into old Mr. King's face.

"I don't know, Grandpapa," she said wonderingly.

"Well, now, my dear, you've had Punch
and Judy, and these nice children," waving his
hand to indicate the delegation from the
orphan asylum. "have sung beautifully for
you. Now what comes next, Phronsie?"

" I don't know, Grandpapa," repeated Phronsie.

" When gifts become burdensome they no longer are kindnesses," said Mr. King. " Now, Phronsie, I have found out — never mind how; little birds, you know, sometimes fly around telling people things they ought to know. Well, I have discovered in some way that my little girl has too many children to care for."

Here Phronsie's brown eyes became very wide.

" And when there are too many children in the nest, Phronsie, why, they have to go out into the world to try their fortunes and make other homes. Now there are so many poor little girls who haven't any children, Phronsie. Think of that, dear; and you have so many."

Phronsie at this drew nearer and stole her hand into his.

" Now what is to be done about it? " asked the old gentleman, putting his other broad palm over her little one and holding it fast. " Hey, my pet? "

" Can't we buy them some children? " asked Phronsie with warm interest. " Oh, Grand-

papa dear. do let us; I have money in my
bank."

"Phronsie," said the old gentleman, going
to the heart of the matter at once and lifting
her to his lap, "I really think the time has
come to give away some of your dolls. I really
do, child."

Phronsie gave a start of incredulity and
peered around at him.

"I really do. You are going abroad to be
gone — well, we'll say a year. And your dolls
would be so lonely without anything to do but
to sit all day and think of their little mother.
And there are so many children who would love
them and make them happy." Now Mr. King's
white hair was very near the yellow waves
floating over his shoulder, so that none but
Phronsie's ears caught the next words. "It's
right, Phronsie dear; I'd do it if I were you,"
he said in a low voice.

"Do you want it, Grandpapa?" asked
Phronsie softly.

"I do, child; but not unless you are willing " —

"Then I do," declared Phronsie, sitting quite

straight on his knee. And she gave a relieved sigh. "Oh, Grandpapa, if we only had the poor children now!" she exclaimed, dreadfully excited.

"Come, then." Old Mr. King set her on her feet. "Clear the way there, good people; we are going to find some poor children who are waiting for dolls," and he threw wide the door into a back passage, and there, presided over by Jencks, and crowding for the first entrance, was a score of children with outstretched hands.

"Oh—oh!" exclaimed Phronsie with cheeks aflame.

"Please, he said we was to have dolls," cried one hungry-eyed girl, holding out both her hands. "I've never had one. Please give me one quick."

"Never had one?" echoed Phronsie, taking a step toward her.

"Only a piece, Miss, I found in a rag-barrel. Please give me one quick."

"She's never had a doll — only a piece," repeated Phronsie, turning back to the family, unable to contain this information.

"Ask the others if they have had any?"

said Mr. King, leaning against a tall cabinet. " Try that girl there in a brown plaid dress."

" Have you ever had a doll? " asked Phronsie obediently, looking over at the girl indicated, and holding her breath for the answer.

At this, the girl in the brown plaid dress burst into tears, which so distressed Phronsie that she nearly cried.

" Yes, but it died," said the girl after a little.

" Oh, Grandpapa, her doll died! " exclaimed Phronsie in horror.

" No, it didn't, Jane," corrected another girl, " the dog et it; you know he did."

" Yes, I know," said Jane, between small sobs, " it died, and we couldn't have any fun'ral, 'cause the dog had et it."

" Well, now, Phronsie," exclaimed Mr. King, getting away from the support of the cabinet, " I think it's time that we should make some of these children happy. Don't you want to take them up to the playroom and distribute the dolls? "

" No, no," protested Phronsie suddenly, " I must go up and tell my children. They will

understand it better then, Grandpapa. I'll be
back in a very few minutes," and going out
she went quickly upstairs, and after a while
returned with both arms full.

" This doll is for you," she said gravely, putting a doll attired in a wonderful pink satin
costume into Jane's arms. " I've told her about
your dog, and she's a little frightened, so please
be careful."

" What's the fun down there now?" asked
Joel of Van, who with Percy could not be persuaded to leave his bedside a moment, " open
the door, do, and let's hear it."

So Van threw wide the door.

" Go out and listen, Percy, will you?" he
said.

" I don't want to," said Percy, who shared
Van's wish to keep in the background.

" You two fellows act like muffs," said Joel.
" Now if you want me to get well, go out, do,
and tell me what the fun is going on down
there."

So persuaded, the two boys stole out into
the hall in time to see Phronsie go down the
stairs with her armful, and carefully using

their ears they soon rushed back with " Phronsie's giving away her dolls! "

" Stuff and nonsense! " exclaimed Joel, " if
you can't bring back anything better than that
yarn, you might as well stay here."

" But I tell you it's true," declared Van,
" isn't it, Percy? "

" Yes, it is," said Percy. " I heard her distinctly say, ' This doll is for you ' — and she
had her arms full, so I suppose she's going to
give those away too " —

" A likely story," said Joel, bursting into a
laugh. At the noise up in the boys' room,
Mother Fisher ran quickly over the stairs.

" Oh, boys! what is it? Joel, are you
worse? "

" No, indeed," said Joel, " I was laughing.
Percy and Van have been telling such a big
story. Mamsie, they actually said that Phronsie was giving away her dolls."

" Is that all? " cried Mrs. Fisher in relief.
" Well, so she is, Joel."

" *Phronsie giving away her dolls, Mamsie?* "
screamed Joel. " Why, what does Grandpapa
say? "

"He's the very one that proposed it," said Mrs. Fisher. "There, Joey, don't get excited, for I don't know what the doctor will say," as Joel sank back on his pillow, overcome by this last piece of news.

When Phronsie went to bed that night she clasped Mr. King's new gift to her breast.

"Grandpapa, dear," she said confidingly as they went up the stairs together, "do you know I really think more of this doll, now that the others are gone? Really I do, Grandpapa, and I can take better care of her, because I shall have more time."

"So you will, dear," assented Mr. King. "Well, Phronsie, I think you and I, dear, haven't made a bad day's work."

"I think my children will be happy," said Phronsie with a small sigh, "because you see it's so nice to make good times for their new mothers. And, Grandpapa, I couldn't play with each one more than once a week. I used to try to, but I couldn't, Grandpapa."

"Why didn't you tell me, Phronsie," asked the old gentleman a bit reproachfully as they reached the top step, " how it was, dear? You should have given them away long ago."

" Ah, but," said Phronsie, slowly shaking her head, " I didn't want to give them away before; only just now, Grandpapa, and I think they will be happy. And now I'm going to take this newest one to bed, just as I used to take things to bed years ago, when I was a little girl."

And after all, there was an extension of time for the three boys' vacation, Dr. Marks not getting up from his sudden attack of fever as quickly as was expected. But there came a day at last, when Percy, Van and David bade Joel " good-by."

" It won't be for long," observed that individual cheerfully, " you'll be back in three weeks."

" O dear ! " groaned Percy when safe within the coach, " we've ruined all his chances. He certainly will be plucked now — with those three weeks to make up."

Van gathered himself up and leaned forward in his corner.

" Don't look so, Dave," he cried desperately.

David tried to smooth the troubled lines out of his face, but only succeeded in making it look worse than before.

"And it will kill Mrs. Fisher," Percy continued gloomily, "if he does get plucked, as of course he will."

"Keep still, will you?" cried Van, his irritation getting beyond bounds. "What's the use of talking about a thing till it's done," which had the effect to make Percy remember his promise to Polly and close his mouth.

But Joel's wound healed quicker than any one supposed it possibly could, and Percy and Van who both hated to write letters, gave up much time on the playground to indite daily bulletins, so that he declared that it was almost as good as being there on the spot. And Mother Fisher and her army of servants cleaned the great stone house from top to bottom, and sorted, and packed away, and made things tidy for the new housekeeper who was to care for them in her absence, till Dr. Fisher raised his eyebrows and hands in astonishment.

"I really must," he said one day, "put in

a remonstrance, wife, or you'll kill yourself
before we start."

"Oh! I'm used to working," Mrs. Fisher
would say cheerily, and then off she would
fly to something so much worse, that the little
doctor was speechless.

And Polly set herself at all her studies, especially French, with redoubled vigor, notwithstanding that she was hampered with the
faithful attentions of the schoolgirls who
fought among themselves for her company,
and showered her with pathetic "O — dear —
me — how — I — shall — miss — you," and
with tears when they got over it. And Jasper
buried himself in his den, only bursting forth
at meal times, and Mrs. Whitney bemoaned all
preparations for the travelers' departure, and
wished a thousand times that she had not given
her promise to keep the house and look after
the boys. And everybody who had the slightest claim to a calling acquaintance, now dropped
in upon the Kings, and Polly had her "good-
by party," and it was pronounced perfectly
elegant by Alexia and her set, and the three

boys came home for the long vacation — and
in two days the party would sail.

"Who do you think is going abroad with
us?" asked Mr. King suddenly, as they all
sat in the library for a last evening talk;
"guess quickly."

"Who?" cried several voices.

"Why, I thought you didn't want any out-
siders, father," exclaimed Jasper in surprise.

"Well, and I didn't when I said so, but cir-
cumstances are changed now — come, guess
quickly, some one?"

"The Cabots," said Jasper at a venture.

"No, no; guess again."

"Mr. Alstyne?"

"No; again."

"The Bayleys, the Dyces, the Herrings,"
shouted Mr. Whitney and Van and Joel.

"No, I know," broke in Percy, "it's Mrs.
Chatterton," with a quick glance to make sure
that she was not in the room.

"*No!*" thundered Mr. King. "Oh! how
stupid people can be when they want to. Two
persons are to meet us in New York to-morrow.
I didn't tell you till I was sure; I had no

desire that you should be disappointed. Now guess again."

"Aunty, do you know?" asked Polly suddenly, leaning back, as she sat on the rug in front of the fire, to lay her head in Mrs. Whitney's lap.

"No, I'm sure I don't," said Mrs. Whitney, stroking lightly the brown hair, with a pang to think how long it would be before she should caress it again.

"How any one can desire to cross the ocean," remarked Mr. Whitney, folding his hands back of his head and regarding meditatively the glowing fire, "is more than I can see. That I never shall do it again unless whipped over, I'm morally certain."

"Are the persons men?" asked Ben suddenly.

"One is," replied Mr. King.

"And the other is a woman?"

"The other is a woman," said Mr. King. "Well, what are their names? Isn't anybody smart enough to guess them? Dear me, I've always said that the Peppers were remarkably bright, and the rest of you children are not

behind other young people. **Go on, try again.**
Now who are they?"

Polly took her head out of Mrs. Whitney's
lap, and rested her chin in her hands. Davie
walked up and down the room, while Ben and
the two Whitney boys hung over Mother
Fisher's chair.

"Dear me!" fumed Joel. "Who ever could
guess. There's such a lot of people in the
world that Grandpapa knows. It might be any
two of them that he had asked."

Little Dr. Fisher's eyes roved from one to
the other of the group. "I couldn't begin to
guess because I don't know many of your
friends," he said quietly.

"You know these two people very well,"
said Mr. King, laughing, to see the little man's
face.

"Now I think I know," said Jasper slowly,
a light coming into his gray eyes, "but I don't
suppose it's fair to guess, for I saw the address
on a letter father was writing two or three
weeks ago."

"You did, you young scamp, you!" cried
Mr. King, turning on him. "Well, then, 'tisn't

a guess for you, Jasper. Keep still, my boy, and let them work away at it. Will no one guess?"

"Mamsie," cried Polly, bounding up from the ring, nearly upsetting Phronsie, who was sitting beside her in a brown study, "can it be — do you suppose it is nice, dear Mr. and Mrs. Henderson?"

"Well, Polly," said Mr. King, beaming at her, "you've done what the others couldn't. Yes, it is Mr. and Mrs. Henderson, and they are going with us to stay until the autumn."

"Good, good!" cried every one till the big room seemed full of joy.

"Oh, father!" exclaimed Mrs. Whitney, "I'm so glad you've done this. They were so kind to Dicky and to me when he was hurt."

"They were kind to Dicky and to you," said her father; "and besides, Marian, Mr. Henderson is a man who doesn't preach at you only once a week, and Mrs. Henderson is a fine woman. So it's a pity not to ease up things for them now and then. Well, how do you like the plan?" He spoke to Dr. Fisher, but his gaze took them all in.

"Immensely," said the little doctor; which being again echoed heartily, by all the rest, old Mr. King began to feel very much elated at his part in the proceedings, and in a quarter of an hour it seemed as if the expedition had been especially planned for the benefit of the Hendersons, so naturally had it all come about.

And on the morrow, the whole family, Kings, Whitneys, Fishers and Peppers, turned their backs on the gray stone mansion and went down to the city.

And Alexia Rhys persuaded her aunt to do her semi-annual shopping at this time, and to take her too; and Mr. Alstyne also had business that necessitated his going, and Mr. Cabot and Mary Taylor, and her father found they must go along too; and Hamilton Dyce was there, and Pickering Dodge, of course, went to be company for Ben on the way back. And at the last moment who should jump on the train but Livingston Bayley.

"Had a telegram," he explained; "must be there at noon. So glad of the unexpected pleasure of meeting you all."

And Cousin Eunice Chatterton went; for, at
the last minute, she had suddenly discovered
that she had visited at the gray stone mansion
as long as she cared to, and notified the family
accordingly.   And Mr. King had so far made
up for his part in the late unpleasantness as
to ask her to go with the party, on her way
to her nephew's in the city.   So there she was
with the others, bidding them good-by on the
steamer.

"Phronsie," she said slowly, under cover
of the babel of tongues, " you are a good child,
and I've done well by you.   This little bit of
paper," putting it into her hands, " contains a
message to Mr. King, which you are to give
him after you have started."

"I will go and give it to him now," said
Phronsie, her fingers closing over the bit.

"No, no," said Mrs. Chatterton sharply,
"do as I say.   Remember, on no account to
let any one see it till after you have started.
You are a good child, Phronsie.   Now, remember to do as you are bidden.   And now,
will you kiss me, child?"

Phronsie lifted her eyes and fixed them on

the long, white face, and suddenly raising herself on her tiptoes, she put up her lips.

"Look at Phron," cried Joel in the midst of the group, "actually kissing Mrs. Chatterton!" and everybody turned and stared.

Cousin Eunice dropped her veil with a quick hand, and moved off with a stately step, but not in time to lose young Bayley's drawl:

"'Pon me word — it's the most extraordinary thing. Phronsie, come here, and tell us what 'twas like." But Phronsie stood quite still as if she had not heard.

"Yes, I hope you'll have a nice time," Pickering Dodge was saying for the dozenth time, with eyes for no one but Polly, "now don't stay away for a year."

Polly with her heart full of the boys, who were hanging on either side, answered at random.

"Oh, Ben! I can't go," she was exclaiming, and she hid her head on his shoulder, so Pickering turned off.

But Joel set his teeth together. "You must," he said, for Ben was beyond speech with the effort to control himself.

"I can't," said poor Polly, "leave you, Ben, and the boys."

And then Mrs. Whitney came up just as Polly was near breaking down.

"My dear child," she said, taking Polly's hands, "you know it is right for you to go."

"Yes, I know," said Polly, fighting her tears.

"Then, Polly, be brave, dear, and don't begrudge me my three new boys," she added playfully. "Just think how happy I'm to be, with six such splendid fellows to call my own."

Polly smiled through her tears.

"And one thing more," said Mrs. Whitney in a low voice, "when you feel badly," looking steadily at Polly and the three boys, "remember what Dr. Fisher said; that if your mother didn't stop working, and rest, she would break down."

"I'll remember," said Ben hoarsely.

"So will I," said David.

"And I will," said Joel, looking everywhere but into Polly's eyes.

"Well, I hope, Miss Polly," said young Mr. Bayley, sauntering up, "that you'll have an uncommonly nice time, I do indeed. I may run across in September; if I do, we shall probably meet."

"Miss Mary Pepper?" suddenly asked a man with a huge basket of flowers, and pausing in front of her.

Young Mr. Bayley smiled indulgently as he could not help reading the card thrust into the flowers. "She will receive my flowers at intervals all the way over, if the steward doesn't fail me," he reflected with satisfaction, "while this boy's will fade in an hour."

"Miss Mary Pepper?" the florist's messenger repeated, extending the basket to Polly.

"It's for you, Miss Polly," said young Mr. Bayley. "Let me relieve you," taking the basket.

"Oh! are they for me?" cried Polly.

"I believe you are Miss Mary Pepper," said young Bayley. "Pretty, aren't they?" fingering the roses, and glad to think that there were orchids among the flowers to which his card was attached, and just placed under the steward's care.

"I suppose I am," said Polly, with a little laugh, "but it seems as if I couldn't be anything but Polly Pepper. Oh! thank you, Pickering, for these lovely roses," catching sight of him.

"Glad you like them," said Pickering radiantly. "Say, Polly, don't stay away a whole year, will you?"

Young Mr. Bayley set the basket in his hand and turned on his heel with a smile.

"Come, Polly, I want you," cried Alexia, trying to draw her off. "You know she's my very best friend, Pickering, and I haven't had a chance to say one word to her this morning. Come, Polly."

"Polly, come here," called Mrs. Fisher.

"O dear!" cried Alexia impatiently, "now that's just the way it always is. It's Polly here, and Polly there," as Polly deserted her and ran off with her basket of roses.

"You don't do any of the calling, of course," said Pickering, with a laugh.

"Well, I'll have her to myself," declared Alexia savagely, "before it's time for us to get off the steamer, see if I don't."

"I don't believe it," said Pickering. "Look at her now in a maelstrom of relatives. You and I, Alexia, are left out."

And the next thing Alexia knew somebody unceremoniously helped her from the steamer with a " Beg pardon, Miss, but you must get off," and she was standing on the wharf in a crowd of people, looking in a dazed way at Polly Pepper's fluttering handkerchief, while fast-increasing little ripples of greenish water lay between them.

And Phronsie was running up to Mr. King: " Here, Grandpapa, Mrs. Chatterton wanted me to give you this," unclasping her warm little palm where the bit of white paper lay.

" The Dickens she did," exclaimed the old gentleman; " so she has had a last word with you, has she? Well, she won't get another for a long spell; so never mind. Now, let's see what Cousin Eunice says. Something interesting, no doubt." He spread the crumpled bit straight and read, Phronsie standing quite still by his side:

COUSIN HORATIO:
I have made Phronsie Pepper my sole heir. You may like it or not, as you please. The thing is done, and may God bless Phronsie.
                              EUNICE CHATTERTON.